SOME KIND of TWISTED LOVE

Siren Sisters, Book 1

Cover Design by Dee J. Holmes. All stock photos licensed appropriately.

Edited by Heather McCorkle

Print Edition ISBN: 978-1-7353743-0-7

Digital Edition ASIN: B08C24HKQM

Printed in the United States of America

SIREN)(SISTERS

SOME KIND OF TWISTED LOVE

RACHEL SULLIVAN

To my daughters,
who inspire me every day,
to break the mold.

There was once a little girl,
who had a little curl,
right in the middle of her forehead.
When she was good,
she was very good indeed,
but when she was bad she was horrid.
HENRY WADSWORTH LONGFELLOW

CHAPTER ONE

My feet skidded to a stop within inches of the cliff's edge. I spun on my heel to scan the forest and confirm that the visitors and my sisters were still around me. The males' scent kept me from catapulting off the cliff in a quick getaway. Evergreens stood proud and tall, creating looming shadows in the moonlight. Water crashed against the rocks below us.

My stomach clenched with hunger. Even if my clan didn't have a list of rules to live by—number two on that list forbid us from revealing our siren species to outsiders—I'd still prefer not to hunt in front of non-siren folk. Call me overly cautious, or guarded, but interacting with non-human boys took some getting used to. Ridding yourself of a lifetime's worth of distrust takes more than the couple months I'd spent around the illusive twins.

I lifted my nose and took another whiff, just to double check. Seaweed and testosterone. Yeah, the twins were following us. Don't ask me why, but for some reason that fact both excited and irritated me.

"What is it, Allura?" my clan-mate, Cara, asked.

"We're not alone," I said as I paused and peered toward the direction the scent was strongest. The three teens who froze beside me were the daughters of my aunts, but I'd never call them cousins. We were more like sisters.

Arlana lifted her nose, and after inhaling she shook her head and her shoulders relaxed. "Not even a moment's peace," she said on an exhale.

Celine's face lit with a flirtatious smile as though she found pleasure in the idea her crush could be watching her. She took one step forward, spun in a half circle, and stopped, facing the two boys who hid behind a tree. "Come out, come out wherever you are, Lover Boy."

The boys were identical twins, but only one had an on again/off again thing for Celine. At the moment they were very much on again.

The object of Celine's taunting ran from his hiding spot with a roar of laughter. He picked her up and planted a wet kiss on her giggling mouth. Very wet. The other boy sauntered from behind a tree, water streaming from the end of the drenched ponytail resting on his shoulder, down over his bare chest. Both sported blond tresses dripping into their blue eyes. Neither their hairstyles nor clothing would blend into this world.

They only arrived a couple of months ago, along with the rest of their family, by way of the ocean. Despite their humanly good looks and charm, the boys were kelpies—males who lived in the water and lured human women to their deaths, sometimes shifting into a horse to earn the woman's trust. As far as I knew, the twins weren't a danger to us—we weren't human women.

The kiss parted for all of a second for Celine's boyfriend to comment on how hot she looked. Traces of an Irish accent filled his words. Celine giggled and they fell upon each other again. She liked his accent more than chocolate, and made a habit of making that fact painfully clear to us by droning on and on about his sexy voice whenever they were apart.

Although, at the moment, you'd think the lips Celine was locked on to were actually made of chocolate, the way she refused to let go. The boy who owned the lips showed no hints of a complaint.

Throughout history sirens and kelpies have had somewhat of a kinship, not that the two species are related in any way. But I supposed their kinship was based on a mutual understanding rather than blood. Both species hunted humans, usually of the opposite sex. Both species lived in or near the water. And both species had a healthy enjoyment of the pleasures life had to offer, oftentimes with one another.

But when humans ran to the sea in droves to harpoon orcas and net up thousands of fish at a time, the siren elders decided the sea was no longer a safe home. Hiding among the humans would be best, they thought, which also meant living as humans. When my ancestors left the ocean and our man-hunting ways behind, they also said goodbye to their kelpie neighbors.

Which was why the boys' arrival a few months back had been such a shock. A shock that Arlana bemoaned, Celine delighted in, Cara found entertaining, and I...well, I wasn't yet sure what I thought about the kelpie boys. They were easy on the eyes. And they gave us more than just each other to socialize with over school lunch. But I hadn't spent much time forming an opinion on the new arrivals.

I caught the non-lip-locked kelpie staring at me and I gave a friendly smile. Despite his Irish roots, he reminded me of a Viking warrior, the way he pulled the length of his hair atop his head back into a ponytail, only baring his shaved sides. His height and broad shoulders completed the look. Once, I almost asked him if he had more Norse than Irish in him, but I figured he could point out the same in me since I didn't at all resemble the country or people the sirens originated from, according to folklore. My hair was dark and my skin tan, like any other person of Greek decent, but my almond eyes and high cheekbones made me look more from Asian ancestry than Greek.

The kelpie responded to my smile with a nod and a smirk. I wondered what secrets he held, what words his mysterious half-smile kept from spilling out.

Cara's stomach growled and each gaze in the group shot to her belly. With our impeccable hearing, we could feel the vibration of sound and decipher the words that vibration created. Her face flushed with embarrassment. Like Arlana and me, she still hadn't gotten entirely comfortable around the boys.

"What?" she squeaked. "I'm hungry."

Celine's kelpie wrapped his arm tightly around her shoulder. He raised his eyebrow. "You guys haven't eaten yet? It's almost dawn, and then there's that thing we do every weekday morning called school."

"It's none of your business what we've done or haven't done tonight," Arlana said. She took a step backwards, toward the cliff. A breeze lifted her brown hair from her face and set it back down over her eyes. She blew it out of the way. "We need to head out, sisters."

None of us moved.

"Our moms said we had to hunt here tonight," Celine answered her on-again/off-again boyfriend, her lips only inches from his. "Something about there being more fish or whatever. They were out earlier, said we'd have more luck over here."

"Well, they were right," Celine's kelpie flirted. "We are pretty lucky to have found these fish-girls, wouldn't you agree, brother?"

Arlana scoffed and rolled her eyes. "Fish-girls? Really, you horse-boys come up with such clever nicknames." She gave a sarcastic thumbs up and fake smile. "Must be all that mane."

We had no clue what the boys looked like while hunting, though human folklore surrounding the shape-shifting, horse-like kelpies gave us plenty to imagine. I highly doubted kelpies still donned mane while luring unsuspecting prey. That's one reason Arlana didn't like the twins; she couldn't trust them.

But I wished she'd at least be nice. Since the boys showed up to school, the unwanted attention my sisters and I received from the human guys had decreased by a lot. We could never fully relax in the presence of humans, but at least we didn't have to walk around acting like ice queens to keep them at bay any more.

The kelpie in Celine's arms whinnied and she shushed him play-fully, mindful of her sister's intolerance for being teased.

"Very funny," Arlana said dryly, and added a fake giggle to get her point across. Looking at us girls, she went on, "Seriously though, dawn is coming and Cara's so hungry she could eat a horse." Arlana raised an eyebrow toward the whinnying boy.

The two boys broke out laughing at my sister's attempt at a jabbing threat. One pulled away from Celine to steady himself with his hands on his bent knees. The other leaned against a tree. Tears welled in their eyes.

The one who'd been staring at me spoke up, "Why fish, though, night after night? A human male would last you weeks."

An awkward silence hit our small group. The topic was one we rarely brought up, but the boys' curious minds couldn't see any logic in our current ways. Apparently they *had* killed, or he wanted me to think they had.

He amped up the awkward a few more degrees. "Honestly, though," he said while running his hand through his long hair. "Sea life used to be more like distant relatives than food to your kind. It's like your great-grandmothers traded one set of relatives for another, turned against the fish and made humans your kin."

Cara's voice grew serious. "As my sister already said, it's none of your business. And unless you're a siren, none of our ways, or our decisions are any of your concern. Besides, if we're being honest, which clearly *you* are, we think your ways are disgusting and we're proud of the decision our great-grandmothers made, the decision to practice self-control. Something your kind knows nothing about."

I eyed my sister. Was she starting to see human males differently, too? Was she having to practice self-control at school, out in mixed company, like me? Did her stomach also secretly growl for more than fish?

Cara and I left the circle of Celine and the boys to join Arlana at the edge of the cliff. Wind blew our hair as we pulled our shirts over our heads.

"I'd better go too," Celine said behind us. "Sit with me at lunch later?"

Thanks to our ability to see in the dark, I spotted Arlana roll her eyes.

My three sisters and I stood in a line, our toes clinging to the edge of the cliff. Scales popped up along our shoulders and sparkled in the hazy moonlight, trailing down our bodies.

The boys pushed past us—splitting our line into two sections—and dove over the ledge, down to the dark water.

Showoffs.

There was no need for me to concentrate on the movement of the wind or to remind myself of the correct footing for this type of jump. Our ancestors were some of the most feared women in folklore; huntresses. And even though our species had weakened since the "glory days" of preying on pirates and sailors, we still pretty much had a knack for all things hunting related—cliff jumping included. Though, back when sirens ruled the seas, they leaped from jagged rocks in the dead of night with hopes of killing much larger prey than fish.

The Puget Sound, an inlet off the coast of Washington state, spread out before us like an endless sheet of onyx glass. Evergreens grew up to the edge, their roots exposed, snaking over the rock and anchoring their great trunks into the cliffside. The four of us shot out from the shadowed tree line where the steep rockface plummeted into nothing but ocean. We soared off the side, over sharp rocks and crashing waves. The night air greeted me with a gush, wrapping itself in my black hair. With chins tucked down, we pushed our hands above our heads, creating arrows of our bodies to cut through the ocean top. My fingers pierced the water. My feet fused together with a numbing tingle and my toes elongated to ten narrow bones connected by a black fin. Changing, for us, was purposeful, not automatic. If we willed scales to rise from our skin, and allowed it to happen in its time, it barely hurt at all.

"Finally," Cara said, the top of her head barely beneath the water's surface. She grabbed the first fish within reach and sunk her teeth into its scales.

I studied our shifting surroundings to ensure we were alone. The boys were nowhere to be seen. Arlana could breathe easy. And I could hunt without fear of being watched.

To anyone else our teeth looked like a human's. But, our tongues glided across a more sinister truth. A hidden reality. Like steak knives, white serrated ridges lined the inside of our pearly whites.

Cara clutched the appetizer to her side as she swam, scanning the water with the intensity of a caged lion released into the zebra-infested tundra. One fish wouldn't do. We needed lots.

We rounded the edge of a star-fish covered boulder, focused on the hunt.

Most animals, land and sea, knew of our existence—knew we were dangerous and to be avoided. It made hunting that much sweeter.

We tucked into a narrow underwater cave and waited, our bodies swaying to the natural movements of the water. A school of unsuspecting fish soon swam by the cave opening. Without warning, four sets of arms thrust from the pitch-black cavern. Each of us clung to our wriggling meal, our nails digging deep, pushing through scales. We exited the shroud of the alcove and enjoyed our meal. Cara, of-course, seemed to enjoy it most.

"That visit with the seaweed boys put us behind schedule. We need to head home soon," Arlana said underwater. The vibration of her words traveled through the liquid in a way only water-folk could discern. Arlana stared up toward the top of the water, where cloud-distilled moonlight danced across the waves.

I bit at the meat stuck under my nails and nodded.

Cara eyed her meal. "I'm still hungry." She examined the remains, searched for any morsel left on the bones. Her head jerked up. "Did you just hear that?"

I craned my neck to study our surroundings. "I heard it too, like something...like a smacking noise or something."

"It's probably just the boys messing with us again," Celine said with a dismissive wave of her hand.

I hoped not.

"No. It's not them. They swam off." Cara released the fish skeleton she'd been clutching, morsel or no morsel, and followed the sound we'd heard and felt. I caught up just in time to see her put a hand over her mouth and gasp. Celine and Arlana stopped short behind us.

7

"This is not good," Cara whimpered, her hand still covering her lips.

An unconscious woman descended through the dark water. A knee-length dress billowed out around her waist. Light brown hair wisped in free-flowing strands above her head. One single thread of red ribbon leaked from her wrist in the most beautiful of ways. The blood twined around her body with each sway of the underwater waves, slowly forming a red cloud.

"We need to turn around and go home. Right now," Arlana demanded in a clipped voice. "The boys did this, they had to of."

Celine put somber words to the thoughts running through my mind. "No. They wouldn't have left any part of her behind." Even though I thought the same thing, her response sent chills running under my skin.

"And they don't slit wrists," I added, transfixed on the woman. "That's a human thing."

Arlana turned her body away from the woman as if she were preparing to race off through the water toward home. "I don't care who did it. We shouldn't be here, it's playing with fire, breaking a handful of our most important rules—rules one and two for starters."

"Arlana's right. If our moms find out we'd even stayed this long they'll be pissed. And anyway," Celine added, "she could come to and see us. Celine shook her head and swam to Arlana as though an invisible line had sprung up between us, separating the righteous from the condemned. "Humans can't see us, or they'll fear us. They wage war against those they fear."

Breaking the rules was an act beyond stupid, and although the list of "do not's" concerning humans, screamed in my head, something stronger, an unbreakable pull, glued me in place. We'd recited our list of siren rules, each created for our own protection, for the livelihood of our clan, since we could talk. Hell, Arlana's first word *was* "rule." But, for the first time ever, I couldn't help myself. And I didn't know why.

Cara's palm rested on my shoulder. "Come on," she said, her earlier food-induced joy stripped from her voice. "Let's go." As a loving gesture of our kind, she trailed her hand down my right arm. She wove her fingers between mine and started swimming away, gently pulling my arm with her.

I allowed Cara to pull me, but gazed back to get one last glimpse. The woman crossed paths with a moonbeam dancing through the water, and a golden charm attached to her necklace sparkled in the moonlight. I zeroed in on the shiny jewelry and eyed the cursive words on the heart-shaped pendant. "DAUGHTER", it read.

I was a daughter once.

I pulled from my sister's grasp. "Go on," I said to Cara, as the gold charm fluttered in the red cloud of water, mesmerizing me. "I'll be right behind you."

My sisters didn't argue. They jetted off toward home and away from the dying human.

I closed the distance between the woman and me, and hesitated for a moment. If she were conscious she'd be staring straight into my eyes. The thought of a human seeing me in this form sent a shiver of excitement and fear through my limbs. Before I could stop myself, I grasped at the charm, not sure if I just wanted to get a better look at the thing or rip it from her neck to keep as my own.

The billow of red encasing the woman ruptured with the force of my movement and vines of crimson trailed away from her body, toward me. The pores between patches of black scales on my arm absorbed the liquid scarlet as they did the oxygen in the water. An unfamiliar thrill shuddered through me.

I dropped the small piece of jewelry as though it had been infused with poison and shook my arm free of the blood. An oily tear welled in my eye as I watched the pendant ease its way back toward the woman's skin. As much as I would have loved to keep the charm as my own and pretend my own mother had gifted it to me, I couldn't steal from the dying girl.

Thoughts of my mother filled my mind and made my heart heavy as if in that instant it had turned to lead. This woman was a daughter. She had a mother—a mother who would miss her, who would be heartbroken without her.

I knew that heartbreak all too well. A new idea popped into my mind, one more involved than merely inspecting a golden charm.

I forced my eyes away from the pendant and shook my head. I needed to do the right thing. Follow the rules. There was nothing I could do for this female.

Except maybe drag her body onto the shore.

I stared off into the darkness, rationalizing letting the ocean claim her, when a quiet thump reverberated through the water. I peered down to where the noise came from—the woman's chest. From the strength of her heartbeat, somehow the hunter in me knew she was nearer to life than death. If I could prevent the severance of a mother-daughter relationship, I had no choice but to try. I pushed all logic from my mind—every possible and probable consequence of what I was about to do—and looped my arm around her waist.

Her blood encircled me, but I pressed ahead. I absorbed fish blood all the time. Why would hers be any different?

I turned to swim to shore. No one would see me unload the body onto a dark beach, especially if I chose a place near the cliffs. I headed south and began to pick up speed when my temples pulsated and my back muscles tightened. Weird. Swimming, or running, or really any activity, had never caused soreness before. Maybe it was the way I was carrying the extra weight. I stopped to readjust my passenger.

Her heartbeat thudded in my ear.

A deep growl ripped through my stomach.

With every pump of her heart, new blood gushed from her wrist. Her wound seemed to be getting worse. Moving her body through the rough water may not have been the best decision.

I started swimming again, slower, more gentle this time. Despite my changed pace, the water around us thickened like crimson satin wrapping around my body. My pores sucked in every ounce she offered. With each thrust of my tail, each push and pull of my free arm through the water, my stomach tightened, folded into a painful knot. But I kept moving. I had to make it to the beach before her heart sounded its last rhythm.

We neared the bend of a cliff. Underwater rocks jutted into the black water and signaled we were close. The crimson satin draped heavier on me, lulling me with its tempting deliciousness. The blood's sweet lullaby begged me to draw-out our time together. To linger in its serenade.

I pushed our bodies through the water. Yes, she was bleeding badly now, but for the sake of her life, I needed to get her to land.

As we rounded the bend, I shifted her weight from one arm to the other and a spurt of concentrated blood surged from her flapping wrist and into my mouth.

I froze.

Acid splashed onto my tongue and my head churned with desire. I had eaten earlier, but now my stomach clenched and throbbed with hunger and an insatiable craving for something I had never tried before. My heart beat hard and fast; my muscles twitched and my tongue slid across the serrated teeth lining my gums.

A growl escaped my clenched teeth.

"I'm sorry," I said through pursed lips. "I've gotta get you away from me." With strong, smooth thrusts of my tail, I shot the two of us up, cutting through the water, pushing us to the surface.

What the hell? Did my pace just quicken...on its own? Somehow, I sliced through the water faster than I'd ever swam before.

What is going on with me?

We reached the pebbled shore. I held her up, above the water, above my head, and thrust her onto the beach. Her body rolled and sank into the forgiving land. Her head lopped to one side and her arms twisted like wet noodles.

I sank back underwater and willed my tail to painfully rip apart, separating into legs. Running from the waves, I hurried to a red, wind-worn emergency phone sitting between the beach and the empty parking lot.

My fingers dialed 911. My mouth screamed into the receiver that I'd found a woman bleeding on the beach. I dropped the phone. My legs shot me back toward the water. Before my toes touched the promising safety of the liquid, I peered back at the woman.

What have I done? What have I done?

Reason flooded into my thoughts as I raced home. My aunts were going to ground me for being late, for not staying with my sisters. And if they learned I'd just saved a human, the price to pay would be much steeper. I swallowed a thick lump in my throat as I pushed through the water.

What would they do if they knew a small part of me wanted to stay in the water, wanted to drown her, wanted to taste the forbidden meal of my foremothers?

CHAPTER TWO

)(

"Allura!" Celine's mother, Aunt Dawn, shouted. "Dinner." From the resonance of Aunt Dawn's voice, I knew the human guests had arrived.

As a source of income, and a tactic to hide our true identities by running a seemingly out-in-the-open type of business, my aunts operated a bed and breakfast out of our home. Yeah, folks in town might have thought we were strange at times, maybe even whispered rumors of witchcraft behind our backs a time or two. But none would take the leap of assuming we were anything other than human, especially not sirens, not when we'd opened our home so frequently.

Of course that was the whole idea: hiding in plain sight.

But as with any type of hiding, it came with its share of difficulties…like having to raise our voices to accommodate human hearing.

Yelling is unnecessary for sirens. But with humans around, we had to behave like their kind rather than our own. Last night though, we had no guests and still Aunt Dawn screamed at me so fiercely I thought she'd blow a blood vessel in her neck or rip one out of mine. While I swam home, my sisters had waited on the beach below our house. We had walked through the backdoor together, as if nothing out of the ordinary had happened. My sisters hadn't told, but somehow my aunts knew.

Somehow my aunts always knew.

Obediently, I made my way to the dining room and found my seat at the table, mentally preparing myself for the show my family would soon put on for our visitors. The large banquet table accommodated the B&B's guests in addition to our own household. As the baked chicken made its way to each human, I eyed the newcomers sitting across from me. The one human boy in the bunch caught my gaze and held it for all of two seconds before I pretended to find my plate more interesting than his chestnut eyes or the way the top button on his Henley fell open.

"Have you gotten a chance to read today's paper?" The father of our group of guests, who looked to be in his forties with a mixture of black and silver hair, folded the newspaper and placed it on his lap as the glassware of chicken was handed to him. "Apparently a twenty-two-year-old woman washed up on the beach last night. The police are reporting this as an attempted suicide. They're wondering who called 911 and fled the scene, though." He speared a hunk of chicken with his fork and passed the dish to his wife. "Who would leave a girl to bleed to death? I think the police should look into it."

I tried to gulp down the knot in my throat and lowered my head. Aunt Dawn's eyes burned into me.

"Just tragic, that poor girl." The mother shook her head and sighed. Dark wavy hair reached down to her elbows and bangs covered her forehead.

Beside the mother sat the daughter who reached out toward her father, trying to grab the printed news. "What's her name, Daddy? Is she going to be okay?" She looked about ten and had her mother's hair.

"Here." The guy at the end of the table, who looked to be about my age, poured milk into the little girl's glass as her mother spooned vegetables onto her plate. "If they just found her yesterday, her name may not be released yet. Especially if she's alive." The little girl gazed into the boy's face. With the way she seemed to adore him, he had to be her brother. His black hair, chestnut brown eyes, and tan olive skin matched the others'.

"She's in I.C.U. right now." The father smiled at his daughter. "And no, they aren't releasing her name yet."

So I'd actually saved her, she still lived…

My relief didn't last long before the dark sinewy shadow of impending doom covered it and snuffed out my twinge of a smile in the process.

My aunts would not be happy about this.

As the older brother plucked a chicken thigh from the casserole dish, he peered up through his hooded lids just enough to catch my eye. Only, this time, I didn't look away. His full lips parted into a smile pointed directly at the casserole dish, but unmistakably meant for me.

"This is Allura," Aunt Anise, Cara's mother, said. She tried to sound light-hearted and friendly, but tension framed her words. She did not however feel the need to tell me *his* name.

"Nice to meet you, Allura," the unnamed, dark-haired guy said.

The family across the table expressed relaxed greetings through chewed food. If the humans knew who they dined with, relaxing would have been the last thing they'd be doing. It might not be fair to think that way, but I couldn't help it. The guy was charming, and I didn't want to be charmed, especially not after last night's incident.

After the mom finished her bite and took a sip of water, she spoke. "So, Allura, we were just talking to your gracious aunts about the high school you girls attend. As soon as we get settled, David will be starting there." She motioned to the boy and then looked back at me. "How do you like it?"

"I like it," I answered hesitantly, keeping the dialog to the point.

"Good." She gave me a smile before moving the conversation to my aunts, oblivious to my discomfort. "We hate having to put the kids in new schools in the middle of the year, but when a better job calls, you've got to answer."

My aunts nodded as though they agreed. As though they even cared.

I munched on the few raw vegetables on my plate and half-listened

15

to the adults' superficial discussion. While I assumed the human adults were being genuine, I knew my aunts were merely donning masks for our guests. Ever the inviting inn keepers.

I popped the last baby carrot in my mouth, swept my plate and glass from the table, and headed for the kitchen. Noticing dirty cooking dishes lining the counter, I rinsed the bowls and pans and arranged as many as I could into the dishwasher. When I reached under the sink to grab the dishwasher soap, I glanced out the little window above the faucet.

Colors of the setting sun smeared across the sky, over the water. Finally!

I stopped to listen for any changes in the dining room. They were still eating and chatting. Good. Hopefully, I'd get a chance to hunt with my sisters before my aunts had the opportunity to remind me how royally I'd screwed up by saving the party-dress woman. I needed to get one last hunt in before they grounded me.

Where my aunts were concerned, added punishments for my rule-breaking wasn't a matter of if, but when.

I squeezed the liquid into the designated soap holder, shut the dishwasher, pressed start, and headed out the back door.

Heavy rainclouds darkened the sky, while farther off, over the water, it looked as though an orange haze held back a raging fire. Sunsets were my favorite. I settled onto a patch of grass to wait for the shadowy darkness to consume the horizon, and watched boats return to their docks for the evening. Water danced as small waves rippled through the now dim, orange reflection. *It's almost time.* My stomach rumbled in anticipation. We could eat regular food, but only meat truly fueled us, and only raw meat would do.

My aunt Dawn used to tell stories of the days our foremothers roamed the seas in search of the ultimate raw meat. While animal flesh kept us alive, the flesh of men allowed my ancestors to thrive. But if you asked my sisters or me, surviving on fish worked just fine. My aunt loved talking about the days long before even her mother existed, when our kind were more powerful in strength and speed. That particular topic had a way of causing her eyes to glaze over, as her thoughts traveled to a far-off place where sirens stood near the top of the food chain, where the humans' worship of us rivaled their fear for us. I'd never wanted to be glorified. I preferred the freedom of anonymity. So, I couldn't understand what my aunt imagined exactly that made her long for something she'd only heard about in stories.

The backdoor shut, and from the sound of the heavy footsteps and longer gait, I knew it wasn't one of my sisters. I absorbed the air around me to double check the scent. My back arched as though a rigid, splintering board shot through my spine.

"It's gorgeous." David, the boy from dinner, stood beside me. I eyed his loose jeans in my peripheral vision. His knees pointed toward the edge of the cliff, toward the ocean.

I sat frozen, silent.

He pulled his hands from his pant pockets and turned. He pointed toward the ground beside me. "Is this grass taken?"

I didn't know how to respond. So I didn't.

He sat beside me anyway, and looked out at the ocean.

I begged my heart beat to slow down, to match the rolling waves.

His movement pushed his scent into me and it took everything not to lift my nose for just a little more. My tongue dragged across my lips before I realized and forced it back into my mouth, against my serrated teeth.

"What do you do around this island for fun?" he asked.

I hesitated. Normally we only allowed newlyweds and other celebrating couples to stay at our bed and breakfast, which meant we barely saw them. I wasn't clear on how my aunts would have me behave in a situation like this, though. They'd always said talking to humans was a necessary evil—if it wasn't necessary, in their minds, it *was* evil. Unless…well, his family were guests in our bed and breakfast and I couldn't be rude; that would be bad business. My aunts had allowed semi-friendly banter at the dinner table this evening. If I kept quiet would I get in trouble for being rude to paying guests? For not playing the role my aunts worked so hard to set the stage for?

Short answers would be best—polite and yet not friendly. They'd fit both the not-befriending-humans rule (number five) and the not-being-rude-to-customers rule (number eight). Worry twisted under my skin, urging me to flex and twitch for release, but I forced my hands and feet to remain still. I had talked to humans before, talked to boys my own age, but this time felt different. Something deep inside me climbed to the surface, excited to be beside this new guy, excited to gain his attention. This thing within hoped he'd like me, a hope I'd never experienced.

I shot a glance at the boy. "I swim."

"Is that all?"

I thought for a moment. What else did I enjoy doing? Other than swimming in the blood of...I pulled myself from the memory, or fantasy, and worked to focus on acting normal. "I hike, too."

My nerves wound and unwound up and down my body, bringing my shoulders forward and slightly hunching them over. I tried to slow my breathing and relax, but my body refused to comply. Apparently the kelpie twins hadn't cured me of my boy-centered discomfort.

Imagining swimming through blood-thickened water didn't help either.

His shoulders eased down and back, and his breathing evened, as though he were chatting with an old friend. Calm.

I envied him.

"Okay, so hiking and swimming," he said. "Probably pretty common around here." He took a deep breath, his eyes still fixed on the waves. "I like to ride my bike."

Despite myself, I let out a little laugh, thinking of a cute, muscular guy like himself on a little bike. I pictured a pink girl's banana-seat with clear and pink glittered tassels hanging from the handlebars. Probably because he had a little sister.

"What's so funny?" He turned and looked at me with an expectant smile on his face as though he wanted in on the joke.

"Nothing, just a bicycle." The words came out of my mouth a little jumbled. I straightened both my smile and my composure to get back on topic. "Do you mountain bike, or..."

He chuckled. "Not a bicycle, a motorcycle."

"Oh." Well that completely changed the image in my head. And not in a bad way.

"Yeah, my dad's always been into Indian motorcycles, so when I got my driver's license he bought a brand new Indian Chief for himself and gave me his 2003 Scout. It's beautiful." He nodded his head. "Definitely my favorite pastime."

I expected anxiety to grow in my chest and intensify from carrying on such a friendly conversation with a human, but the more David spoke, the more I noticed my shoulders ease down away from my ears. I'd never conversed with a guy like him.

The air of unfriendly indifference my sisters and I put off at school worked well in keeping humans away, but once in a while a particularly arrogant guy would have the cockiness to ignore and push past our icy boundaries and approach one of us. David seemed bold too, only not in the same way. His confidence seemed rooted in friendliness not a self-proclaimed status as God's gift to women.

"Have you ever been on a motorcycle?" he asked, meeting my eyes.

I held his attention for a breath, noticed the specks of gold in his eyes, and found myself wanting to know more about him. I caught my thoughts in a pretend jar, screwing the lid on tightly, and lowered my gaze to the ground. "No. Never ridden a motorcycle." My fingers played with the blades of grass near me.

The sun had moved below the horizon. I could leave soon to hunt, and forget all the questions flooding through my mind about David's arrival to the island and what that meant for me. I pulled myself up to start heading down the crest of our yard, to the beach. But David got up too, and then we just stood there together, not talking. Awkwardness suited the boy just as much as confidence.

"You should come riding with me some time," he blurted out. "I promise there'll be no tassels."

I grinned, picturing him riding that banana-seat bike again.

"What? Were there tassels?" A smile played in his voice.

"Yes. Pink, glittery ones."

"Hey," he said with a chuckle. "The last time I rode a bike with pink tassels I was too young to have put myself on it, or get myself off it."

"No, you liked it," I teased before remembering where I was and who I was talking to—a human. I took a step backwards, away from David, away from the human boy I'd found myself getting too friendly with. One of my feet caught the other and the ground seemed to shift beneath me as my balance took a short vacation.

I shoved my arms out behind me to break the fall.

David did too.

He reached for me and his fingers skirted along my skin. "First day with your new feet?" he said. The dark blue fabric of his long sleeve Henley brushed against my cheek.

I gasped at the physical contact. Touching two humans in two days, must be some sort of record. I seized my body from his arms and spun around to see Cara's wide eyes watching us.

When Cara finally blinked, she shook her head and walked past us, heading for our beach with our waterproof drybags in tow.

I looked from Cara to David, who stared at me with questions in his eyes. My empty waterproof drybag hit the ground with a light thud near my foot. Soon it would be stuffed with my clothing and I'd be in my siren form. "Oh." I bent to grab the small backpack that I should have been able to catch from my sister without a problem.

"I'll get that." David swooped in, grabbed my bag, and handed it to me before I had completely reached an upright position.

I tried to say something—give some sort of statement of gratitude or let him know I had to go. But nothing audible came out, so I abandoned the whole talking idea and just stood there. I heard Cara make a noise between a cough and a snort, and the reality switch flicked on like a blaringly bright light bulb. I didn't belong here, standing next to a human boy. I belonged on the beach with my sister, the water lapping at my toes, anticipating a night full of stalking and eating.

"Sorry, I've got to go," I muttered.

I looked away before he could respond. I jogged to Cara who had vanished down the side of the hill where she followed the trail, making her way to the darkening shore.

"So," I asked, trying to act like this night's hunt preparation didn't differ from the others, "are we supposed to hunt anywhere in particular tonight?" The night prior we'd been given instructions from our aunts where we'd find the most fish. I assumed they'd have opinions about where we hunted tonight as well.

She shrugged and pulled her pack a little tighter to her shoulder. "They weren't able to discuss tonight's hunt in front of the humans."

I dropped my backpack on the pebbles and inched toward the water to dip my feet in the refreshing liquid while we waited for Arlana and Celine.

"Stop, Allura." Aunt Dawn's furious voice trailed down the side of the cliff. By the way she whispered, David must have already gone inside the house.

I lowered my head and whispered back, "I wasn't going to leave my sisters. I just wanted a little drink."

Aunt Dawn's red hair resembled an angry torch as she crested the top of the cliff. The moment she was beyond view of the guests in our home, she sped down the trail and caught my upper left arm in her tight grip. "What would make you think you should enjoy the rewards of our kind when you refuse to follow the rules we hold to?"

Her hand still encircled my arm like a vice as she pulled me away from the water's edge and backed me against the rocky cliff. A light whiff of oily tears changed the scent of the air around us and a sharp pain tightened my heart at my sister's sadness. The tears were falling from Cara's downturned face.

"My sisters thought the stern warning you received last night to be good enough, but I highly disagree." Aunt Dawn leaned closer to my face; her lips opened just enough to expose her teeth. "And now the girl still lives?"

"She didn't see me," I squeaked.

"I don't care if you *think* no one saw. You shouldn't have broken the litany of rules in the first place! You essentially trusted someone outside of our clan by helping her; you showed your siren form to a non-siren." She shook her head before resting her glaring gray eyes on me again. "You'd better be thanking the stars and the moon the Council didn't see you pull that stunt."

21

I worked up the courage to speak through a tightly shut throat. "The Council is here?"

"They were passing through last night." She took a step back, away from me, but continued to squeeze my arm. It felt like the bones of her fingers were going to leave a permanent imprint. "The Council is about to revolutionize the way our kind lives, and no unpledged teenager who values human life will get in their way. Do I make myself clear?"

"Yes, Aunt Dawn." When she released her grip on me, I tried to walk around her toward the water, but her arm flung into the air, clotheslining me and shoving my back into the cliff. The sharp rock fragments cut through my shirt and stung my skin.

"Allura?" Aunt Dawn almost smiled, which I trusted less than her furious voice.

"Yes?" I stared at the pebbles beside my feet.

"Who were our foremothers?"

"Powerful huntresses."

"And what did they hunt?"

"Animals." I knew where her questions led, and I didn't want to get to the part where she made her point.

"But what did they *live* to hunt?" Her lips curled up, over secretly serrated teeth.

"Men." My heart beat faster. I could never picture my sisters and me tracking a man with one goal: to eat him. But just thinking of how I could never do such a thing, made my stomach growl.

"What *type* of men?" Her right arm shot out beside my head and her palm smacked into the rock behind me. She didn't so much as wince.

"Human men." A drop of acid swirled in my mouth and my stomach clenched, anticipating. As though she'd just mentioned a drug I'd tried and loved, my mind buzzed with ways to get another fix.

"That's right, human. So if we *ever* catch you going against nature and defying your own kind to save one of theirs, I will personally see to it that you never again enjoy the gifts nature has bestowed upon us."

I nodded, the pebbles in my line of sight now a blurred backdrop to my thoughts. I shook the dangerous fantasies of luring men to their deaths from my mind and peered up. Whether in my head or real life, I had to stay away from humans. The threat of never being able to hunt the seas with my sisters again wasn't worth breaking even one more rule.

The normal cadence in Aunt Dawn's voice returned. "Cara?"

Cara's head jerked up and she wiped the tears from her cheeks.

"Bring your sister something to eat when you come home tonight." Cara nodded and looked at Celine and Arlana who were removing their shirts and stuffing them into their backpacks.

"And, Allura." I pointed my face to Aunt Dawn, but she still focused on my sisters as she spoke to me. "You can go to your room now. Aunt Rebecca has something special waiting for you per my recommendation. Something to put my mind at ease, so I'll know you haven't disobeyed and left your room to hunt."

I snatched my drybag from the wet pebbles and started making my way up the side of the cliff when I heard the last pieces of Aunt Dawn's instructions to my sisters. "Make sure you kill the fish before it leaves the water. You can cook it when you return home. If she wants to sympathize with the humans, she can eat like one too."

CHAPTER THREE

)(

I lay alone in my bed, depleted of energy, desperately trying to sleep, as the scent of cooked fish stole any droplet of hope I'd had left. The punishment hours earlier had pushed my body to a threshold of pain I'd never endured before. Even now, as I wished to disappear into the darkness of my room, recent memories of my aunts holding me down, tying the fireweed, transforming the braided green leaves into hand and leg cuffs, plagued my thoughts.

The achingly painful flashback sent a rush of heat through my arms and legs—remnants, body memories.

Aunt Anise and Aunt Rebecca had been waiting for me when I entered my room as Aunt Dawn had directed. I followed every instruction they gave. Disobeying hadn't even entered my mind as an option. Two adult sirens against one teen? Plus, disrespecting our clan leaders would heap more shame on my shoulders. With my mother's disgraceful decision years ago, and now my genius idea to save a human, shame already weighed me down. I didn't need an ounce more.

As instructed, I sat on my bed, rolled up the bottoms of my pants, and crossed my ankles. Then we waited. Aunt Rebecca paced the room as she clutched a clear mason jar holding my punishment: fire-weeds. While temperature failed to affect us, fireweed taught our kind what scalding felt like.

Aunt Dawn burst through my bedroom door, all excitement and smiles. "You ready?" she said as though we were about to light birthday candles.

Each of my aunts found a place beside my bed.

I tried to be strong. I tried to stare ahead in silence. But the moment Aunt Rebecca's gloved hands tied the puke green fireweed around my ankles, I lost it. At first, I'd only dug my fingers into the bed and bore down, tearing small holes in the comforter. But then she added a second layer and screams tore from my throat as someone shoved a pillow over my mouth. I gnashed my teeth into the soft cotton, ripping and shredding. The plant had been moistened, so it stuck to my skin, its panic-worthy residue mixing with the liquid, smearing wherever it touched, absorbing into my pores. My body shook and writhed with pain.

Yet again, thoughts of my mother flashed through my mind. Would she have stepped in to protect me?

My pain deafened their whispers, but I thought I heard murmurs from Aunt Dawn and Aunt Anise calling me a sympathizer as my three aunts left my room.

"What is this generation coming to?" one of my aunts asked as she held the bedroom door open for her sisters.

I bore my head into the torn pillow. Shame fought pain in a battle of what hurt more.

"Is it not enough to weaken us, now our own seek to expose us 'till we're hunted down and killed off?" said another, once the door shut behind them.

*Aunt Rebecca returned hours later, after my sisters came home from hunting. After a newly lit linen-scented candle did little to mask the cooked fish smell wafting through the bed & breakfast. Her gloved hands made quick work of untying my ankle restraints, placing the weeds back into the glass jar. Her eyes refused to meet mine while she gently applied a stinging salve where the fireweed had been.

My aunt opened the door to leave my room, allowing a gust of putrid charred fish stink mixed with fake candle smell to billow in. I moaned inwardly. Accepting the punishment meal would break Cara's heart and turn my stomach, so I didn't wait for Cara to come to our room, cooked fish in hand. Instead, I had curled into a ball and pretended to sleep.

"How badly does it hurt?" Cara whispered after returning the fish to the kitchen and climbing into her bed.

I didn't answer. We both knew I wasn't sleeping, but somehow pretending felt easier.

"I hope you're not mad at us, we didn't tell. Arlana and Celine feel really bad for you." She waited before continuing. "I'm sorry if they act like they don't care. You know how they can be sometimes. The fact that they have to leave soon must weigh on them every moment of every day. After they graduate, life as they know it comes to a screeching halt. Scary."

I rolled to face her bed in the pitch-black room and whispered. "We're only a year behind them."

Cara seemed able to come up with excuses for each person in our clan, and our older sisters were no exception.

"But are you mad at us?"

"No." I dropped my voice to barely audible to keep others from listening in. "I just hate being the one your moms scrutinize, waiting to mess up. If you watch anything long enough, you'll find what you're looking for."

"They aren't waiting for you to make a mistake. They watch because they care."

Cara and I agreed on most things, and I could talk with her about any issue, but this one she just didn't understand. Why would she? She assumed her mom, Aunt Anise, loved me the way she loved her own daughter. But Aunt Anise didn't. Unlike my sisters, I didn't have a blood-bond with our leaders—a birth mother who helped govern our clan. Cara had no clue what it felt like to always have one foot in the door, but never allowed to bring the second foot across the threshold.

A heavy silence hung in the darkness between our twin beds. I sensed the weight between us...Cara had something else on her mind. "Spit it out so we can go to sleep," I half-groaned, half-whispered.

She exhaled. "It'd be real shitty of me to bring it up tonight. I just worry about you."

"But?"

"Be careful with that David boy. I saw the way you looked at him," she answered.

My breath caught in my throat. "Did you tell the others what you saw?"

"No, I want to avoid the drama it'll bring."

I let a heavy sigh fill the quiet. "All I did was trip, and he caught me." I felt the need to defend myself, which wasn't a normal tendency with Cara.

I sat up as new frustration crawled up my back. "Be careful with what?"

"Siren's don't trip. We aren't exactly klutzy. You lost your focus because of him."

I snorted a response.

"Tomorrow morning the Hudsons will be told that we had a water pipe issue in the middle of the night and they'll need to find another place to stay. So as long as you don't talk to him at school, David can be a thing of the past."

"David was never a *thing* to begin with," I grumbled. "Absorbing that woman's blood and feeling the sudden urge to bite people, that's a *thing.*" I flung my hand over my mouth. "I didn't mean to say that."

"Seriously? Is that what happened?" Cara shifted in her bed, suddenly interested in the topic. "I knew I should have been more pushy that night and made you come home with us. And now you're actually talking about...biting humans. Do you fantasize about it too?"

"Just when the subject is brought up," I said, partly in defense and partly in a desire to share my secret with someone before its weight burst me wide open. "Not all the time."

"Sick."

"Not helpful," I said, wishing I'd kept my mouth shut.

Cara slithered from her bed.

I opened my covers and she crawled in beside me. "Don't worry," she comforted, "sirens haven't eaten men since before our grandmothers were born. I doubt we'd even know what to do with ourselves if the opportunity arose."

When Aunt Dawn had tried to make a point earlier and reminded me who my foremothers were, my imagination had a pretty solid idea of what I'd do with a male prey.

"Am I gross for fantasizing about it?" I let the conversation pause for a bit. I had already mentally pieced the puzzle together, at least part of it. Now it was time to find out what Cara thought of my assumptions. "Obviously the fantasies didn't start until after the whole human blood incident. I don't understand though, it was a woman's blood, not a man's."

"I think human blood is human blood. But still, I guess it would make sense if you absorbed and ingested it once, that your body would want it again. I know after my first time eating tiger shark, I craved it like nothing else." Cara grinned and ran her tongue along her top teeth.

"You and tiger shark," I said with a quiet laugh. I could always count of Cara's bubbly personality to lighten the mood.

"Either way, if I were you I would keep this little turn of events between the two of us. At least until you know more about it."

"Yeah. If your mom and our aunts find out, they'll watch me more than they already do." A new anxiety clung to my thoughts.

"I already told you," Cara said on a sigh, "they aren't looking for you to screw up. But yes, you might make them worry more."

I considered a thought for a moment, staring into Cara's eyes. How could I learn more about something that hadn't been experienced in decades?

"What about Aunt Rebecca's books? You think any of them would have that sort of information?" A glimmer of hope burned away the anxiety and coursed through me.

If an explanation existed for what plagued me—for the tantalizing fantasies the woman's blood must have created within me—then it'd be in Aunt Rebecca's books.

"Her books are about healing ailments caused and cured by nature. But maybe back in the day a tincture or two involved humans in some way. I guess it's worth a shot." Her passive response put a damper on the hope I carried, but didn't dissuade me. "Wait," she added as an afterthought.

I perked up.

"I know it's risky, and totally breaks the no-trusting-those-outside-our-clan rule, but our kelpie friends Kaven or Sean might have more answers about this stuff than a book of healing."

"You're right, they already get to hunt humans," I blurted before thinking.

Cara scrunched her eyebrows at me. "*Get* to? You seriously need to deal with your sudden obsession-with-eating-people...before you slip and say something like that to god knows who."

I assumed Cara worried I would slip and mention my newest desire to our aunts. If they found out they would probably lose their shit and lock me away from all humans to keep our clan safe from the judgment of the elders, the leaders of all siren kind. I didn't blame Cara for her concerns. To break a clan rule would require clan justice, like not being able to hunt with my sisters. But to break an elder rule...that would require a consequence decided upon by the elders. For sirens, hunting humans was against the rules. Period. And the punishment for hunting humans was death.

"I know," I muttered. "I know."

It wasn't like I ever planned to hunt them. Wanting a thing based off a primal instinct and actually doing it were two very different things. But the elders wouldn't see it that way. I desperately needed to understand this new desire and find a way to either control it, or get rid of it.

CHAPTER FOUR

))((

Cara and I sat on the backseat in our little car, with our older sisters in the front, on our way to school. It'd been three days since my talk with Cara and no bloody cravings had entered my mind. Hope that the worst was behind me had become my new go-to emotion. Maybe just getting my thoughts out there had been all I'd needed to purge them. I'd decided not to bother Kaven or Sean with my non-issue. Clan business should stay clan business.

Celine and Arlana carried on from the front seats about their next year of freedom during their *nadu*. Cara and I listened in on what we knew would soon be our fates as well.

While each siren clan held varying preferences on where to hunt, what animals to eat, and where to live, they all agreed on the basics of our kind. One of those basics was pledging. For as long as sirens have existed, our clans have been like small tribes. And when a siren reaches the age of adulthood, she must leave her tribe in an attempt to find herself. To decide what she believes, how she chooses to hunt and live. We call this a *nadu*. What she did, where she traveled, and how she behaved while she was gone, would remain a secret. But when she was ready to return, a choice had to be made. Pledge as an adult to her original clan, or to the clan of another.

My two older sisters agreed they intended to return to our clan, but they had a difference of opinion as to what they'd do while away. Arlana, the more practical one, wanted to visit other clans and glean any wisdom they'd be kind enough to afford her. Celine, on the other hand, had a less dignified proposal in mind. She wanted to find men... and play. They weren't obligated to stay together during their *nadu*, but most sisters did, for comfort and safety.

"I still think that's unwise, Celine," Arlana scolded after Celine made a joke about the unsuspecting college boys who partied at spring break destinations.

"Why? It'll be fun. I won't hurt them or anything. I'll just stalk and taunt. It'll be torturous for them. But in a good way for me." She pulled the visor mirror down and applied her lip gloss. "I've always wondered what it'd be like to actually hunt men."

I made eye contact with her reflection from the back seat. "Are you talking about torturing them with your teeth or your body?"

The car exploded in laughter. I joined in, half hoping she would answer my question.

"Celine," Arlana joked, "If we lived a couple hundred years ago, you'd be the one in our clan on a protruding rock, calling the men on shore to wade into the sea and visit you for a snack."

"I know. I was born too late," she quipped with a devious smile as she snapped the visor down.

Laughter filled the car again. I needed this, the light-hearted banter of sisters. But in that moment, I couldn't fully absorb the warm fuzzies. Something distracted me.

An image of Celine, long hair draped over her naked curves, luring the town's fishermen to join her in the deep water and then lashing out in ravenous hunger, painting the waves red, filled my mind.

I didn't need warm fuzzies at the moment.

I needed someone to smack the siren out of me.

Cara laced her arm in mine as we walked through the large doors of the beige and white school building. "What are your thoughts?" she asked after our sisters left us for the senior hall.

"About what?"

"About what Celine and Arlana were saying. Did your "fantasizing about biting people" issue rear its ugly head again?" We stopped at my locker, a dark purple rectangular shape among hundreds of others exactly like it. Rows of them lined the walls of the hall. Purple and gold were our school colors. Home of the Fighting Wolverines.

"It started to, but I pushed it back down. Whenever the topic comes up, I try to distract myself and just not think of it." I turned the black dial until I heard the lock pop open. I unzipped my backpack, and shoved the books I didn't need into the locker.

If I'd had my way, the inside of my locker would be covered with pictures of my favorite things, like how the others at my school decorated their lockers. Only, my pictures would be of the gorgeous views only seen from ocean depths foreign to human eyes. Instead, I'd adorned the inside of my locker door with the necessities: a single magnetic mirror in a black frame.

"Good. I'm proud of you."

I shoved the last textbook into my locker and turned to look at Cara just in time to see her beaming grin.

"I try," I said, giving a slight curtsy.

I pulled my strawberry tube of lip gloss from the small pocket at the front of my backpack and examined my reflection in the mirror as I applied the light pink, shiny substance to my lips. I smacked my lips in the mirror before turning to Cara to remind her that talking about my issues, however innocent, only made me think about them and I preferred to pretend they didn't exist. Digging them up every few days wouldn't keep them buried.

But before I could speak to change the subject, a tall, blond-haired football player, Jason, sauntered by in his purple and gold letterman's jacket. He smiled in our direction and we glared back. He spun his head in the other direction and walked away from us, laughing.

He whispered, "Watch this," to a buddy before smacking the butt of a nearby girl. The unsuspecting girl yelped.

My legs flexed in response. My hands begged me to catch up to Jason and allow them to strike him back—see how he liked it. As my fists unclenched and prepared to feel Jason's skin sting across my

33

palm, my heel pushed off from the floor, using the resistance to cata-pult me ahead. I made it about one foot before Cara's arm blocked me like a seatbelt restraining my body before the impact of a car crash.

"Seriously?" Cara hissed, shaking her head.

I fell backward and into a locker from the collision with her arm. "What?"

"You know what." We watched the boy and red-faced girl walk away in separate directions. "Someone would see."

"He needs to be taught a lesson." I turned to face my locker.

"It's not your problem. If she doesn't like his chauvinistic attention, she'll do something about it."

"She's too timid to stick up for herself." A smile twitched across my lips. "But, I can do it for her. He wouldn't see me coming."

"And then what?"

"I'm not going to actually do it, Cara. And I know what you're getting at. If I teach him a lesson, he'll fear me and when people fear things, they wage war against them." I repeated the quote I'd heard too many times before.

Cara put her arm around my shoulder and walked beside me. "It's sweet—in a twisted way—how you want to help people, but that's not what I was 'getting at'." She cleared her throat and whispered, "This not thinking about your issues thing is *not* working."

"That boy being an asshole has nothing to do with my *issues*," I whispered harshly.

"No, but your reaction to him does. You looked like you were going to tear him apart and drink his bone marrow. Seriously, Allura, if you start eating people, Aunt Dawn's fireweed will be the least of your worries. The elders won't let you live. And even if they did let you live, what if Aunt Dawn's right, and the humans do find out and hunt us down? I know we can handle a few of them, but can we handle a torch-wielding mob after our existence goes viral?"

My shoulders slumped and Cara sighed. "I can't come up with any other way to manage my urges."

Talking to the kelpie boys reemerged on my to-do list.

"Thanks for the arm restraint, though." I mimicked a seatbelt across my chest with my own arm.

"You're welcome." She chuckled as we parted ways and headed to our classes.

The morning flew by. Lunch found my sisters and I at a little round table picking at sushi and complaining about dead food. The kelpie twins sat with us, each sipping on their salt water filled thermoses for lunch. When he wasn't smashing lips with Celine, Sean teased us about our food choices for not only our mid-day meal but our nighttime ocean diet as well. It would have made a great opening into my probing question about controlling human-hunger, but it was neither the time nor the place.

In fifth period P.E. the teacher wanted to enjoy the sun while it graced us with its rare presence, so we ran on the track outside. Thankfully, stretching my legs made that period also pass quickly. And although I didn't run as fast as I possibly could, I made sure to stay ahead of every student, even as they huffed and puffed toward the end.

A benefit of being the first to complete the assigned laps around the track was getting to change in the empty locker room while the rest of the girls finished. I found the corner in the alcove of lockers where I had stored my jeans, long sleeve cotton shirt, army-green fitted button-up jacket, black flats, and backpack. After pulling off my purple sweat pants and faded gray t-shirt with the white wolverine emblem plastered on the front, I slipped into my regular clothes and flung my backpack over my shoulder. On my way out of the locker room the high-pitched sound of voices coming in from the track echoed behind me.

As I pushed the metal door open another sound greeted me—the oddly shallow breathing of a guy. I didn't even bother to see who I'd just passed, assuming he was waiting for his girlfriend.

"You were acting weird at lunch today," Kaven, the other half of the kelpie twins said, touching the back of my elbow. Ah, now the shallow breathing made sense. For some reason—I assumed the lack of water in the air—the twins rarely took deep breaths.

I eyed the few students walking the hall before the bell rang, and pulled him to a more secluded spot beside the glass cabinet of sports trophies. His smile dropped slightly when I released his muscular arm from my grasp.

Was it in my head or was he upset that I'd pulled away from him? I really didn't want to discuss this at school, but when else would I ever get a chance to be alone with him? Every time I hung out with the twins, my sisters were there.

"I have a question," I said, examining his green eyes, gauging how deep his trustworthiness extended. Rule one pounded in my head: trust no-one outside our clan.

"Then I have an answer," he said. Kaven's confidence danced between cocky and sexy in a way that only a kelpie could pull off to this degree.

I sighed and reconsidered searching through my aunt's books before allowing the words to fall from my mouth. "I can't stop thinking about hunting people; men. Killing them. It makes me so hungry." That last part I whined a little without meaning to.

His smile grew, showcasing his perfectly straight, white teeth. He nodded approvingly. "Then don't stop."

"I have to. My kind aren't held to the same rules as your kind. If I kill someone and the elders find out, they'll kill me." I canvased our surroundings for signs of my sisters and then returned my focus to Kaven. "How do I stop?"

"Come live with us." His offer shocked me. For as much as we hung out with the kelpies, we barely knew them. "Suppressing your instincts will only make them more volatile," he continued. "I'll show you how to control them, but first you have to release them. I'll protect you from any backlash." His voice, his demeanor, they weren't cocky, but rather filled with genuine concern. Something I'd never seen from a kelpie, much less Kaven.

And I believed him.

But believing and doing were two very different things. "I can't leave my sisters. I have to fight it. Can you help me?"

"I know I joke a lot, but..." Kaven grazed my temple before

cupping my cheek in his hand. The tingle of scales pushed up from beneath my skin in response to his touch. His forearm flashed a kelp shade of green. He cleared his throat to continue.

David came around the corner and stopped short. "Allura!"

My abs tightened. I hadn't noticed how many students now rushed through the halls on their way to class.

Kaven dropped his hand to his side and I shifted my hair to cover the scales on my cheek slowly melting back into my skin.

"David? Hey, how have you been?" The words flowed from my mouth as if we were old friends reconnecting after months of being apart.

Awkwardness can do that.

Kaven raised an eyebrow at me and I shook my head. I shouldn't have been so friendly with David, a human. When the ol' kelpie presumption returned to Kaven's smile I figured I knew what he was thinking: That my siren was luring David. I wasn't sure if I agreed.

"I'll just leave you two," Kaven said with a wink in my direction. "But Allura, remember, fish don't poop where they eat. Well." Kaven looked down the hall and then met my eyes again. I swear, even his eyes smiled. "Fish do, but we don't." He sauntered toward his next class and away from David and me.

"Hey, I'm glad to see you," David said, ignoring Kaven's oddness, his brown eyes fixed on my face. I scolded myself for noticing his eye color and how it darkened around the edges of his irises. For noticing their unique beauty.

His black and dark gray striped fleece hoodie fit him in all the right places. His shoulders and pecs pushed the soft fabric out just enough to notice they were there, but not in a steroid-jock sort of way. His deep brown, almost black hair lay perfectly tousled in waves atop his head. A smile twitched on my lips as I thought about how much I loved waves—all types of them.

"We're all moved in now, at least mostly," David explained, snapping me out of my self-loathing for comparing his hair with my love of oceans. "We live in the historic district of town."

I forced my lips to move and the tiniest ounce of voice came out. If

37

my sisters heard us talking they'd give me shit. "Oh," I whispered. I knew the area he referred to, but saying so would only stretch out a conversation that shouldn't have started in the first place. Kaven was wrong. I could fight this. And keeping away from David would probably help more than hurt.

"I spent most of last night cleaning my bike," David added, as though he were searching for a topic I'd respond to. "It got dusty during all the packing and moving, but you should come by and see it. I'd like to take you for a ride around the island."

I'd always wanted to ride on a motorcycle. "Um." I tried to lean toward him so I could drop my voice to a quiet lull. "I don't think that's going to happen."

"I can come pick you up. I don't live too far." His smile widened. "Is it even *possible* to live too far away from anyone on this island?" He laughed and watched me for a response. His humor was so dry it made me want to laugh.

But I didn't.

Ice queens don't laugh.

"Oh, you're afraid of motorcycles," he assumed.

If I said yes to end the conversation, he'd only suggest another activity.

"Listen, David." I scanned the hall for any prying eyes…or ears, and leaned in. "I'm not allowed to talk to you, or visit you, or even know you."

David tensed and his voice lowered. He turned to make eye contact with me, his cheek only centimeters from my own. "Are you with that guy you were just talking to?" Anger flashed through his eyes. "Is he *that* controlling?"

I almost laughed. Again. Though, this time he wasn't joking.

I pulled away to get some distance. "Oh, God no, I'm not with him. I'm not with anyone. And I don't want to be with anyone either." I raised my eyebrows. Hint, hint.

He backed away another step or two. "Oh, you think I'm hitting on you?"

Wasn't he, though? Or had I just made myself look like a dumbass?

I had to save face and I had to do it quick. "No, I just don't hang out with people like you." Humans.

If words were planes, mine just crashed hard. And burned. In the worst way ever.

Ice queens were cold, not cruel.

What was left of David's smile faded. He shook his head and turned to walk away.

I knew I should let him go, let him think whatever he wanted about me. It'd probably be best for him to assume the worst, that I was a hideous bitch, to believe what most guys had believed about us. But I couldn't. Not David. How could I repay a genuine kindness and warmth with counterfeit hostility?

"David please, it's not like that." I didn't want to tell him I was thinking of his safety as well as my own.

"No?" His shoulders lowered and his jaw released as though he'd quickly contained whatever he'd been feeling. His relaxed confidence returned and he spoke as though he'd dialed the wrong number. "I thought you were someone that you're clearly not. That's my mistake. It won't happen again."

He left me standing there, beside the glass-encased golden plastic trophies and team photos.

I watched David walk away as I stood silent, still, with a stab of remorse. Why did following the rules feel like such a mistake lately?

CHAPTER FIVE

)(

As I pulled the thick, worn history book from the locker it hid in, I repeated to myself, *One more class, one more class.*

In my irritation, I accidentally smacked the locker door shut with a little more force than usual. The flat surface slammed into the metal clutches, bending the bottom corner. A chunk of purple paint chipped from the edge.

Relief swept through me at the realization I'd just marred something.

I shouldn't have even been nice to him in the first place. This is why. This is what happens. I shouldn't be made to feel guilty for being myself. I told David I couldn't talk to him, but he just kept pushing.

I shook my head at the messiness of it all and made my way to class.

Mr. Moore's lecturing voice boomed into the hallway. I lingered outside taking a deep breath. I swung the door open.

One more class.

David's scent smashed into me like an angry wave crashing into a rocky cliff. But before I could mentally cuss myself out for noticing his scent above the others, something else caught my attention. The boy sitting beside him, or namely the boy's bloody leg.

Oh crap.

I turned to leave, and almost made a clean escape until Mr. Moore called out to me in a patronizing tone. "Miss Allura, a little later than usual, but at least you made it, right?"

I stood in front of the door that had just shut behind me, my fingers in a vice grip on the shiny, metallic knob, fighting back the onslaught of want. Acid dripped in my mouth in preparation to quickly break down raw meat. The release of acid before a meal was normal, but not like this, not this much.

I clamped my jaw, the sharp inner edges of my teeth grinding against more sharp, serrated edges. If I could sweat, I would have been soaked. At least there was that one mercy.

My eyes scanned the room for a seat, bouncing from face to face assessing their expressions, looking for traces of fear, hoping my monstrous urges weren't outing me. Mr. Moore shot me a stern "sit down" look and continued with his lecture.

I slid into the closest empty chair toward the back of the room.

As I dropped my backpack, without thinking, I instinctually lifted my nose just slightly into the air and inhaled the earthy, yet coppery, deliciousness that wafted from the boy to his predator.

Blood.

Delicious.

My eyes focused solely on him; the skater boy beside David, whose leg dripped with blood.

Mine.

I didn't care about the skater's unkempt brown hair, or his rock band t-shirt. Shoot, I didn't care about him at all, but what I did want, what I did desire, trickled down his right leg from a fresh cut on his knee.

Acid dribbled in my mouth like a tiny leak. The longer I stared, the faster that leak dripped. I licked my lips and swallowed down the extra liquid swimming over my tongue.

I had to stop. I had to control this...whatever *this* was. We sirens weren't supposed to hunger for men anymore. We weren't supposed to feel like this. I closed my eyes, but my sense of smell only intensified. My heart pounded with deep, heavy thuds. Blood pulsated through my temples. I had to keep my eyes off the boy's leg, shoved out into the isle between rows of desks. But I couldn't control the way his scent swirled across my skin.

My fix.

It was here.

In the room with me.

I fumbled in my jacket pocket for my cell. I had to text Kaven. Or Cara. Maybe I needed both to come get me. I couldn't leave on my own; I was afraid to move. What if I accidently ran toward the skater boy instead of the door? What if I ran out of the class and into another human and lost control?

I needed help.

But when I unlocked the home screen Mr. Moore rested his gaze on me and shook his head. No cell phones allowed during class time.

I sat still as a statue and tried to pretend I didn't have flesh-disintegrating acid flowing through my mouth. My legs clenched beneath me, readying to spring from the seat and pounce on my prey. "Stop," I whispered under my breath, but it didn't help. My fingers clenched and unclenched.

Oh God. My stomach churned and screamed with desire. My head pounded. The hunger was worse than I'd ever experienced before.

Way worse.

From some distant place I could still hear Mr. Moore. I could still sense a room full of bodies, like through a haze or as though they were all behind a glass wall and the only two beings on my side of the glass were the boy wearing skater clothes...and me. Would they even notice through the clear wall, if I devoured their classmate?

Suddenly moving pictures played behind my closed lids. *I see myself, spring from my seat in one leap and land on Skater Boy's desk. I crouch down to stare him in the eye. His goofy grin falls from existence. Terror flashes through his face and his fear fuels me that much more. He freezes for a quick second, but then realizes what I've come to do.*

He grabs his skateboard leaning on his chair leg and swings it at me. I leap from his desk before the painted board makes contact with my skin, and land behind him. He jumps from his chair, but not quick enough. My fingers clasp at his shoulders, and fling him across the room. His body slams into the gray cupboards lining the wall and he scrambles to get up. I move too fast for his weak efforts to stop me. My teeth sink into his skin, too quick for him to see, biting him all over his body. In the same way I'd learned to drain my larger prey quickly, I drain Skater Boy until he has no more fight left in him. But it isn't blood I'm after. Blood is only the appetizer, the drink before the feast.

"Allura," Mr. Moore called out.

My head shot up and I wiped my mouth. "Yes?"

"Glad to have you back." He addressed the rest of the class, "As I was saying..."

I tried to slink lower in my chair, but my rigid muscles kept me upright. I scanned the room again. Did the others notice I'd been drooling? Well, salivating...but still.

They all stared forward, even the skater boy, who I tried not to look at. But one set of brown eyes watched me, and when I noticed them, David mouthed, "Are you okay?"

"No," I mouthed back, shaking my head as my taut muscles trembled. *Not at all.*

When the release bell finally rang, I sprang from my seat with my backpack already draped over one shoulder and walked as fast as humanly acceptable to the little red car. Except, as my feet hit the pavement outside the school doors, so did Skater Boy's skateboard wheels. He sped past me, toward the back of the school.

Blood-tainted oxygen shot through my nostrils and swirled across my pores.

Mine.

My nose led the way as I skipped behind him, far enough back to keep anyone from noticing he had a follower. My lips pursed to let out a silent whistle, like a school-girl anticipating a lollipop. Only, I didn't wear pigtails and I wasn't interested in licking to find out what was in the center of my tootsie roll pop. I also wasn't interested in luring him, waiting for him to come to me.

Skater Boy rounded the corner to the back of the school. I slowed my pace and scanned our surroundings. We were far from the student parking lot and there were no teachers around. We were alone.

Perfect.

I edged closer to the corner. His scent stirred nearby. My heart pounded. A thick drop of acid fell onto my tongue. I savored the taste. My fists clenched and the muscles in my legs twitched with power. I gripped the wood slats of siding my body pressed against. My nails dug into the forgiving surface.

I pushed my body from the building and leaped into the path of Skater Boy. He eyed me skeptically before pulling something from his pants pocket. Old green trash dumpsters boxed him in between the building and me.

"What do you want?" he asked, lighting a blunt.

I eyed the muscles in his forearm as they contracted and stretched with every flick of the lighter.

"Smiles won't get you anywhere with me. I don't share."

I took a step closer to him, not realizing I was smiling.

He shrugged and breathed out a puff of dense smoke. "Fine. But I only accept three methods of payment. Grass, cash, and ass. And since I clearly already have grass, and don't need cash, I'll take some ass." He eyed my chest and licked his lips. He took another drag and blew it toward me.

Billows of red clouded my mind. Blankets of scarlet wrapped our surroundings like fabric. I no longer saw the dumpsters or the school. It was just me and Skater boy and the promise of a blood-filled embrace, the assurance that a perpetual emptiness would soon be filled. The knotting and twisting of my stomach would be calmed. The painfully loud pulsating in my temples would be quieted.

I lunged. I didn't know if he screamed because all I heard was the thudding in my own chest. I tasted blood and felt flesh between my teeth.

"Stop!" The booming voice came from behind me.

Out of instinct I jumped up and crouched between my prey and Kaven, ready to fight the incoming predator for what was rightfully mine.

"Allura," Kaven crooned. "I thought we went over this; no hunting where you live, where you go to school. You know, don't poop where you eat…"

"Help!" my prey yelled to Kaven. "The crazy bitch bit me!"

"Allura," Kaven called again, clearing the red clouds in my mind, bringing me back to reality.

I swung around and zeroed in on Skater Boy. He clutched his forearm as blood wound down his fingers and the back of his hand.

"I didn't—" I started to protest, but then stopped. The taste of fresh blood tinged the very lips I used to argue my innocence.

Skater Boy bolted from me and I froze, wordlessly begging Kaven for help.

"Stop," the kelpie commanded. The human froze. "Come back here." The boy reluctantly returned.

Kaven grunted and strolled toward me. "No, I won't finish him off for you. I don't swing that way."

I cleared the tightness from my throat until my voice worked again. "Ugh, no, that's not what I wanted."

"Good. Then what do you want?"

I threw my hands in the air, thoroughly embarrassed and ashamed, and thankful it was Kaven who'd caught me and not someone else. But what was the likelihood that Kaven just happened to walk this way when he had a car waiting on the opposite side of the school? "Did you follow me?"

Kaven neared the Skater Boy to assess the damage. "Damn, you meant business. Not too shabby for your first time."

Skater Boy started to speak again when Kaven put a finger to his lips and stared into his eyes. My prey froze, mid-sentence and stared back at Kaven like the sun revolved around the kelpie.

"I can't transfix him forever, Allura. Tell me what you want. We can leave right now, with him, where no-one will see us. You can finish the job with my guidance. Release your hunger, learn to work with it, not against it." Kaven spoke to me, but kept his eyes on Skater Boy's.

Tears rolled down my face, giving away my inner struggle. No, I couldn't. I...I wanted to. And I hated that part of me with a burning passion at the moment. But it would destroy everything—my sisters, my aunts, my life. The elders would have me killed if they found out. Not to mention, it would mean crossing over a threshold that I never imagined I would want to cross. I would become a monster, a destroyer of lives. Sure, maybe Skater Boy lacked potential, but who knew, he could become president some day. Simpler than that; he was someone's son, grandson. People would miss him, mourn him.

The shock of what I'd just done crashed into me and I shook uncontrollably. I'd almost killed someone. What if Kaven hadn't stopped me? Kaven. My focus cleared to see his dirty blond hair tied back in a ponytail, his gaze still fixed on the boy I'd tried to make my prey.

"I want option two," I said with a shaky voice. "Give me an option two." I wanted to be closer, to speak to Kaven face-to-face, but I didn't dare move any closer to my bleeding victim. I didn't trust myself.

"Option two it is," Kaven said before his voice deepened and crawled over his next words. "What is your name?"

"Brian," Skater Boy said.

"Brian, you came back here to get stoned, and someone must have laced your weed because you're high as fuck."

"I am, man. I'm high as fuck and that chick bit me," Brian said, slurring his words.

"Nah, Brian, no-one bit you. That's how high you are. Your front wheel hit a rock, you flew from your board, and when you landed you bit yourself. You bought some strong shit."

Brian gave a goofy laugh. "That was some strong shit, to make me bite myself."

Kaven nodded and slowly backed away, keeping eye contact with Brian. "And you didn't see anyone else, Brian. And no one saw you. You're alone right now. But you want to go home."

"I do. I gotta sleep this shit off. I'm so high I'm seeing people that aren't even here." He shook his head, stood, placed his board under his foot, and skated away. "They're not even here," he mumbled to himself as the distance between him and the two predators grew.

Kaven stretched his shoulders and exhaled a shallow breath. His black t-shirt pulled across his chest and thick biceps. He cleared his throat. "You've got something, on your chin." He motioned to my face.

I took my jacket off and wiped my mouth on the sleeve. Blood streaked across the green fabric. I wiped again and again, eager to erase any evidence.

"You got it," he said. He rested his arm across my shoulders and started walking toward the school parking lot.

I pulled away and bundled my jacket into a ball. "Where are we going?"

"To my car."

"Why?" I asked.

"For option two. You wanted option two, so I'm giving it to you." He reached his hand to me and while I begrudgingly walked alongside him, I didn't accept his offered hand.

"Would you like to know the details of option two?" he asked as we hurried away from the scene to duck into his car.

"Does it matter?" I was a siren who'd agreed to a kelpie's unknown conditions that involved keeping me out of trouble with the humans, a kelpie I barely knew, who could literally demand anything of my clan and me. Wars between folkloric creatures had been fought over less.

We passed by the little red car where my sisters waited for me. Celine leaned against the trunk running her fingers along Sean's lips as he pressed himself into her.

"Aye," Kaven called to his brother. "Go take your girlfriend and her sisters to the movies. In their car."

Sean nodded knowingly and moved to the side of the car to open the door for Celine.

Cara mouthed, Are you okay?

I tried to give an assuring nod. "Don't worry, have fun," I said under my breath, knowing she'd hear. I did worry, though, about more than what option two entailed. Could Kaven transfix me the way he transfixed Brian?

"It's times like these I wish my dad carried a cell," Kaven said the moment both doors of his Ford Ranger truck slammed shut.

"What does your dad have to do with anything?" I asked, nervously. Did option two have to do with leaving my clan and moving in with his? Avoiding that was one of the reasons I didn't choose option one.

"Because I'd really like some backup when I present to your aunts, their fully actualized siren niece along with an ultimatum." He turned off the main road and toward my house.

"You're going to do what?"

He offered me a smile. "That, my gorgeous siren, is option two."

CHAPTER SIX

)(

"Allow Allura to learn the old siren ways or we'll report her," were the first words out of Kaven's mouth.

My three aunts sat on the front room couch while Kaven and I rested in separate high-back chairs. Well, he rested. I attempted to press my rigid self into the stuffed cushions behind me, but probably looked more like a straight board leaning vertically up the length of the chair. My worst fear had come to fruition. My aunts knew my secret, that I'd been craving the old ways.

But for some reason, their reaction didn't quite fit the enraged screaming I'd imagined in my head.

Instead, they were discussing me, my purpose, my future, without including me in the actual conversation. It both enraged and terrified me. What were they holding back in front of this kelpie?

"Report to whom, your dad?" Aunt Dawn asked, clearly offended by Kaven's brass attitude.

Our clan had met with our new kelpie neighbors, but never in our home. And now Kaven sat in our front room like he was a human guest, seemingly oblivious to the danger surrounding him—outnumbered by sirens. And it's not like he beat around the bush either. He'd followed me into the house, waited while I called down my aunts, and then immediately sat across from my aunt Dawn to give the leaders of our clan an ultimatum.

When Kaven and my aunt Dawn began their current stare-off.

Finally, Kaven ended the staring contest to give me a nod. "Kelpies like sirens, we really do. But when a young siren starts killing humans with the finesse and sophistication of a three-year-old finger-painting, right on our doorstep, we take issue."

I scoffed, my offense trumping my discomfort. "Finger-painting?"

He shot a glance at me. "It wasn't bad for your first attempt."

Kaven's focus shifted back to Aunt Dawn. "I admit," he said with a sigh, "we aren't the most governed species, us kelpies; we don't like to live by rules outside the main ones surrounding humans. But imagine the lengths males will go to when they perceive a *right* is being taken away from them." Kaven folded his hands on his lap. "My uncles and father believe exactly that will happen if sirens begin killing, unbridled, untaught. The humans will know there's monsters among them and practice more caution, which will cut down on our *right* to hunt them."

It unnerved me that my aunts weren't shocked to hear about my new siren tendencies. In fact, they showed no emotion at all. Maybe that explained their lack of reaction. In a way, they could have been practicing rule one: don't trust those outside our clan.

Aunt Rebecca stood and motioned to the front door. "Well, while we appreciate you stopping by, it's time for you to leave."

"Kaven," I interjected with desperation, for fear of being left alone with my aunts.

My other aunts stood, glaring at him.

The kelpie stood and made his way to the door. His focus gently shifted from my aunts to me, as though he had no clue that the moment he left, all hell would reign down on me. "Allura, I'll see you later. For all of our sakes, I hope you'll seriously consider my proposition and give me your clan's agreement when we meet again. I'll be in touch." He gave a slight nod, walked from the house, and closed the door gently behind him.

All three of my aunts seemed to exhale at once as they turned to examine me from the entry way. I escaped from the confines of the high-back chair to stand in the middle of the front room, to give myself the ability to run.

But rather than turn their disappointment and anger on me, they ridiculed the kelpie.

"Supernatural males are as entitled as human males," Aunt Anise commented. "They need to be brought down a notch or two."

"We aren't strong enough to fight an army of kelpies, not even if we called for help from other siren clans," Aunt Rebecca reminded. "They've maintained their strength from the days of old by eating what they were born to eat—humans." She sighed. "We haven't."

I waited for one of them to actually speak to me rather than one another while staring at me. With each passing second fear knotted my muscles tighter. They didn't seem mad at me for trying to kill a human. Why? I'd broken a major rule. Gotten the kelpies, outsiders, involved. Where was the fireweed punishment?

"Well, there's no time like the present," Aunt Dawn said. A smile crept up her face and devious intentions sparkled in her eyes. I knew that look. She eyed me from head to toe and back again.

Aunt Rebecca shot her a scowl that quickly faded.

"No time like the present to do what?" Aunt Anise asked.

"You mean, to do whom," Aunt Rebecca said dryly.

Still, my aunts stared at me. Unnerving.

"It's the only option that makes sense." Aunt Dawn squinted her eyes as though deep in plotting mode. "It's not exactly how we'd planned it, but it still works. We can use this to our benefit."

"Oh," Aunt Anise said under her breath.

"Planned what?" I found my voice to ask.

It made no difference, though. I didn't get an answer.

"If we do nothing, who knows if the kelpies' next step will cause a war between our two species, a war we know we'd lose," Aunt Dawn explained to her sisters. "If they bring other supernaturals in, we're as good as dead. But I won't allow an outsider to teach our daughter a damn thing about her own nature." Her tone changed, lightened, as though she were getting to the good part. "If we pretend to go along with their demands, revert back to our old ways, train Allura, we will be calling the shots and their threats would be just that, threats. Meaningless. We'll be back at the top of the food chain, living stronger than our kind has in generations. Impenetrable by the kelpies or any other species who wants to tell us how to live. Perhaps humans will bow down to us once again."

"Yes!" Aunt Anise gushed.

"It's risky, and you can forget about being worshipped, Dawn," Aunt Rebecca said, shaking her head. "If we do this, the humans can't know. They'll hunt us down and wipe us out. Not to mention how much it'd upset the kelpies."

"Screw the kelpies." Aunt Dawn finally looked me in the eyes and met me in the middle of the front room. "Have we ever told you about Providers, Allura?"

I shook my head. "No." After I answered I realized I'd heard of them a time or two in old siren stories told to me when I was little, but nothing in detail.

"Of course not," she said with a smile and a shake of her head. "They've become obsolete. But back when sirens hunted men, each clan had a Provider. She was the strongest and most cunning of the group, a force to be reckoned with, really. We've always participated in a type of family style dining. It's why your sisters and you hunt together nightly, why I hunt with my sisters. But when hunting human males, a clan of sirens descending on one man does more to scare him off than entice him."

"That's where the Provider comes in," Aunt Anise spoke up, almost giddy. "She hunts the man and when the time is right, she lures him to her sisters to share."

I tried to ignore the uninvited images of my foremothers' "family-style dining" but, the drop of acid on my tongue signaled my failure.

"But," I whispered under my breath to myself, to sort information without actually having enough to sort it all. "The woman in the water..." None of this added up. I'd been punished for the possibility of showing my siren self to a human. How was their request any different?

"I stand by my decision." Aunt Dawn's response startled me out of my thoughts. "You tried to save a human's life." She spoke the last statement as though the words alone should make perfect sense. But they didn't. Not to me.

"And anyway," my aunt said with a brush-off tone. "Circumstances have changed."

I'd felt like an animal with the skater boy. The woman's blood had triggered my siren, started all these urges, and now what my aunts were asking of me...would it only get worse? Would these thoughts and the churning hunger in my gut only intensify? Would I become a murderer? A monster?

"You want me to prey on innocent humans," I said in a non-threatening whisper. "I can't do that."

"You can and you will," Aunt Dawn snapped. "We're sick of living like this. Someone needs to step up and provide the meals that'll make our clan stronger, unstoppable. I'd like to see the kelpies threaten us then."

I took two steps backwards, away from Aunt Dawn's reach. "No, I won't," I heard myself say, as if I had a choice. I'd heard Kaven earlier. I'd gone too far with Brian, the skater boy, in a public place. I'd lost control. And now there was no going back. But every decent fiber in me protested my aunts' proposition.

It was wrong. "Why can't *you* do it if you're so eager?" I demanded.

Aunt Dawn cocked her head and eyed me threateningly, as though she were equal parts shocked and offended at my response. "Because *I* want you to do it."

I blinked back the tears in my eyes, suppressed the urge to cry in frustration. "But hunting humans is against the elder rules," I reminded, grasping at excuses to disobey their orders.

"We will deal with the elders," Aunt Dawn snapped. "And you will deal with us."

"Celine would be willing," Aunt Anise offered to her sister.

"And I wouldn't be prouder if my daughter was our Provider," Aunt Dawn answered. "But she leaves this summer for her *nadu*. Seeing as we can't be sure how long the training will take, or even how exactly this is going to work, Celine and Arlana are off the table."

"I'm sure Cara would step up for the good of her clan," Aunt Anise said of her daughter.

I knew Cara would, too, even though it'd go against everything I knew about my sister. If I thought this Provider thing would mess me up, possibly erase what bits of humanity I had, it'd annihilate Cara. She was too kind, too soft, to be Provider.

It would break her.

I gulped down the knot in my throat to agree to a plan that half of me loathed and half of me yearned for. "Fine. I'll do it. When do I start training with Kaven?" A weight dropped onto my shoulders and queasiness set in.

"We're not going to let some male species tell us how to live and hunt. No." Aunt Dawn tapped her fingertips to her lips. "We'll figure out the training ourselves. In the meantime, this stays between the four of us. No sense involving your sisters until the details are ironed out." She walked past me, probably toward the office to begin planning. She paused, but didn't turn around. "Oh, and you can tell your kelpie friend that we've decided to train you in the old siren ways, but on our own terms. The assistance of his kind will not be needed."

*W*ater danced at my knees as I waded into the waves. Moonlight glided across the liquid as though it had trouble deciding where to land. It was mid-November, so I assumed the air had to be frigid, but as I couldn't feel temperature, it felt fine to me.

My sisters laughed behind me, oblivious to our new clan dynamics decided upon earlier today. I felt deceitful keeping such big news from them, especially Cara. Out of guilt, I hadn't said more than five words to her since they returned home from the movie theater. It was unlike her not to ask me about my mood, although I was sure she noticed. I assumed her mom instructed her to keep the prying questions to herself. But what reason did her mom give her?

I willed scales to spring forth and my transition began instantly, quicker than normal. My onyx and emerald-colored scales started like a narrow, quick-growing vine from my right ear and down the nape of my neck, sending tingles along my skin. Scales increased as they crossed my back. They peeked out from under my left arm. As though a bottle of black ink spilled on my skin, the scales swept across my body, multiplying over my chest and down my stomach. As they descended, they also spread out, scattering across my arms. Intermixed colors of black and deep greens dusted them. The colors scurried downward, and covered my thighs, merging my legs together in a painful type of pleasure, an aching soreness, as I plunged into the sea.

Absorbing the salt water cured the ache in my legs.

I swam hard, past the schools of halibut, and the starfish clinging to enormous rocks. My regular meal choices wouldn't do tonight. I needed something bigger. I'd lost my control with the skater boy earlier…and then I'd lost more as a result.

Tonight, I needed to fight.

To win.

My sisters caught up to me, and Cara grabbed at my hand. "Slow down, why did you just pass a ton of food?" Fish hid between stalks of green and brown sea plants, waving in-sync with the ocean.

I didn't look back to respond. "I'm not hungry for that right now."

"What are you hungry for?"

"Something that'll put up a fight." I jetted out in front of Cara, leaving her, Celine, and Arlana trying to keep up, trailing me.

Power pulsed through my being. I sensed a speed within me that even my aunts wouldn't be able to out-run or out-swim. Strength shook me to my core.

We had to swim farther out than usual to find what I craved, but once the ocean floor plunged deeper, and the dark water became more cavernous, I sensed my prey nearby. Fewer plants reached the surface here. The moonlight failed to stretch this deep. My senses heightened automatically, on the prowl for my prey, as though my body and I had already discussed our plan of action. I didn't have to think, I only had to feel, to know, and trust that knowing.

I had only hunted shark with my aunts and sisters once or twice before. Technically we weren't supposed to even hunt shark without my aunts. But then again, technically I wasn't supposed to be learning the art of luring men to their deaths, and *that* was going to happen. Even if it tore my heart out and replaced it with callous blood-pumping organ of a monster, void of guilt and remorse.

I rounded an underwater cliff and my eyes scanned the water, searching for out-of-the-ordinary movement among the swaying seaweed or a tailfin past the group of starfish clinging to the black rock. My shoulders shot up and I hovered, frozen in the water.

Dinner time.

The animal I sought focused on its own meal, a school of fish in front of it. Its slender body and long pectoral fins hid a white, smooth underside.

Without thinking, or strategizing with my sisters, I sped toward the blue shark, arms outstretched. My prey swung its head around, noticing me for the first time, and darted in my direction. We collided, head on, and I flew back. I landed only inches away from a jagged underwater stone, and spun around, using the sharp rock as a pushing off point. On each side of its long conical snout sat round black eyes studying me.

The blue shark raced to close the gap between us, and for an instant, fear shuddered through me. But only an instant, because the moment it looked certain I'd be its next meal, excitement replaced the fear.

The preparations my body made before the decided attack pounded through me with excitement. My head thudded. My stomach twisted and churned. My muscles flexed and loosened, sending volts of anxious yearning throughout every last centimeter of tissue within me. Damn it felt good to hunt, to *really* hunt.

"Allura!" Cara screamed from behind.

"I've got this!" I shouted back, not for sound but for an increase of vibration strength to get the message across.

I stopped swimming and waited.

If sharks could smile, this one would have.

I could tell I was dealing with a mature female, from her large size and the bite scars scattered along her thick skin. The shark careened into me, pushing me back again, but I instantly regained my place in the fight. I reached out to catch it, to claw its skin, but the scratches didn't seem to slow it. It bit down, tangling my hair in its mouth, and pulled. My neck torqued in pain, and I twisted around to dig my nails deeper in its scarred blue skin.

With my dark tresses still in its mouth, its pearly whites flashed again, this time targeting my skull. I whipped my head back, yanking my hair out of its teeth, and swung my body toward a rock. The shark tried to work out of my grip, but I refused to let go. I noticed how dangerously close we'd moved to the sharp cliff edges. Perilously close.

In one, powerful thrust, I bashed all two hundred pounds of the shark against the pointed shards of rock and raced far enough away to give myself a second to think while the animal regained its position.

But it was no use. The shark recoiled quickly and thrust its tail harder and faster, heading straight for me. Blood floated out from its skin as it moved through the water. Beautiful, red, ribbons of blood.

Skater Boy jumped through my mind and ravenous instincts replaced thinking. I thrust my tail in smooth, strong strokes until I was almost on top of the shark. I reached my arms out, wrapped them around its head to close its mouth, and sunk my face into its skin. Over and over again, I hurled my teeth into its flesh. Numerous, circular red patches spread across its torpedo shaped body as I worked to weaken my prey.

Its tail slowed, and I knew it was safe to release its mouth. The blue shark still tried to chomp at me, but with barely any gusto. With every ounce of frustration, and hunger, and confusion, and anger, I pressed my face into the shark's slippery skin, finally delivering the fatal blow. The fatal bite.

As its body slackened, I called for my sisters to help me. "Hungry?"

I turned to see their shocked faces peeking from behind the jetted-out cliff.

I didn't have to ask twice. My three sisters raced to their meal, and without a word, we devoured our prey.

"I'm not gonna lie, you scare me a little," Celine said as we walked up the shore. "But I also kinda like this new angry, angsty side of you." She rustled through her bag, pulling out a folded black sweat suit. She slid the pants on.

We had finished our meal and swam toward home in a wordless euphoria. Now that our night of feasting had come to an end, it seemed my sisters had found their voices.

"I feel so strong!" Cara exhaled as she emerged from the water. "Ah, I could just scream! I love shark!" Cara skimmed the top of the water with her fingers as she waded through the waves, her tail already separated into legs. Her green scales sparkled along her skin. Despite the fact that sharks were generally more filling than fish, I suspected Cara's sense of strength came less from the meal and more from the battle beforehand.

Even within the tamest siren lived a warrior.

Speaking of warriors of the water, I breathed a little easier after the twins didn't show up during our hunt tonight. I couldn't be sure when the whole Provider thing would become more than an idea shared between my aunts and me. Anticipation for my talk with Kaven—revealing our agreement to have me trained, but not by the kelpies—hit me again as I scanned the beach for his shadowed form beside the dark cliff or at the top of the cliff's edge, standing in my back yard. He hadn't told me when we'd meet again, just that we would. I wished I'd had the forethought to schedule a date and time, not wait for him to appear at any moment.

I sat, shoulders-deep in the water, as black and green scales absorbed into my skin. Once my legs separated, I stood and walked toward the beach.

"You already did scream, like ten times under water," Arlana teased Cara, allowing the water to drip down her newly separated legs. Her white and ice blue scales still glimmered along her thighs in the moonlight as they faded into her skin.

"This is what it's all about sisters. This right here." Cara raised her green-scaled arms and spun around, the waves smacking at her knees. "Us four, acting as a team to take down our prey, rip it to shreds and feast upon it." Her wide eyes shone excitedly until they rested on me. Then they dimmed a bit. "Sorry Allura, I didn't mean that."

Celine laughed. "You just get crazy when it comes to food."

I swallowed hard, thankful Celine hadn't understood Cara's real reason for apologizing—because she'd mentioned ripping through prey, possibly triggering my man-eating fantasies. I hoped Arlana hadn't caught on either.

"At least it wasn't tiger shark, you're favorite, Cara," Arlana said. "But seriously Allura, next time you're having a bad day, let me know ahead of time and I'll skip lunch." She rubbed her hand across her full stomach, all traces of scales gone.

I found my drybag on the beach, grabbed my clothes out and pulled the yellow long sleeve shirt I had been wearing earlier over my head. I caught a waft of David's scent mixed with a bit of blood clinging to the cotton. I closed my eyes with a deep inhale before allowing the fabric to slide over my nose and under my chin. When my lids fluttered open, Cara's brown eyes bore into mine as though she knew what I now worked desperately to conceal.

If she could only see the movie playing through my mind at that exact moment, she'd have wished our meal had been fish and seaweed rather than what she now picked from her teeth. I thought hunting and killing a fiercer animal would turn the inner movies off and somehow satisfy the new strength pulsing within me. I hoped it would use it up or something, and dial back my cravings, or at least give me a break for a few days. But the opposite held true.

My newfound strength? Yeah, that didn't seem to be going anywhere. I had enjoyed the hunt, too much maybe, because now the movie was even brighter, the sounds louder. More real.

A part of me fought to turn the images off, but a stronger, more insistent part yearned to keep watching, begged to see how it ended. The pictures now flashed across the screen of my mind—a dark-haired girl attacking her prey, burying her mouth into its flesh. Only, she didn't stop after one bite. She kept going, making quick work of her meal. As her prey twisted, desperately trying to pry itself from her grasp, its dark eyes pleaded from the screen and into the audience of one. That's when my shriek cut through the damp night air and the fantasy came to a thrashing halt.

I peered past my sisters, up the hill, and toward where I knew he lived. Where my fantasy victim now called home—the historic district of the island. A sickening dread filled me. The images clung to my mind as wind whipped at my bare legs. Not even a hurricane had the power to blow away my newest desire to sink my teeth into David.

CHAPTER SEVEN

)(

My sisters had wanted to fill our rainy Saturday afternoon watching movies, but I couldn't just sit and be entertained by the unrealistic simplicity of some character's life, when my own life felt so real and exciting. Plus, I already had movie overload going on...in my head.

And I couldn't wait around the house any longer for Kaven to show up. The anticipation of telling him news he probably wouldn't like ate at me. I needed to get it over with. I'd tried his cell when I woke up, but as usual, he didn't respond. The twins only carried their phones when they were on land and wearing clothing. The location of where they stored their land items had been kept a secret from us, so searching for Kaven on the beach would do no good.

There was a chance I'd stumble across him in the forest where Sean had once said the boys liked to don the appearance of horses and meander through the woods. I had to give it a shot, get our talk over with.

I slipped my feet into my canvas shoes and crept out through the back door of the house before anyone could stop me to ask where I was heading off to before noon, or why.

When I arrived at the edge of the woods, I peered left and then right to make sure I wasn't being watched. The coast was clear. I double checked, real quick, before running full speed into the forest. At about twenty or thirty feet into the woods, past the curtain of trees, I stopped again, becoming still as a statue as I assessed my surroundings, smelling the air, and listening for others. Birds had been chirping when I'd entered the woods, but now an eerie silence swept through the air.

They sensed the presence of a predator.

Me.

I smiled. Just knowing they feared me made my teeth feel sharper. I could use a snack. Small land animals weren't my preferred choice of meal—and technically, according to rule four, we weren't allowed to hunt alone—but nobody would notice if I helped myself to a quick goodie. Not many animals roamed the woods in late November, but if they were out, I'd find them.

I sped past trees and ferns with the new strength I'd gained from my moments with the skater boy behind the school. It had waned a bit since the shark attack.

So, this was the reality behind my aunts' stories of how our ancestors hunted men for increased abilities, how my foremothers had to continue hunting to rebuild their strength. I cringed, inwardly. I'd only had a bite. One. Bite. And yet the potency of my forbidden snack still hummed throughout every piece of me, down to my fingertips.

I paused to examine my fingers. How much more were they capable of now? I shook my head. I shouldn't think that way. Increased power at the cost of another sentient being's life was wrong, no matter how intensely my aunts disagreed. Ugh, I didn't want to think about it, because then I'd have to figure out a way to obey my aunts while disobeying them. To stay in our clan, I had to obey my clan leaders. But to live with myself, I had no choice but to disobey them.

I sprang into a run, mostly to outrun my racing thoughts. Wind whipped at my face. The damp air recharged my senses.

Beads of rain dripped down my forehead before absorbing into my skin. Every type of water had its own unique taste, and water syphoned by evergreens held a fresh, hint of pine flavor. If it weren't for the now gnawing hunger in my stomach, I would have been content to just enjoy the woods for the pine water they provided. I paused, resting my back against the wide girth of a tree trunk. Lifting my nose into the air, I closed my eyes and breathed in deeply.

A faint, yet familiar scent, mixed with the pine surrounding me. I stood rigid when I heard the nearby branches rustle. Immediately my feet moved me toward the animal I'd heard, and my stomach tightened with anticipation.

It was something big, that much I could tell. But, it wasn't a bear or a big cat. I sped through the woods as my body pushed past bushes and low laying tree branches. Not wanting to run straight into the presence of a fierce animal without first knowing what I'd be up against, I lifted my nose again as I ran and breathed deeply, searching for an exact scent. Pine. Yes, duh, there's pine everywhere.

I sniffed again.

And some sort of soap.

And, wait...soap?

My lowered leaning body arched upright, and I came to an abrupt stop.

"Allura?" The voice cut through the tall, overgrown fern separating us.

I stood on my tip-toes to peer over the scraggly shrub.

"David," I sighed, or whined rather.

A branch snapped a few hundred feet away and I jerked my nose toward the noise. I inhaled deeply. A full grown deer. *Now the animals choose to come out.*

I noticed movement from David and peered back at him. He pushed his sleeves up, giving me a glimpse of his brawny, tanned forearms. My eyes lingered on his arms and before I knew it, words escaped my mouth.

"You aren't cold?" The leaves protected us from the rain, but that didn't change the fact that we were on an island off the coast of Western Washington in the later part of fall.

"No." His voice sounded frigid enough.

The abundant fern leaves spread out, heavy with moisture, drops dripping from the edges onto the damp dirt beneath.

David stopped mid-step, his eyes still looking to the growth-covered ground. "What are you doing here?"

I wanted to turn and run in the other direction, but I wanted to stay too, to be near the boy in the woods. I pushed my way through the lush bushes, and walked toward him, being sure to leave plenty of room between us.

"Hiking." *And hunting, as it turns out, for food and a kelpie or two.* My stomach growled loudly as if to remind me of my new main focus this afternoon. Not only did a meal in the form of deer wander nearby, but a delicacy stood in front of me.

Had Kaven set this up? I peered around to search for the kelpie, but not so much as a whiff of seaweed met my senses.

David's boot kicked at the dirt. My attention zeroed in on the human boy in front of me.

"Huh." He gave the ground another kick, looked up at me, and walked over to the wide trunk of an evergreen. He leaned against the bark as he pulled one leg up to rest his boot on the tree. "Well, seeing as you're the one with the rule that you're not allowed to be near me, I think you should be the one to leave."

My fists clenched. I was *this* close to having deer for lunch. And he had to come along and ruin everything. "You know...about that rule...I made it up." The words squeezed their way past my gritted teeth. My breath caught on the lump in my throat and I swallowed it down. "I'm just psychic and knew you were a jerk before you had the chance to prove it. Look, you've confirmed my supernatural ability."

My chin jutted out as I separated my feet a bit and added, "I'm not going anywhere."

"So, is this the real Allura?" He shook his head. "Was the friendly girl I met that night at your bed and breakfast just an act for paying customers?"

"You don't know what you're talking about." I tried to loosen my fingers, pretend he wasn't irritating me, but they only clamped down tighter.

Where was Kaven when I needed him?

"I just mentioned your name at school, and the response was pretty unanimous," David said, nodding his head with a smirk.

One of my eyebrows rose in question, but I already knew what he had heard. It was the same thing they all said about us. The same thing they were supposed to assume of us for their own safety. Still, I didn't want David to agree with them; he wasn't like them. But the tone in his voice told me he believed everything he'd been told. That fact alone pissed me off.

"Apparently you and your sisters think you're better than everyone else, except the G.Q. twins for some reason. Although, with me you chose a new technique to prove your absolute disregard for others. And then the lie about not being able to know me is the cherry on top of the façade pie." He mumbled in a low voice as though he said the rest to himself. "Didn't know staying at your bed and breakfast came with a free pie."

"Don't act like you know me from *one* conversation!" The words spat from my mouth as I tromped toward him quicker than any human should see me walk. First, I had a kelpie threaten my clan if I didn't embrace my inner monster, then my aunts went ahead and decided for me that I'd be the clan's Provider, and now this human had the audacity to assume he knew me?

Why did everyone suddenly feel entitled to have a say in my actions and personality, as though I were nothing more than an empty vessel, waiting for them to tell me who to be?

"It was *two* conversations. That last one was where I got to know you." His tone was solid, not shaky or angry; he wasn't even fazed by how pissed off I was, which infuriated me.

Maybe I was just pissed, period. Maybe I wanted something or someone to hate. The past week or so had been a whole mess of painfully confusing crap. And it's not like I could direct my anger at my foremothers, the ones who kept our species alive by doing exactly what I now fought.

Yeah, I had enough crud of my own. I lacked the capacity to put up with someone else's. Right here, right now, David was in my line of sight and with words like his, I wasn't about to back down. Backing down wore on me like a pebble in my shoe.

I'd been nice to him! I'd treated him better than any human, ever, and this was what I got? My mind screamed with a growing rage. Blood pushed through my veins urgently, and thudded in my ears. A trembling rippled through my body.

"You don't know sh—" Acidic saliva swam throughout my mouth and a haze of crimson satin seemed to drape over the ferns and trees in my mind's eye. My inner siren made her way to the surface. *Oh no!* "Just get out of here, David!"

I prayed a horse would show up, or even Kaven in his regular form, to intervene.

David kept his stance against the tree, watching me. He shook his head and stood his ground.

I took a step back away from him. Screw my resolve to not back down. One of us had to go.

Now.

I tried to concentrate on leaving, on the movement of my feet, on the ground, but my siren fought to stay.

My tongue slid across my teeth as I forced myself to step back. My teeth pricked it. The taste of blood mingled with the acid in my saliva. The combination of the two flavors sent a shock pulsating through my muscles. I froze. My jaw quivered as the flurry of tastes assaulted my mind and worked tirelessly to unearth the bloody images I had fought so hard to bury. Skater Boy. On the ground. His blood smeared across my lips. Deliciousness.

My hands ached and my stomach growled. My head throbbed.

I stood a few feet from him and tilted my head to meet his gaze. A sharp smile tugged across my tightly closed lips.

I gulped down a mouthful of delectable acid and lunged forward. In one fluid movement, my arms snatched his shoulders and shoved them into the tree.

"Don't worry." The words seethed from my salivating mouth, my siren gaining control. I stood on tip toes, staring straight into his deep brown eyes. "I'll *show you* the real me."

CHAPTER EIGHT

)(

My shaking body heaved my chest against his, causing David's breath to wheeze from his lungs. The ringing in my ears grew deafening. Instinctually, my lips parted. My body screamed for him. This wasn't some fantasy, some movie playing in my head.

This was real.

Very real.

The impulses I'd been struggling to control were now ten times as strong. They were beyond my rational brain to dial back. My own mind was siding now with my body, operating on something more intense than pure animal instincts. My rational side created reasons and justifications to follow through with what I had started. I was the Provider, right? Shouldn't I practice providing?

Without warning, my mouth went in for the kill. Exhilaration shrilled through me. Finally. Finally, no Kaven to stop me. No people to worry about. I could take what I yearned for. As much as I wanted.

Wait. Why was I giving in? I had to fight this, or else who knew what could happen. *He's a person. He's David with the love of motorcycles who made me laugh.*

He gasped as his fingers laced around my waist and squeezed my hips. His hands worked their way up my back, clawing me as they moved. His lips softened and his mouth opened. I lost my focus and stumbled back, pulling my face away from his. I tripped on a dead branch and tumbled to the ground, my butt thudding into the moist dirt.

"Wow." David propelled himself from the tree and reached his hand out to me.

"What did I just do?" I asked, knowing full well I'd just kissed the guy. I thought for sure my siren had been preparing to attack him.

"Besides completely confusing me?" David asked with the hint of a laugh. "Not that I'm complaining or anything." The corners of his eyes rose, matching his mouth in a warm smile.

He reached toward me again, but I still couldn't accept his gesture of help. I scrambled back on my hands until my feet were steady enough to stand upon.

My mind went blank as though the overload of shit I'd just gotten myself into by kissing a human could not compute. I didn't even want to touch the idea that the whole interaction with David had been a product of what I really wanted, of my letting go and giving in. Or had it been what my siren wanted?

"I gotta go." I turned my back to him and ran.

___

*A*bout a block away from home I realized my supernatural speed and slowed to a humanly acceptable jogging pace.

"What's my problem?" I scolded myself, wishing my mind could just stay blank until everything worked itself out: like the kelpies left for another town, and my aunts let go of the whole Provider idea, and David magically forgot that we'd kissed.

Unless Kaven removed the memory from David. He could do it, I knew he could. It was one of their creepier powers. Come to think of it, all their powers were creepy.

No, then I'd have to tell Kaven what I'd done. Kaven would probably give me another kelpie ultimatum as my payment for his help.

I needed my mom—some motherly advice from a source of

unconditional love. I'd never missed her more. I passed through the yard and made my way down to the empty beach. The waves tossed as the sun set. Pink clouds covered the sky. Wind whipped my ponytail across my cheeks. I pulled the rubber band out of my hair and wrapped it around my wrist, then bent down and slid my shoes from my feet.

I didn't bother rolling up my jeans; I couldn't wait to feel the salt water against my skin, like the comforting "welcome home" a loyal dog gifts its owner with at the end of a tough day.

I stared out into the thrashing ocean. A single tear escaped and slid down my cheek.

"Why did you want to leave me? I have so many questions and you aren't here to answer them," I screamed to the waves. I'd gone my whole life without my mom's advice, and now I needed her guidance more than ever. I took two more steps into the water until it danced at my knees. My vision blurred as tears poured down my cheeks.

My chest heaved with each sob. I kicked and smacked the water before allowing myself to fall backwards into the liquid. Pulling my knees close into my chest, I cradled my face between my knees and wept as the waves pushed and pulled the sand around me until darkness covered the beach.

My long sleeved shirt hung drenched upon my shoulders. My ragged breathing calmed. The ocean didn't give me the magic answer; it only reminded me that I didn't have to have one. The waves never stopped to consider which shore they'd wash up on, and yet they survived, lived to ebb and flow as the ocean inhaled and exhaled, as it lived and breathed.

Just *being* was enough for the waves. It needed to be enough for me.

Everything would sort itself out. I had to believe that.

As the liquid washed over my skin, a peace fell upon me.

"There she is!" Cara shouted.

I turned to see my sisters pulling shirts over their heads and sliding pants down their legs.

"Should have assumed Allura would be here," Arlana joked.

"We've been texting you all afternoon. You are so going to wish you didn't go missing in action today, Allura," Celine said as she folded her shirt and placed it in her bag. "Our moms got word that we're getting a special guest in the next week, so they made us shut off the TV and get to scrubbing. They've been turning the house upside down in preparation. Meaning we weren't allowed to go anywhere."

"We've been forced to clean all day," Cara whined.

"She's from another clan, just finished her year away and is on her way back with her decision to pledge. I wonder if while she was away, she lived out Celine's dreams of playing with college boys." Arlana snickered and Celine pretended to hit her.

I exited the water and walked to the shore where I'd left my shoes. Pulling my shirt up, I tugged the water-soaked and clinging fabric from my arms and flung it onto the pebbles. My sisters stared at me as I started unbuttoning my plastered-on jeans. Celine raised a dark, arched eyebrow. Arlana's mouth opened as though she were about to speak but found herself absent of words. Cara took a step toward me but stopped. My chin jutted out. I didn't care. They could stare at my darker than normal scales all they wanted; I wasn't going to tell them anything about today. I refused to relive even a second of it.

I finally pried the metal button of my jeans from its entrapment and looked up at my sisters. "Hungry?" I asked in a nonchalant sort of way.

"Of-course," Cara crooned.

I pushed my soaked jeans down my legs and kicked them off without taking my eyes from my sisters. "How does shark sound? I could really use a good kill." Something with skin to bite into.

CHAPTER NINE

)(

Monday morning, after we arrived at school, I told my sisters I needed to stop by the school library to drop off an overdue book and try to talk the librarian into not suspending my library card as punishment. Arlana—the research and library lover that she was—agreed I should take care of it. Of course, I didn't have a late book, and had no intentions of talking to the librarian.

My eyes combed the halls for David. When I spotted the back of a dark gray Henley, the thudding in my heart quickened and I started to hurry over to the boy until he turned and revealed his true identity: not David. Idiot, running around after a boy. Gah!

Just having a relationship with him, even a friendship, constituted betrayal to my sisters and aunts. And I couldn't just turn off my distrust for humans in general, human men in particular. They were domineering and full of pride from what my aunts taught us. Only, that first time I talked to David, he didn't seem like either of those things. Of course our little encounter at school hadn't began or ended in friendliness either. But even then, he wasn't full of himself. Even when I yelled at him, he exuded a calm, humble confidence.

I had to talk to him. Just to clear a few things up. It would be fine. I decided to take the reins in this conversation—get what I needed, assurance that he understood the whole kiss in the woods couldn't happen again. I'd march right up to him, and tell him there could be no confusion over the rules. We were just going to be semi-friends, get to know each other. No public displays of even knowing each other. The last thing I needed was for the kelpies to think I was hunting humans close to their home. Assuming the kelpies were still on the island, which, since the boys' truck wasn't in the parking lot this morning, I wondered.

As I rounded a corner listening for his smooth voice, I heard my sisters down the hall. They had to be huddled around Celine's locker. If they saw me, they'd wonder why I wasn't in the library. I made a U-turn away from their direction and headed toward the library.

Staring into the big windows that separated the rows of books and desktops from the hall, I slowed my pace. Where was he?

A hand wrapped around my right bicep from the back and a voice melted into my ear, "There you are. I've been waiting for you." His scent covered me and lit little fireworks inside my stomach.

I did a half turn to my right and looked up at him. "Waiting?" I choked out.

"Yeah, I know your first period class is around here. I need to talk to you."

While I enjoyed his touch, the fact that he had stolen my thunder kind of irked me a bit. *I* wanted to be the one who came from behind and told *him* we needed to talk. I had planned it all out in my head. In addition, I also wanted to pull him into the supply closet and inform him how this *relationship* was going to—no, not a relationship. Never a relationship.

"Let's talk in here." He moved his hand from my arm to the small of my back, directing me into the library, past the computers and a few rows of books to the back where the reference materials covered the shelves.

"Listen," he began, looking into my eyes.

"No, you listen." I backed away from him a few steps until a book-laden shelf stopped me.

"I will," he interrupted, "but I really need to get this out." His eyes appeared genuine, teetering on sad.

Fine. I'd listen to what he had to say.

"You are the most beautiful creature I've ever seen," he started.

I almost told him to stop right there, but I loved that he called me a creature.

He paused and watched me for a moment.

"Ever since I first saw you that night at your house over dinner, I couldn't stop thinking about you. I wanted to get to know you. And then you completely blew me off." He smiled, reached forward, and picked up a small cluster of my dark hair resting on my shoulder, intertwining his fingers through it. "There's something about you. I don't know, I guess I can see it in your eyes. And when you kissed me Saturday, I was pleasantly surprised...no, I take that back, I was pleasantly shocked." He dropped my hair and took a step back.

My muscles loosened and I relaxed, leaning against the shelf behind me rather than feeling trapped by it.

"But, as hard as I try, I can't get one fact out of my mind." His arms crossed in front of his chest.

"Fact?" I asked, perplexed by the sudden chill emanating from his stance.

"All yesterday I kept trying to tell myself to forget about you blowing me off, to pretend like our kiss erased it all and started a whole new beginning, but I can't. I need to know what you want because honestly, reading you is more confusing than trying to read a book written in hieroglyphs." His eyes bounced from me to the floor, and back to me. "And just to be crystal clear, I don't know hieroglyphs." A muscle jerked in his forearm. Why were his sleeves always up? His arms were so distracting.

"Hello, are you even listening?" his voice sank an octave deeper. I looked up from his folded forearms to see his eyes searching me.

I didn't know what to say. This friendship with a human thing was already too hard, and we'd only just started. But the way his eyes exposed an inner tenderness he now worked at protecting, I couldn't just walk away.

Hmm. What did I want from *him*? I didn't know. I didn't even know why exactly I was standing here talking to him when every rule forbade it. Honestly, though, I wanted to smell him, to watch him, and part of me still wanted to bite him. "Yes, I heard you. I'm just thinking. I want you." Yeah, that about summed it up.

David closed the distance between the two of us in two steps. "I *want* you, too." He shook his head and peered down at his feet. "I don't mean I want you like *that*. Well, actually—"

"I know what you meant." Seeing as we were talking about our wants, I might as well act on one of mine. I reached down to pull his arm closer to me and with a slight shudder of worry, I ran my fingers across the exposed skin of his forearm. It felt even softer than it looked. "I'm not supposed to be talking to you," I whispered, while the words pounded in my head with demanding screams.

I had to think clearly. I needed to say what I'd intended. "We need to be just friends and keep it a secret," I added.

His fingers glided up and down my right arm. My eyes widened to pierce his and my breath caught in my throat. To siren-kind, rubbing the right arm was a show of deep affection, connection.

"How did you know?" I mouthed, as his hand against my arm shot bolts of electricity into my heart, melding an invisible titanium rope from me to him. A flurry of pleasure spun within me followed by a layer of tranquility.

"Why aren't you *allowed* to talk to me?"

I blinked and pulled myself from the ocean of enjoyment he had created by easing my arm from his touch. "It's complicated."

"That's a generic answer like 'I don't want to talk about it,'" he said.

"Pretty much," I half-whispered, half-spoke.

David's gaze lingered on my hair and then my eyes.

"We're late for first period." He placed his arm around my shoulders and directed me toward the library exit doors. His arm didn't feel foreign against my skin, as I assumed it would.

"The final bell hasn't rung yet."

"Yeah, it just did. You didn't hear it?" he asked.

"Nope. Lost in thought, I guess."

Before we passed the last row of shelves and faced the windows leading to the hall, I stopped and looked up at him. "We're just friends."

David nodded with a slow smile. I'd have given anything to read that boy's mind.

"I'm not supposed to be talking to you, or really be seen with you," I reminded.

"Right. The whole complicated thing."

"I kind of played that down a little. It's more than complicated. If my aunts ever found out about us, you'd probably never see me again." He chuckled a little, but I was dead serious.

"Okay, so I'll just pretend I'm not in the process of learning hiero-glyphs." With a smirk, he released me from his half-embrace and walked out of the library.

He didn't look back once.

I'd know, I was watching.

CHAPTER TEN

)(

My sisters and I shuffled out of our red Ford Focus parked in our driveway around the side of the B&B, and grabbed our bags from the trunk.

"Yeah, they're saying he's losing it, that he might have to go to rehab," Celine said. My sisters had spent the whole drive home from school discussing the latest gossip.

Hell, I'd spent the whole day hearing people talk about how Skater Boy, Brian, went on a drug bender and bit himself. Everyone was whispering about it in first period. Guilt and remorse filled me to brimming. And if I was honest, embarrassment too. By fourth period I'd heard the forced drug rehab part and decided that maybe something good had come out of it after all. What troubled me more, though, was that Sean and Kaven hadn't shown up to school either.

"Celine, did Sean say anything about going on a trip?" I asked, glad to change the subject.

Celine turned from the front passenger seat to answer me. "No. It's weird. He hasn't tried to contact me, and he's not answering my texts. I have no clue why he wasn't at school today."

With my backpack strap hoisted over my shoulder, I followed Cara around to the front of our home, situated on a cul-de-sac type street with no other houses nearby, while Arlana and Celine chatted outside.

All three of my aunts sat in the front room, waiting. Two of them, Aunt Dawn and Aunt Rebecca shared the white and dark green pinstriped couch while Aunt Anise sat on the matching love seat. My three aunts stood when Cara and I entered the room, waving us to take a seat. They did the same when Celine and Arlana walked through the door.

I stared into each of my aunts' faces, trying to read their expressions. Our clan meetings were infrequent at best and usually the result of a broken rule or devastating news. Had the kelpies finally reached out? Did my aunts know about David and me in the library? Who would have told them? Or were they about to spill the beans about the whole Provider thing? I wasn't sure which idea terrified me more. I clamped my lips together and wrung my hands in my lap, anticipating the worst.

Cara shared the loveseat with her mother, Aunt Anise. Celine sat between her mother, Aunt Dawn, and Aunt Rebecca. I sat in one of the high-back chairs nearest the window while Arlana sat in the other.

"How was school today, girls?" Aunt Anise asked in her usual, friendly tone, which didn't necessarily mean all was well. She resembled Cara, or should I say Cara resembled her? Aunt Anise wore her wavy blond hair in a ponytail while wisps of golden strands framed her delicate face. Her eyes were brown like Cara's, but unlike Cara, she had specks of hazel on the outer rims of her irises. While she spoke, she rested her hand atop Cara's thigh.

"Good, Mom. But, glad to be home." Cara repaid her mother's warm smile with one of her own.

"Yes," Celine agreed. "Glad to be home. And glad I won't have much longer pretending to be one of them."

I yearned for the friendly banter to be over so the real reason we were called together—sitting in a semi-circle—would be revealed.

"Yes, the winter and fall will fly by in no time," Aunt Anise said with a laugh.

"And soon honey, things will be different." Aunt Dawn brushed strands of her hair from her shoulder. She looked nothing like Celine. The only trait they had in common was their complete self-assurance. While Celine's eyes were blue, her mother's eyes were gray. Aunt Dawn's hair was a deep shade of auburn, unlike the black locks her daughter so stylishly pinned up with little silver sparkly clips. Both had full lips, but they were shaped differently, and even their noses differed.

"Which is exactly why we wanted to talk to you," Aunt Anise added. "Ladies, we have something of a private nature to discuss."

Aunt Dawn stood from the couch to pace the floor. "My sisters and I have decided to take part in something that will change the way we live." A smile stretched across her face and her eyes glimmered. "Normally, we don't like leaving you for more than a night or two, but we think you're old enough now, and have proven yourselves to be mature and ready to handle this responsibility." She eyed her daughter with satisfaction.

Excitement twinkled in all three of my aunts' eyes. Even quiet, introspective Aunt Rebecca, Arlana's mom, sat at the edge of her seat in anticipation with her hands on her knees.

Wait. This wasn't about me. The lump made its way down my throat, helping me to breathe easier.

"Where are you going?" Arlana watched Aunt Dawn pace the room.

"To the largest gathering of our kind in many years, and all three of us must attend. They're taking a vote, and we want as many in favor of this new change as possible." Aunt Dawn picked up a mermaid statue from a bookshelf along the wall and eyed it for a moment, smiling.

"I don't understand, Mother. What's so big that there's going to be a vote for it?" Celine asked, playing with strands of her dark hair.

Aunt Dawn stole a glance from Aunt Anise and then Aunt Rebecca. "I wish I could tell you, believe me. More than that, I wish you four could join us in the vote, but you're still underage and have yet to formally accept this way of life, so you're not allowed to know until the decision has been made official." She gently placed the statue back onto the shelf.

"Does this have something to do with the Council visiting a while back?" Arlana asked.

"Yes." Aunt Dawn thought for a moment before continuing. "They were on their way to visit the clan of our soon-to-be guest, Vanessa."

"Which reminds me," Aunt Anise added. "We'll be gone a week, so during that time the bed and breakfast will have no guests, other than Vanessa of course."

"And," Aunt Dawn's eyes bounced to each of my sisters and me, "we want you to be extra cautious about your hunts, the rule to always take a sister applies more so while we're gone. In fact, we'd prefer you only go for a swim when the four of you can go together, otherwise, don't risk it. You could be hurt or spotted, without us to help you. Four sets of eyes to watch out for danger is better than two." She paused.

"And Allura." Aunt Dawn's gray eyes caught mine. "No shark-hunting while we're gone. We'd hate to think of what would happen if the hunt took a turn for the worse."

"Okay." When I'd told my aunts about killing the shark, they were almost giddy with excitement, asking if I'd planned my attack or just moved from instinct, and from what part of the body did I take my first bite.

Aunt Rebecca spoke up, "And if any of you do accidently get injured, you know where to locate the laso plant that will heal just about anything."

We nodded.

Every now and then, my aunts would take my sisters and me on a type of field trip with one lesson in mind: the art of survival. When we were much younger, they taught us what not to touch in the ocean and whom to stay away from. Then the instructions progressed to how to find a quick snack, then to meals, and then matured to more complicated kills. Only recently had my aunts moved past the "eating" part of teaching and onto the healing practices of using medicines of nature.

One night about a year ago, while deep in the dark cave crevices offered by the Puget Sound, Aunt Rebecca brought us to a particular kind of seaweed: one that was so rare, she refused to pluck even a strand of the poky, but otherwise plain-looking plant. She insisted we take turns inspecting it while its roots still clung to the ground, noticing the tiny details and how it differed from other sea plants. She'd called it Iaso, after the Greek Goddess known for healing and recuperation.

"One leaf from this plant," she had whispered as though her voice could render it useless, "may save you someday." When she had continued, her eyes were cloaked in sadness. "You are sirens—fast and fierce—but never believe you are invincible." She had swallowed hard and continued. "If ever a day comes when one of you is outnumbered and overpowered, whether on land or in the sea, only place one strand, textured side down, onto each one of her wounds. Her skin will absorb the medicinal properties it carries and completely heal within hours."

As we sat in the light green-painted living room sprinkled with white book shelves, I thought of the dainty little sea plant, hidden from the world. "I understand," I answered. "We will be careful not to need the Iaso plant. While you're gone we'll eat mussels, and only the fish who are dying to be eaten."

Cara giggled.

"Good." Aunt Dawn took her seat again beside Celine. "Now, onto some lighter news." She smiled and as though she couldn't sit still. She popped up from the couch again to stand and address us. "Vanessa should be here any day now. She called today from Seattle, very happy to soon be an official member of her siren clan, and would still love to stay with us to rest for a day or two before going home to California. You will meet her at Deadman Island and lead her here."

"So she's not just passing through?" Celine jumped up to hug her mother. "I'm so happy for her. I can't wait to meet her."

I chuckled. Celine's face glowed, but I was pretty sure her excitement had more to do with coveting Vanessa's stories from a year of freedom and less to do with Vanessa becoming an adult member of her clan.

Aunt Dawn gently grasped her daughter's elbows. "This is definitely cause for celebration. We wish we could welcome her personally, but she understands." She wrapped her arms around Celine and squeezed. "I love you, darling. I'll miss you."

Arlana sprang from her seat and threw her hands out in front of her. "What, you're leaving now?"

In one quick movement Aunt Rebecca stood and wrapped an arm around her daughter's back. "Calm down. We were waiting for you to get home from school before we left."

I scanned the room until I saw three dark blue, almost black, waterproof drybags resting against the wall near the kitchen.

"But why so quick?" Arlana still looked at Aunt Dawn even though her own mother held her close.

"It's a meeting we've been waiting years for, but because of outside forces, it couldn't have been planned for more than a day out." Aunt Dawn released Celine, walked to the door and grabbed her bag.

"What do you mean "outside forces"?" Arlana's voice spiked as her eyes tightened. "Shouldn't we know what's going on with our own clan?"

Aunt Dawn, still holding her bag, moved to Arlana, now in the middle of the living room. She placed her hand on Arlana's left shoulder. "Don't worry about it. It's not necessary that you know everything. I completely understand that you want to be in the know and therefore in control, and I even find that a commendable quality under most circumstances." Aunt Dawn's smile dropped from her face. "But your inability to remember your place in this clan seems to go hand–in–hand with your need for control, which will only hurt you and irritate your aunts."

Arlana's eyes widened before her head dropped. "Sorry, Aunt Dawn. I was out of line."

But was she? She'd only asked a simple question. Aunt Dawn had always been the controlling one out of us all. Lately, though, she seemed to be getting worse, more insistent that everyone in the house take her lead and not question her.

Aunt Rebecca squeezed her daughter tighter, but wouldn't look at her sister. She only stared at her own daughter.

"Realizing your faults is important in the process of changing them." Aunt Dawn removed her hand from Arlana's shoulder and turned toward the kitchen, leading to the back door.

"Oh, and no kelpies in the house," Aunt Dawn turned to say.

"Why would we ever let them in our house, our territory?" Celine asked as though she took offense that her mother would imply she'd allow Sean into her room while the adults were away.

Of course I knew the real reason behind my aunt's words. A kelpie had already graced our front room. I wondered if Celine had smelled his presence that day after she'd gotten home.

Aunt Anise hugged Cara tightly and kissed her cheek before retrieving her bag. My two aunts walked through the kitchen and exited the house.

I heard a delicate whisper behind me, "Keep them safe, Allura." Aunt Rebecca's hand grazed my right arm as she walked past me to join her sisters.

Keep them safe? I'd already promised not to hunt shark while my aunts were out of town. Was this another veiled instruction involving the kelpie twins? The boys who'd mysteriously disappeared?

Before Aunt Rebecca closed the door behind her, she gazed at her daughter for a split second, and then winked at me.

Silence echoed through the green and white living room as the four of us simultaneously listened for the older sirens, their steps light and dainty as they made their way across the back lawn and down the cliff. Once we were sure they had submerged in the ocean waters, Celine slapped her knee and rolled back into the couch.

"I can't believe you said that!" Celine shook her head and snickered.

"I know! I have no clue what came over me, but as soon as the words came out, I wished they hadn't," Arlana said, her eyes still wide with worry.

"You may be able to talk to your mom that way, but my mom won't take it. I wouldn't dare raise my voice to her or question her." Celine smiled and shook her head.

"Seriously." Arlana fell back onto the love seat and let out a big exhale.

"Well." Celine stood with a twinkle in her eye. "We're free for a day or two before Vanessa comes. What do you want to do?"

"You guys go ahead. I've got homework." I grabbed my backpack and headed toward the stairs, thankful to have the house to myself long enough to collect my thoughts. Maybe I'd try to get ahold of Kaven again, for the umpteenth time.

"No you don't." Celine followed after me until I stopped and turned to look at her. "You'll have plenty of time to do homework when Vanessa's here babysitting us. Today, we play." Her eyes narrowed as one side of her lips turned upward.

She grabbed my wrist and pulled me to the living room. "You still have the car keys, Arlana?"

"Yup." Arlana produced them from her pocket and jiggled them in the air.

"Then let's go have some fun, sisters." Celine turned on her heel and sauntered to the front door.

Before rescuing the drowning woman, "fun" with my sisters lined up pretty well with the meaning of the word. Now, though, as my sister pulled me from my tornado of thoughts and self-containment, I hoped their idea of fun didn't end up with another nearly-dead human and all eyes on me.

CHAPTER ELEVEN

)(

After school, and a day of pretending I didn't know David, I finally found myself at home. Alone. Finally, I had the time I'd craved the day before, when my sisters whisked me off to hike that turned out to be mundanely enjoyable.

My phone had buzzed with a text from David when I'd walked in the door. I promptly deleted it, after checking it of course.

He'd only said "Hey", but I didn't want my sisters noticing even one text from a human boy and then deciding to stay and give me the third degree.

Since Vanessa hadn't arrived yet, my sisters figured they were still on homework hiatus and had decided to go hiking. I bowed out, with an excuse about being behind on calculous handouts.

Cara put up a semi-fit, but her toddler moment didn't last long. She probably figured I'd join them when I finished. And maybe I would...if they were still hiking by the time I completed my phone conversation with the human boy I couldn't get out of my head.

After the door shut behind my sisters, I ran to my room and peered out the window, watching them drive off. It wasn't enough to hear them leave; I wanted to see it too. I opened my textbook and binder to lay homework paraphernalia on my bed. I had to start on my calculous in case they forgot something or came home and Cara asked me about an assignment. I motored through most of the first half of math, only having to skip one problem I couldn't quickly figure out. I didn't particularly love math, but I wasn't horrible at it either. I did, however, hate having to show my work on each equation.

The second half took a little longer as the equations got progressively complicated.

My eyes wandered to my phone. Maybe I'd done enough for now to prove I'd actually worked on homework if my sisters checked.

As if the phone knew I was considering picking it up, the thing buzzed. The screen flashed that I'd received another text from David. I unlocked the phone to retrieve the message.

I missed you today.

Oh, I responded.

His next text came right after I pressed send.

I know I got to see you, but I want to talk to you.

I didn't know how to reply. Did that mean he wanted me to call him?

Can I see you? he asked as though he'd read my mind.

Now? I texted back.

Is there a better time today?

I thought about his question for a moment. No. My sisters would be home later and then Vanessa would arrive sometime tonight or tomorrow. I wouldn't be able to just slip out with a house full of super-hearing sirens. And honestly I wanted to see him, too.

My phone buzzed again and I pictured him texting me. In a Henley. With his sleeves pushed up.

Allura?

The tips of my fingers grazed over the screen, responding almost effortlessly. Where do you want to meet up?

I waited a second. I began reading his next text before my phone even had time to buzz.

I want to show you a place I found in the woods.

The forest was out, at least while my sisters occupied it.

No. Can't go to the forest right now.

Not the forest, he answered back. Meet me outside Clover Woods.

Clover Woods was a privately owned piece of property filled with huge, ancient trees. I'd gone there with my sisters once before, but seeing as it was private property, my aunts instructed we stay out.

No one's allowed in Clover Woods.

His answer came quick, like he knew I'd argue with him. Oh, I didn't know. But you've got to see this place.

I thought about it for a minute. Privacy was a good thing when it came to me being with David. Plus, it's not like the owner lived on the property to somehow catch us.

Okay. I'm on my way.

I slipped the phone into my back jeans pocket and left the house.

The closer I got to our meeting place, the quicker my legs moved. I had to consciously slow myself a few times because I'd look down at my legs and notice they were moving inhumanly fast. I couldn't tell if this urgency was from my inner siren. I'd never met up with a human boy before; I'd never wanted to.

It was as though the closer I got, the more he pulled me to him.

I slowed as I came to the thick line of evergreen trees bordering the property. I scanned the area for people. No one. Good. I walked deep enough into the woods to not be noticed by a random car driving past, and leaned against a tree trunk. When I heard a crack, I pushed myself from the tree and searched for the source of the sound, absorbing the air around me.

David came out from behind a moss-covered tree, his smile wide and eyes twinkling. I breathed his scent in and held the woodsy-clean smell in my nostrils longer than usual before exhaling. He took a few steps toward me, and while I'd meant to stay right where I stood and wait for him to come to me, I found myself closing the gap between us.

I almost hugged him, but stopped myself. His left arm swooped behind my back, and his fingers pressed lightly into my side as he pulled me into him.

"Glad you could come." His hand slid from my side to my right arm. A quiver swept through my body.

We're just friends. We're just friends. I prayed my inner siren would behave herself.

"You ready?" His fingers laced mine and he led me to a tree with two beige towels hanging from a low branch. He grabbed the towels and headed farther away from the street, deeper into the woods.

"So, where are we going?" I asked, staying in step with him.

"A couple days ago I found this amazing lake. I almost went right past it because it's so well hidden. When you told me yesterday, in the library, that we needed to stay a secret, I thought of this lake and wanted to bring you here." He smiled as he faced forward.

He walked quickly and I thought of pretending to have a hard time keeping up since my legs were shorter than his, but decided that although I wouldn't share who I really was with him, I also wouldn't pretend to be someone else. I'd be myself…to a degree.

"Why the towels?" I asked, eyeing the beige terrycloth he held in his other arm, the one that wasn't attached to me.

"I'm kind of weird." He looked at me and then went back to staring ahead. "Have you ever heard of those old folks who like to get together and swim in ice cold water in the dead of winter?"

"Yes."

"I wonder if maybe my birth parents were related to them somehow because the cold just doesn't bother me. It's like a shock to my system, in a good way."

"So, you want to go for a swim? In the hidden lake?" I didn't have to make my voice sound skeptical; it went there on its own.

"I know, it sounds crazy. You don't have to do it if you don't want to." He pushed a low hanging branch full of dark green needles to the side for us to walk through. The branches grew denser as we walked and the tree trunks closer to one another.

The temperature of the water made no difference to me, but the idea of absorbing stagnant water…brown, stagnant water. It disgusted me just thinking about it.

I decided to tell him it was too cold, but not yet. Not until he saw me cringe from dipping a toe in the murky water. Plus, there was something else I wanted to talk about besides cold and murky water.

"Birthparents?" I asked.

"Yeah, I'm adopted."

"I had no idea," I said with a laugh.

"Really? My parents and sister look nothing like me. They're Italian and I'm very much not."

"I guess I hadn't noticed," I said.

"You know," he admitted, "I actually assumed you were adopted, too, because you look nothing like your sisters."

I arched an eyebrow.

"Are you half islander, or Asian or something?" he asked.

I shrugged my shoulders because I honestly didn't know. If I had to guess, though, my facial features matched the Filipino kids in school more than any others.

"Well," he said, "you're not completely white, that's obvious."

"With us, race isn't a big deal," I finally said. We shared the same siren culture no matter what shape our eyes resembled. We were more interested in the colors of our scales than the color of our skin. The men whom our mothers chose to conceive us with weren't given more than a moment of thought, so their ethnicity never mattered either.

"My mom says she thinks my birth mother was Hispanic." He swept his hand out in front of us to remove another branch from our route. "But my parents are great people. And my little sister's fun. I couldn't imagine life without them, so I'm okay with not sharing genetics with them." He moved behind me and wrapped his hands around my waist to lift me over a dormant blackberry bush.

I tried not to swat his hands away.

Once I was safely over the bramble, he jumped over.

I wanted to ask a question, but couldn't find a tactful way to do it. I gave up the quest and muddled through. "So, when were you, why were you, I mean…"

He laughed. "I was adopted when I as a baby. A newborn from what my mom tells me. She worked with my birth mother. My mom said it was weird because the woman acted really happy about the pregnancy, excited, and said she had plenty of help and support to take care of me."

"What changed?"

"I don't know. Right after I was born, someone brought me to my mom's work. The lady told my mom that my birth mother had changed her mind. She handed me to my mom and then left. My mom never heard from her again. She tried to find her." He pushed another branch from our path. "We're almost there."

"That must be hard, being adopted."

"Not really. How can I miss what I never knew?" I watched his face as he spoke, as he looked forward along our path. His eyebrows furrowed for a quick second.

"I never knew my mother, and I miss her more than words can say." I didn't mean to say that, but I didn't regret sharing it either.

"Did she leave you?"

"Sort of."

"That's why you live with your aunts." His voice was steady, as though respecting the depth of our conversation, without making it into an emotional event.

"Yeah. They raised me, but none of them feel very motherly to me." I shouldn't have let that personal tidbit slip.

"Well then our situations are different," David assured me. "My mom stepped up and loved me, took care of me like her own. No one stepped up for you."

His words hurt and made sense at the same time, like rubbing ointment on a raw wound. No one had ever stepped up for me. I loved my clan and I knew they loved me. But I wasn't blind to the reality of our household situation. Each of my sisters had a mother, and each of my aunts had a daughter. We all had each other. But unlike them, I didn't have someone who was just mine.

"Here it is." He pointed to a wall of thorny blackberry bushes covered by tall, old fir trees whose branches hung low and touched the tops of the bushes.

"Where?" My eyes scanned from side to side. Nothing but plants and dirt, although the scent of water called to my skin and nose.

"Here." He reached forward with both his hands and parted the scruffy bushes.

I watched his arms a little too intensely, waiting for the thorns to cut him, to expose a hint of what hid beneath his skin.

I licked my lips in anticipation.

Embarrassed, I bounced my eyes away, to the ground, to my feet, and then to the bush.

"Allura?"

My eyes darted to his. "Yes?"

He motioned with his head for me to look through the chasm he'd created. "It's through there."

CHAPTER TWELVE

)(

I stepped closer and peered through the opening in the branches David had created. "Wow," I whispered on a breath.

Ten feet beyond the bushes lay an oval lake, its serene top interrupted by gentle ripples with each breeze. Huge, smooth rocks jutted out from the water's edge on the long side and an old, barely-there dock stood at the center of the lake's shorter side. Tall surrounding evergreens reflected their presence, turning the water into a huge mirror, with the rocks as its frame.

"I know," David commented.

We both gazed in silence a while before David spoke again. "Here, let me help you." He pushed himself into the small opening in the bush and stretched his arms wide to create a space large enough for me to fit through.

I lowered my head to climb through the leafy branches and under his outstretched arms. Brushing against his skin made heat dance along mine. I wanted to linger and run, kiss and bite, at the same time.

"Thanks," I muttered, stepping quickly through. I breathed deep, trying to gain control of both my hormones and my instincts while watching the water ripple and glide before me. "How did you find this place?"

"I was hiking one day and came across it. It reminded me of you, of that first day we met when you were sitting on that patch of grass staring out at the water," he said. A sweet smile came over him. "That's when you told me your favorite things to do are swim and hike, and when I saw this place I thought you'd like it, hiking to get here and then swimming once we arrived." He pushed and twisted his way through the bush to stand beside me. "When you said we had to meet in secret, I figured this place would be perfect."

David interlaced his fingers in mine. I nearly jumped at his touch and moved to part our hands. But he only gave a reassuring squeeze as he led me to the rickety dock.

"Don't worry, it'll hold us, I've already tried it."

The dock didn't scare me. What would happen? I'd fall into the pristine water? Just seeing the glasslike blue, smelling the freshness, I couldn't wait to be submerged in it. If it smelled this amazing, how much better would it taste? Mucky and stagnant this was certainly not.

"Let's just dip our feet in at first. If you think you can handle it, we'll dip the rest of ourselves in." David set the towels down and pulled the hiking boots and gray socks from his feet.

I gave a little kick with each leg to toss my canvas shoes off. I wanted to rip the clothes from my body and run into the water. But rather than pound the wooden slats and jump into the air, my foot pushed my empty flats together and I took a seat on the dock beside David.

Behave like a human. Behave like a human.

Slowly, I sunk my feet into the water. The moment my skin touched the liquid it flowed into me, through me. A human I most certainly was not. And in this moment, I couldn't be more thankful for that fact.

I sighed.

It tasted amazing. It reminded me of freshly cut slices of cucumber.

"You like it?" he asked, touching my hand as it rested against the splintery wood of the dock.

"Very much. Thanks." I sighed again, thankful for the opportunity to pause and just be. It was a need I didn't know I'd had.

"You want to jump in?" He arched his eyebrow and smirked as though he'd just issued a challenge.

"Yes!" I stood and started unbuttoning my pants, excited to see what the lake held under her watery-glass top. Yes, a body of water is breathtakingly beautiful, but no matter how gorgeous it appears on top, you can bet it's ten times more underneath.

"Whoa, what are you doing?" His eyes bounced from my face to my fingers, now pulling at my zipper.

"Oh, sorry." I zipped and buttoned my pants back up. *Duh, act like a human.*

"Sorry," David said as he cleared his throat and pulled himself to stand at the edge of the dock. "I spaced on the whole bathing suit part. Have you ever swam in your clothes?" He exhaled and met my gaze.

"Um, I didn't know that was a thing." Who would want to swim in anything more than skin? I mean, of course I've seen humans in bathing suits, but even those looked uncomfortable to me.

"Let's make it a thing. Come on, we'll do it together. You game?" He walked near the beginning of the dock, where broken boards rested on dirt, and reached his hand out to me.

"Sure." I skipped over to him and placed my hand in his. This time my body didn't feel the need to pull away at his touch.

Apparently, getting naked was out of the question, but at least I could run into the water, or in this case run and jump into the water. Hand in hand, we sprinted, our bare feet pounding the wooden slats, thudding the planks in unison. Right before the wood came to an abrupt stop, we pushed off, the resistance flinging us into the air. Our hands held tightly to each other as our bodies splashed down and the water rose to meet us.

My pores absorbed the sweet liquid. Swimming every inch of the lake, experiencing all of it, became my new goal. I wriggled my hand free from David's to explore...until I noticed him paddling his legs, pushing toward the surface to breathe.

I'd forgotten, I was supposed to need to breathe too.

I copied his movements. Once we reached the surface, he took in a deep breath and I followed suit, careful not to choke myself on too much air. I'd never had to gasp for breath before; it didn't feel natural, though I prayed to the Goddess that it at least looked natural.

David leaned forward in the water, his legs kicking to keep him in place. "How do you feel? Okay? Too cold?"

"Perfect," I said on a breath that, in my opinion, looked incredibly human.

We floated silently in the water for a few moments before David asked another question. "So, does your mom ever call or anything?"

I watched the liquid beat gently across his chest and slink back again. "She killed herself when I was a baby." A twinge of guilt shot through me for revealing my mother's secret. I never liked admitting she'd committed suicide.

"Oh, I'm so sorry."

I didn't respond, I only watched the water and listened to David's breathing.

"That's rough," he added.

"How could it have been that horrible, though?" I asked in a moment of too-honest reflection. "She'd just had a baby girl." A tear welled in my eye and I blinked it back, out of existence. "She should have had a happy life with a new baby, full of hope. I should have been enough for her."

"You never know." David exhaled, his voice gentle. "Depression makes people do things they wouldn't normally do."

"Maybe." I pictured my mom holding me while weeping. Had she been depressed? My aunts had never mentioned her having any issues like that.

"Did your aunts ever tell you why she did it?" he asked.

I shook my head. My mom's death wasn't something we talked about. Everyone knew about it, at least every siren I came into contact with. They had to. Our kind was spread out, but everyone still knew each other's business.

"I think that's why my birth mother gave me up," David said, picking a strand of seaweed from his chest and releasing it at arm's length away from him. "I think she had postpartum depression. And you probably know this, but I have to say it because for a long time I didn't know it." His kicking legs slowed and he leveled a concerned gaze at me. "Your mother's act had nothing to do with you. Just like my birth mother giving me up had nothing to do with me." He reached for me until his fingers rested on my shoulder.

I nodded and fought the urge to run the back of my hand across my eyes.

"Trust me." His eyes sparkled with playfulness again. "I mean, what woman in her right mind would give up a guy like me?" His hands outlined his frame as though he were for sale.

"Please," I scoffed with a crack of a smile.

"What? I'm a catch! Complete with no friends, no sports hobbies, and an addiction to junk food. This right here," he motioned to his whole body again, "will be damn sexy in thirty years. Like I said, a catch."

I laughed out loud and splashed water at his face. "You're not friendless."

"Oh, you're right. I do have a friend. Who I have to pretend...isn't."

I splashed David again and slithered down under the water. He dove after me. I raced around the rocks to the center of the lake when I realized it should be time for me to need to breathe again. I pushed to the surface and looked around just in time to see him barreling toward me.

"Ah!" I screeched. "You are mine!" I dunked back under the water to meet him head on.

He swam directly past me, flashing a teasing smile as he passed.

I twisted my body around and swam after him, kicking my soaking wet jean-clad legs.

I caught up to him and reached to grab his foot, but he was just out of reach. Cupping my hands and pushing them through the water, I sprung forward to wrap my arm around his waist. Suddenly he stopped and pulled his body upright while still under water. His arms opened wide and before I could change directions, my body glided into his chest. Playfulness left his expression and seriousness took over. I peered up into his eyes, and hovered, our clothed chests barely touching. His left hand came down slowly, his fingers drifted through my hair, brushed my shoulder, and then smoothed across my right arm before resting on the small of my back.

David's head tilted down until his lips caressed mine. The kiss was so soft, so affectionate, I couldn't pull away. When it ended, I opened my eyes to see light glistening in streaming ribbons, dancing through the water and framing David's face. He nodded to the surface, grabbed my hand, and we both kicked our calves to push our bodies up.

"Wow." His fingers ran through his wet, now jet black hair.

"Can most people hold their breath underwater that long?" I asked, before realizing how un-human that question sounded.

David didn't seem to notice, though.

His brown eyes reflected the water glistening below his chin as his soft gaze kept trained on me. His head tilted for a quick second toward the largest group of mostly-submerged rocks along the side of the lake. "What do you think? Sit with me for a while?" He flashed a cheesy don't-you-want-to-sit-with-me smile and started swimming to the rocks.

As we neared the shore, he crawled to the point where his shoulders barely broke through the surface of the water. Turning to lean on his back, he brought his hand above the water. The inviting look he gave me drew me in. I made myself comfortable in the opening under his arm, right against his side. Slipping in next to him felt so comfortable, so natural, that I did it without thinking.

"It helps to keep most of your body submerged in the water."

"What?" I asked, not sure what he was referring to. "Why?"

"It's cold. So to stay warm, it helps to keep your body underwater." He looked down and my eyes followed his. Our bodies were completely submerged, only our heads and shoulders peeked through the surface. "Is it working for you? Or are you too cold? If you're cold I can get you a towel."

"Uh, no thanks, I'm fine."

He raised one eyebrow and lowered the other.

"No, seriously, I'm perfectly fine." *More than perfect.*

He rested on his side, facing me. Lake water wrapped around his shoulder protruding from the surface. He shook slightly, the cold starting to set in. "Swimming in a lake in the middle of winter. Yeah, we're weird." He kissed my forehead. "We can be weird together, though."

"I want to get to know you." His voice was low and quiet, as his mouth hovered near my ear. His fingers wove in and out of my hair.

I wondered if I should remind him of the friend agreement, although the kiss in the water pretty much smashed that regulation to pieces. And the more time I spent with David, the more I was okay with throwing that rule out.

"Okay." I watched my hand swish back and forth under the water between us.

"I think you and I have a lot in common." He watched my hand too.

"Is that a question?" I asked.

"More like an observation."

"Then I have a question."

"Go for it." He watched me, waiting.

"Why did your family move to Friday Harbor?"

"What, that's the big question?" He laughed.

"I never said it would be profound."

"Then the answer is work. My dad's a pathologist at the hospital. He travels between here and a few other hospitals, but his office is here."

"Wow," I said. "Wait. What's a pathologist?"

David laughed. "He basically examines causes and effects of diseases," he answered. "Most people think that sounds cool, but if you hear him talk about it, you wouldn't think it's very interesting."

"So then I assume dinner talk is scary boring?" I asked with a short laugh.

He gave a half snort. "No, he doesn't bring his work home with him. But my mom, she's a different story."

"Oh? What does she do?"

"Since we moved? Lots of scrapbooking."

I let out a belly laugh and rolled onto my back, keeping my head above water.

I gazed at how the lowered sunlight slid across the evergreens in the distance, shifting their colors from fresh greens to dark blues and grays. The sun was setting in an hour. My sisters would be looking for me soon, if they weren't already. They wouldn't think to look for me here, but even if they saw me walking home they'd question where I'd been and why. Especially because I'd told them I couldn't join them on their hike so I could finish my homework. And seeing as I didn't bring my textbooks and a backpack, lying about being at the library wouldn't work.

"It's getting late," I stated, shifting to sit up.

"Here." He stood from the water and jumped from the boulder to the shallow shore of the lake. I could only stare at the Henley plastered to his upper body. "Let me get you a towel."

He jogged around the lake to the dock, grabbed the folded beige towels, and walked back toward me. I rolled from the boulders to tread water while I waited. At the water's edge he held the towel out, extending it as he took the few steps into the shallow end to meet me. With each hand holding the top corners of the outstretched towel, all I could see was his fingers, legs, and the tops of his shoulders and head.

I pushed myself from the pebbles. The water grasped at my clothing. I thought I saw his eyes waver from my face to my chest as my drenched body rose from the liquid. He wrapped the soft, inviting towel around my body and picked me up out of the water enough to take me to the dry shore and set me down.

Rubbing the towel against my arms, he said, "Here, let me warm you up."

I wanted to tell him he couldn't, that it was impossible, but I only smiled and stared into his eyes.

"You planning on walking home in wet clothes too?" I asked, to break the Hallmark movie moment, to say something…anything.

"I'll ride my motorcycle," he answered. "The wind will dry me. Did you need a ride?"

"No, I'm fine," I said, brushing off his offer. "Isn't that cold, though, riding your motorcycle while wet?"

"Yes it is. When can we do this again?" he asked, holding me in a tight embrace.

"Uh." I thought about our company coming. My aunts said Vanessa should be arriving either tonight or tomorrow. Either way, tomorrow was out of the question. It'd be too difficult to elude my sisters with a new guest in town. But, after she'd been here for a day, maybe Vanessa's presence would keep them occupied long enough for me to slip out for a few hours. "The day after tomorrow," I suggested. "How does that work?"

"It isn't ideal, like tomorrow would be, but it works." He gave me a wink. "And next time, bring another set of clothes, dry clothes. Or a bathing suit; there's an original idea." His mouth edged toward my own, but I lowered my head and his lips landed on my forehead.

He backed up. "What's up?"

I had to go. "I'll text you." I peered back up at the sun, now hiding behind the clouds. The moon would be coming soon. I had to get home.

"Hold on. This day can't end like that," David said. He looked away and tapped his foot before explaining. "I can't keep starting from the beginning every time we hang out. You're distant when we first see each other and then you slowly warm up to me and then pull away and say goodbye and it starts all over again the next time. Now you're pulling away and saying goodbye. But I don't want you to be distant when we meet up again."

"Please don't push," I said softly, but with a slight edge of warning.

"I haven't once pushed myself on you," David said, throwing his hands in the air.

"In the lake?" I took a step away from him and shook out my arms, not sure if my body was preparing to lunge at him, or trying to loosen my tightened muscles. I'd never gotten this close to a human; I had no idea where this intense reaction of mine was coming from. Or his.

"Calm down." He motioned to my arms. "I'm not the enemy here."

I took a deep breath in, and exhaled loudly. My arms stilled. I hadn't realized where these irritated feelings came from until they started to dissipate.

He was right.

He wasn't the enemy.

He wasn't the one who kept me from allowing myself to like him.

"You okay now?" he asked.

I nodded.

"Listen, in the lake, I initiated the kiss, but you accepted. What, do you regret kissing me?" He ran his fingers through his hair and waited for my answer.

"No, but life would be easier if I hadn't," I said. "Celine's right. I taunt danger to the point of stupidity." I watched my toes dig into the ground.

"I thought you wanted to start a friendship, and I did too," he started, moving toward me again. "But you're hard to resist. I've never felt a pull like this to another girl. I don't want to lose you, though, so if a friendship is seriously the farthest you want our relationship to go, I'll fucking try my hardest."

I didn't answer. I wanted to, to tell him I had meant what I'd said in the library. Friends only. But if I said that now, I'd be lying.

David's hand drifted across my skin as his fingers lightly brought my chin up. My eyes met his. "Do you only have friend-type feelings for me?" he asked.

I closed my eyes and shook my head. There it was—the truth. I didn't want him to just be my friend. And apparently, I was the last to know of this revelation.

"So, if it's okay with you, I'm going to kiss you now." The corners of his mouth lifted. "Hopefully, third time's a charm."

I thought about my sisters, about my aunts, even about the elders. I knew what they'd say if they found out about us, and I could guess what they'd do, but I had already crossed that line. In their eyes, even befriending David was fraternizing with humans. Male humans.

The seed of rebellion took root deeper within me. I enjoyed

David's company. And shouldn't I be allowed to enjoy myself? Being with David wasn't some curiosity I'd gone too far with, like the woman in the party dress. It was something more—a choice. A decision I should have every right to make on my own.

"Yes," I said, my voice strengthening with each breath. "Kiss me."

CHAPTER THIRTEEN

)(

I turned the corner onto my street to view our big white bed & breakfast in the distance. Tucked between fir trees, it had nothing but a garden and water at its back border. No little red car sat in the driveway.

Good.

I jogged into the house and up to my room. After peeling the wet clothing from my body and pulling on soft sweat pants and a short-sleeve shirt, I threw myself onto the bed.

Just as I plopped the open binder onto my lap, the sound of a motor—less of a rumble and more of a whine—alerted me to the Focus pulling into the driveway. My sisters came through the front door chatting.

"What were you guys thinking about for dinner?" Cara asked the group.

"I don't care," Arlana said. I listened as she threw the car keys into the glass bowl resting on a low table near the front door, the same table Kaven had leaned against the last time I saw him, when he'd promised to check in on me for a final decision. A promise he had yet to uphold.

In less than five seconds Cara stood beside my bed, staring down at the books strewn around me.

"You're so good, Allura." She touched my math book with one finger as though it was contaminated, and turned to fall onto her bed. "Humph. I hate math."

"I don't exactly love it either." I looked over at her staring at the ceiling. "Tired?"

"Kinda." She let out a sigh. "I'm gonna be sore tomorrow."

"I bet." Running in the woods, darting through blurs of greens and browns sounded fun, but I got to enjoy the forest from the water.

With David.

I fought to keep the smile off my face.

"Sisters…" The word floated into the room along with Celine. She looked at me, books everywhere, and shook her head. "You hungry, study girl?"

"I am…" Cara let out a pitiful moan, "famished."

"As long as we don't have to carry your ass from being too hungry to walk, Cara," Celine said. "Plus, I wasn't asking you."

"No, as soon as I hit the water I'll feel better. I think I can drag myself at least that far," Cara said. "And I *was* answering you, whether you asked me or not."

"What do you think about dinner, Allura? Shark sound good?" Celine licked her lips and raised her eyebrows. Celine acted like the obedient daughter when my aunts were around, but when they weren't, her unapologetic wild girl came out in full force.

"Oh, shark would be perfect for dinner after our day of hiking. I need sustenance that'll fill me up. Like, all you can eat style." Cara rolled onto her side and looked at me, her eyebrows raised.

"Not a chance," I answered. "It's fish and clams tonight, ladies." Both sets of eyebrows dropped. "What? You heard your moms. No shark hunting."

"Oh, please," Celine scoffed. "Our moms won't find out."

"Yeah, and I could so sink my teeth into a fleshy shark. Umm." Cara licked her lips. "I'm salivating just thinking about it."

"Sorry." I shook my head. "If they *do* happen to find out, which they have a knack for when it comes to matters involving me, I'd be the one paying for it, not you." I gently pushed the binder from my lap and moved a textbook out of my way so I could get up from the bed.

The three of us met Arlana downstairs in the kitchen near the back door. She had already taken off her shoes and socks and had her water-proof bag slung over her shoulder. "Are we going?"

"Yes, but it'll be boring, wimpy fish for dinner," Celine complained.

"What else were you expecting? We need to be careful while they're gone." Arlana looked over at Cara, shoulders slumped and all. "Seriously Cara, fish was always good enough for you before."

Arlana opened the door and led us down to the dark, empty beach where she placed her drybag on the mist-moistened pebbles. Celine tossed hers and Cara sauntered over and dropped hers onto the pile.

After a quick check to make sure we were alone, we shed our clothing. As I stared out to the welcoming water, David popped into my mind. Part of me wished he were with us, swimming alongside me, hunting with me. But then again, life would be much easier if he were the supernatural hunter rather than the human at risk of being hunted. I shook my head; no, he's not the hunted. He's just not the hunter either.

He didn't have to be one or the other.

Right?

"So," I asked Arlana, right before we jumped into the choppy ocean water. "When will our guest get here?"

"Vanessa?"

"Yes. Is there another guest I should know about?"

"Sometime tomorrow." As soon as the water hit her knees, Arlana's white and light blue scales spread across her shoulders and she jumped into the waves.

I took a couple more steps until the water splashed into my thighs. Turning toward the beach one last time to confirm we were alone, I looked back out at the Puget Sound and immediately slid under the water.

J was the last of my sisters to wake the next morning. Somehow I must have found my way under the covers in my sleep. Probably reliving the towel moment with David in dreamland. I pushed the covers down to my shoulders.

"What's that smile for?" Cara's head pushed through the bedroom door. I gazed sleepily at her. "Oh, I heard you moving around." She answered as though she understood the question on my face.

I folded myself out of bed, first placing my bare feet on the carpeted floor and then pushing my body to an upright position. After I stood for a moment to collect my thoughts, I turned to pull the covers over my pillow and neaten my sleeping mess.

"We've decided it's a lazy day, so grab your pillow," Cara said as she removed her own pillow from her bed.

"What about Vanessa? Shouldn't she be here soon?" I pulled my pillow from under the comforter and followed Cara down the hall.

"No, she called this morning. By the way, you know it's almost afternoon right?" She tilted her head to me and I knew why. Our kind didn't sleep much. We needed maybe a few hours a night of complete rest, if that. I had just slept in. Not normal.

"When is she coming then?" I pretended to ignore her head tilt.

"Tomorrow morning, early, while it's still dark. She's leaving tonight and seeing as every siren on the west coast knows where Deadman Island is, we'll meet up with her there and guide her through the Sound."

Deadman Island wasn't far from us, an uninhabited piece of land in a string of larger islands. A sandy beach covered half the island, while a dense forest and jagged cliffs covered the other half. The Native Americans had legends about the island explaining why they used to find the remnants of men's bodies on it. We had our own stories of Deadman Island, only ours were true.

When we made our way to the living room, Arlana and Celine were sprawled on the green and white striped couch with their pillows balled up underneath their heads, watching a movie. Cara sank into the matching loveseat and curled up with her pillow.

"Movie day?" I asked my sisters as they stared like drones at the television.

"Yup," Arlana and Celine answered in unison.

"I need to go to the library," I said a little too quickly. My sisters continued staring into movie storyland, unphased. "I need to pick up a book for a report."

"Okay," Cara chirped as she repositioned her pillow. "You need a partner to accompany you?"

"Nah, I'll have my cell phone on me if I need anything."

"Okay," Cara answered again.

I loped up the stairs to my room, grabbed two pairs of jeans that looked almost identical, pulled one of them on, and pushed the other into my empty backpack. Rummaging through my drawer, I found another white shirt, similar to the one I wore, and stuffed that into the bag too. Slipping my flats and jacket on, I grabbed my phone and headed out of the house.

While walking toward the woods, I texted David.

Busy?

After a minute he answered back.

No. Want to hang out?

Yes, meet me at the lake. Bring towels.

As soon as I entered the forest, hidden by its own trees and bushes, I sprinted toward the lake. Ferns and wild blackberry vines smacked at my legs, but only for split seconds before my fast pace snapped them from their roots. The deeper I ran into the forest, the darker it became as though I were pushing through layer after layer of curtains that got heavier and thicker as I moved.

Dark emerald fuzzy moss grew up the russet tree trunks, and sage-green porous moss hung from the branches. Little round birds cocked their heads to stare at me and squirrels scurried away to find a hiding spot.

I heard the cawing of the birds David had told me about and ran in that direction until I reached the gangly bush he had helped me climb through the day before. The rangy shrub grew in front of me, shielding my view of the lake.

I grinned as I backed-up a few paces to get a running start. David had been sweet to open a passageway through the bush for me. And while his assistance spoke volumes of his concern for me, it had been unnecessary. My body crouched, pulling me closer to the dead pine needles carpeting the ground. In a burst of power my legs impelled my body up, springing me into the air and over the bush, clearing it by three or more feet. With the lightest of thuds, my feet landed gracefully onto the dirt on the other side of the plant.

I walked to the creaky old dock and pushed my flats from my feet.

I rolled my pant legs and took a seat on the edge of the dock, letting my bare feet hang into the water while I waited. David lived farther from this property than me.

"Ah," I said as my toes wiggled in the liquid.

Bush branches rustled behind me and I shot to my feet to inspect the origin of the sound. David ran from the bushes, sprinted toward the dock, and dropped the towels onto the wooden planks, without stopping. He flew past me and jumped off the dock. His laughter filled the air before he hit the water with a splash. In a hurry, I plunged into the water after him, chasing him.

My arms pushed through the clear water; my legs kicked me forward. My body absorbed the fresh fluid, fueling me. Instinctually, my arm reached out to his foot when I closed in on him. My smile morphed into a serious frown as I fought the water to reach my target. As David moved his legs, his foot came into my grasp and my fingers jetted out, wrapping around his ankle tightly. I yanked on his jean-covered ankle and his body whipped back from the force. A cloud of bubbles escaped his mouth. He stopped swimming and turned to stare at me with wide eyes. My fingers still gripped him. He looked down at my hand and began prying my fingers from his body. As though I were merely a spectator, I watched his hands work against mine.

David wrenched my pinky finger from his ankle and without moving his eyes to my face, he pushed to the surface and coughed, his chest heaving in and out.

I jerked my arm to my side as I gawked at him from below the surface. What just happened? I was playing at first, but then…I wasn't.

Without even a glance in my direction, he swam with his head above water toward the dock.

I wanted to escape, run home and never speak to him again. How could I have done that? One minute I yearned to touch him, and then next I sought him out the way a dog chases a cat. Embarrassment mixed with confusion and a strong dash of what-the-fuck whirled in my mind.

My predator drive was bordering on ridiculous. And yet Kaven was nowhere to be found, still hadn't answered any of my texts or calls. I dreaded the moment he showed up out of the blue to retrieve my clan's response to his ultimatum, but I also kinda needed him.

In the meantime, I had to apologize. Then, if I still wanted to leave, I would.

I paddled to the surface and silently followed David to the dock. He clutched the edge of the wooden slats hanging out over the water and hoisted himself up. I did the same and sat down beside him.

"I'm so sorry, David."

He just looked at me, and what's worse, I couldn't decipher his expression.

"Did I hurt you?" I asked, sure he saw right through me, to the siren lurking beneath my surface.

"What? No, but you shocked me a little," he answered, studying my face as though he couldn't understand my worry.

I beat myself up inwardly for losing control. Since befriending David, I'd assumed that I had the most to lose in our relationship—if we were caught—but now I realized David could lose more than his freedom. It wasn't that I suddenly figured out I was a predator, but I did—for the first time—care deeply for my potential prey.

I gulped down the lump in my throat, expecting the taste of acid to swirl through my mouth. Only, there was no acid. My stomach felt fine too, not churning or burning with hunger.

I almost laughed out loud with relief. I wasn't pursing him to eat. That was good news… In a weird, distorted way.

"I didn't mean to grab you so hard. I just wanted to touch you and lost control a little," I said, still apologetic, but not so embarrassed.

"You're strong." The indecipherable look dropped from his face and he reached his arms to me, pulling me into him. His chin rested on my head. "You're cute…in an intense way."

Cute? Wrapping my hand around his ankle and tugging him toward me under water didn't exactly classify as a cute move.

He took a breath and finished his thought. "Uniquely cute," he said with a laugh. "I've heard of people losing control when touching the one they like, but you just took that to a whole new level."

"Is uniquely cute a good thing?" As I asked the question out loud, another bubbled up inside: why did I care so much what he thought of me?

"It's not boring, so it's a very good thing." A grin shone through his voice.

I tilted my head to kiss his smiling lips, but when my hair brushed past my ears, I heard something else brush against a tree branch in the forest surrounding our lake. My head jerked toward the sound. It was faint, light, gentle, like a bird landing or a huge squirrel scurrying up a tree. My eyes widened.

David must have seen the look on my face. "What's wrong?" he asked, staring off in the direction my eyes led.

"Let's get back in the water." I jumped up and grabbed his hand.

"Wait, why?" He stood, still holding my hand and turned again to look at the forest.

"Because I think it would be fun to run and jump in the water together, holding hands." I peered up at him anticipating, impatient. I didn't want to pull him with me, not after what had just happened with my apparently intense, unique cuteness.

He nodded, and before he could speak, I started running toward the water, his hand still wrapped around mine. My feet pushed off the edge of the dock, shoving us into the air and in the second we hovered above the water, I shouted, "Race you to the big rock!"

I hoped the sound I'd heard wasn't who I thought it was, but I couldn't chance it. I couldn't chance them seeing David, knowing about him.

The water welcomed us with a splash and my legs shoved the water behind us, causing our bodies to collide through the water. I didn't want to let go of his hand. What if he couldn't keep up? I knew he couldn't keep up, but what if he didn't make it to the rock in time? My free arm pulled us while my legs moved in one synchronized motion, impelling us toward the biggest rock along the lake's edge. I could have moved faster if I weren't wearing those damned jeans.

The muffled sound of three gentle thuds on the ground resonated from somewhere near the dock. *Crap.*

Before we reached the rock, while still underwater, I peered at David; his free arm stroking through the liquid with strength. We slinked behind the huge, protruding rock, and broke through the surface of the water. His mouth started to open, but I couldn't chance them hearing his voice, so I kissed him. As my lips pulled away from his, I brought them to his ear and whispered as quietly as possible while still allowing his human ears to hear me.

"Please, I'll explain later." My breath panted the words as fear wound its constricting tentacles around my throat. "Hide behind this rock. When I cough, crawl up onto the bank and stay hidden behind the rock. Don't make a sound, and I mean not a peep. They'll hear you." I pulled my mouth from his ear to look gravely into his eyes. "Don't let them hear you."

I turned and pushed my feet off the rock like a torpedo through the water.

"Allura, we know you're here." Celine's voice wafted from the dock, and down through the lake water. "We heard you talking about racing to the rock."

I popped my head above the surface to see my three sisters staring straight at me.

CHAPTER FOURTEEN

)(

"What are you doing?" Arlana scanned the lake with a look of disgust.

"Swimming. What does it look like?" I wanted so badly to turn and make sure I couldn't see David from where my sisters stood, but that would be too obvious.

"Why would you swim in lake water?" Arlana eyed the water as if it were poisonous.

"Actually, it tastes amazing—almost fresh and a little citrusy. It's hard to explain." I snapped my mouth shut when I saw Cara slowly bend down toward the water. I should have told them it was disgusting and that I was weird for swimming in it. Maybe they'd have gone home.

"It doesn't look like most lakes." With hesitance, Cara barely dipped her pointer finger in the lake. "Wow, she's right."

Celine started pulling her shirt over her head and removing her shoes at the same time. "Smells good, too."

"But why are you in your clothes?" Cara asked, looking up from her crouched position at the edge of the wooden dock while her whole hand now dangled in the water. An eyebrow rose on her face.

Celine pushed her shirt back over her head and stood still, waiting for my response. The three of them stared at me. I looked down at the sopping wet t-shirt hanging from my shoulders.

"It's in the middle of the day," I said, as though that statement alone should make perfect sense.

Apparently, my general reasoning didn't work because Celine went back to unbuttoning her jeans. I knew I had to think of something better or else I'd have three naked sirens jumping into the same lake my... I didn't know what to call him. The same lake David had the perfect view of.

I considered my surroundings, searching for a better excuse. "And...this is a lake. It's not like if someone came I could swim away out to sea. I'd be kind of stuck. So I jumped in with my clothes on."

"But then you can't change into your tail," Cara said.

"Yeah, I'm not swimming with legs," Arlana spoke up.

My breath caught. How well could humans hear, exactly? I prayed David still hid behind the rock, out of view of my sisters.

"Seriously." Celine slid her jeans from her body. "Me neither." As the last word left her lips, she ran the short distance to the edge of the dock and dove into the water so seamlessly she'd left barely a splash in her wake. Her empty clothes lay in a pile on the wooden slats, only feet away from the pile of towels David had left for us. Did she just assume both towels were mine? Or maybe she hadn't noticed two lay in the crumpled pile.

Cara quickly stood to kick off her shoes and socks, following my example by leaving her clothes on. Jumping high into the air, she did a summersault before falling into the water. She and Celine were still underwater when Arlana, naked as the day she was born, walked to the edge of the dock, and as though she meant to take another step on solid wood, she stepped right off into the lake.

When all three sisters were enjoying themselves under water, I let out a loud cough to inform David it was time to move from one side of the rock to the other, from water to land. So far so good. He was completely silent and invisible. Unfortunately, he was probably also freezing.

We couldn't see or hear him, but how much had he heard from my sisters? I wondered what was going through his mind. How much had he pieced together from my sisters' comments on tails and legs?

"I can't believe you've been holding out on us, Allura." I turned to see Celine's head bob above the water.

"I just found this place," I answered, hoping she wasn't planning on doing what I knew she was going to do.

"Well, I'm glad you did. Ah," she exhaled as cobalt and ice blue scales multiplied across her chest and chin. "That feels so good."

I hoped David didn't pick this very moment to peek at us from behind the rock.

Celine's straight, black hair framed her face and glistened against the water with hints of blue like spilled oil. I stared at Celine and wished David weren't nearby, as I watched the transformation take place. Her blue eyes fluttered with enjoyment.

Celine reached her left arm into the air and turned it from side to side, inspecting herself. "I never get over how beautiful I am," she said.

"Yes, yes we all know your self-proclaimed splendor far surpasses that of any fish." Arlana's unconvinced voice joked underwater as her scaled arm broke the surface. Her face soon followed, with a smile.

In an instant, Celine lay her body back slightly and flung her strong tail into the air in a blur of blues and browns, and with force, smacked it back down against the water, spraying Arlana with a wave of lake water. Celine turned and dove down to the depths of the lake. Arlana chased after her.

Arlana's tail was the lightest of our group of four, but her mother had the lightest tail in the whole clan. The tip of Arlana's tail peeked above the surface before she dove after Celine. The body of her tail—a faint pink, almost white color—had iceberg blue scales scattered lightly up to her fins where the blue showed strongest. A solid, thick vertical line of ecru stretched along the tips of each side of her fin. Her tail matched the clear lake water better than any of ours.

"Who do you think will win the race they're clearly having?" Cara swam to me, naked, with a wad of soaked clothes in her hand. "Sorry."

She motioned to the clothes. "I just couldn't do it. Swimming in clothes just isn't right." Her long, blond, curly hair straightened with the weight of the water and appeared even longer, flowing effortlessly in an inverted umbrella around her.

"I don't know," I answered, trying to act calm, but failing miserably. Any minute David could get tired of hiding and reveal himself. For all he knew, there were just four girls swimming in the lake. Why not join in?

"Why haven't you gotten rid of your clothes and changed yet?" Cara asked. "I was going to wait on you, but..." She shook the wet bundle out in front of her.

I almost let out a grunt. I wanted to turn and look at the rock, David's rock, but with Cara watching me so closely, that would be stupid. I wished I could magically make them leave, pretend none of this had happened, and hope David still believed I was who I wanted him to think I was. I looked down at my shirt and thought for a moment. What if I told my sisters I heard someone coming? No, then they'd stop to listen closely and hear David breathing. Then it hit me, and I rolled my eyes at how my panic-brain left out the best explanation.

"When I got here," I explained to Cara, "I saw a few shoe prints, so I'd just rather be safe." I paused, guilt growing in my gut for lying to my closest sister. I added a truth to keep the guilt at least partly at bay. "With everything going on, I didn't want to take any chances."

"Well, now that you know we're alone, are you going to swim or not?" Cara asked.

I looked up at my favorite siren. She wanted to take an afternoon swim with her sister. Poor Cara, she was so loyal and transparent with me. Lately, I couldn't give her the same in return.

"Yes, let's go swimming." Under the water, I peeled my pants down my legs and finished undressing until I too held a wad of sopping fabric in my hand. Cara and I threw our clothes at the same time. Releasing the dripping cloth left a heavy pit in my stomach.

There was no way David didn't know by now, hadn't pieced

together who really swam in this lake by what he had seen. But I still couldn't let my sisters spot him. They weren't killers, but if they thought he had seen us transform, I wasn't sure what they'd do. Or more importantly, who they'd tell.

If David were watching, he'd already seen my sisters and could assume I was the same, but I still didn't want him to see me change. So as the scales prickled across the back of my neck, I stopped treading water with and allowed the fresh-tasting liquid to engulf me. Cara and I sank down deep enough to keep us well hidden among the green lake plants.

"How was the library?" Cara asked. Her green tail flitted back and forth beside the plants, making it almost invisible among the deep green strands of lake life.

"I haven't gone yet. Sort of got preoccupied." I looked around as though the lake was what kept me and not the amazingly handsome guy waiting for me up top. Small talk was the last thing I wanted to do in the moment, but I had no choice. "What about you guys? I thought it was movie day," my words vibrated through the water.

"After a movie and a half, Arlana said we should take advantage of our last day without supervision and turned off the T.V.. Apparently, you had the same idea." She wove her scale-covered arm through the lake weeds, watching how it camouflaged enough to disappear and reappear.

Arlana and Celine swam up behind Cara and she turned to greet them.

"So, fresh water fish are gross." Celine stuck her tongue out and rubbed it as though she were cleansing it from the nasty taste.

"Yeah, there's a weird flavor to them." Arlana batted at a lonesome little fish minding its own business. It quickly swam away, tucking itself behind a patch of stringy lake weeds. "Have you tasted the plants, Cara?" She watched Cara weave her arm in and out of the shades of green.

"No, but they're pretty," Cara said as she stopped weaving.

"They're probably disgusting too." Celine blew a strand of green vine away from her face. "This is definitely no place to hunt, but a great place to swim for fun." Celine turned to look at the other side of the lake. "Do you see those rocks?" She pointed and my body jerked to attention. Celine gave me a questioning look before turning back to the rocks. "Can you imagine just lounging on those? They're huge, and probably flat on top."

"And we could bring combs and mirrors and brush our hair while we waited for the loves of our lives to ride up on horses and rescue us from our horrid scaled condition," Cara played along.

My pulse slowed a little, hoping Celine didn't actually intend to nose around the area where David hid. I hoped she'd just been joking like Cara.

"I'd actually like the mirror part," Celine chided. "But the rest sounds hideous."

"The rocks are pretty, though." Cara's tail pushed her above the reach of the green vines as she hovered over us.

With a flick of her tail, she started to make her way over to the biggest rock that was both submerged and protruding from the lake. David's rock. With nothing better to do, my sisters waved their strong tails and caught up to her.

Shit.

I panicked. What could I do? Tell them to stop? What reason would I give? In one hard stroke of my tail I brought myself close behind them. Thankfully, they were in no hurry, but unfortunately I had to be. I couldn't tell them the rock was a stupid idea; I had wanted to see it too when I first came to the lake. Its monstrous stature commanded attention.

Thoughts, questions, rushed through my mind as we neared the hiding human boy. If they saw David—when they saw David—was I willing to pretend I didn't know him? Hand him over to whatever Celine had in mind with the support of my sisters while not even batting an eye?

No. But how far was I willing to go to protect him?

Within ten feet of the rock and quickly closing in, I decided to scream and pretend something bit me. I could lead a search-and-kill party on a living being under the water rather than the one above and right behind the now incredibly interesting rock. But, before I could open my mouth to let out a fake shrill of pain, another shrilling sound screeched through the air and penetrated the water.

CHAPTER FIFTEEN

)(

Celine, Cara, and I hovered in the water, our eyes barely above the surface, scanning the horizon for the intrusive noise.

"Ah, we have to go," Arlana said with a scoff at our sudden defensive stance. "That's my alarm." She flitted her tail at us and ambled to where the mound of clothing lay near the water.

"Alarm for what?" Celine asked as she followed.

I followed too, trying to pull Cara's attention in a new direction, away from David and the rocks. It worked—she swam directly behind me.

"I set the alarm on my phone. The sun will set soon and we still need to clean up our mess from movie day."

When we neared the edge of the lake, Arlana's fins retracted smoothly along the sides of her tail. Her blended light pink scales made it harder to see the transformation on her skin compared to my other sisters. But I still noticed the scattered line of scales melt away as though someone had taken an eraser to her torso and erased the shimmer. As her color dulled, her tail pulled apart, separating into two pale legs. Arlana didn't so much as flinch when her tail separated; she simply continued waving her legs in unison back and forth.

When she made it to the shore, she crawled up the pebbles, only having to expose her back to the outside air, before checking to make sure we were alone. "Weird," she said as she stood naked along the shore and held her shirt over her head. "I smell humans, but there are none here."

I froze…for two reasons. One: she scented David. And two: David had more than likely just heard her refer to humans as though she were nothing of the sort. We were nothing of the sort.

"It's a good thing we brought the car." Arlana pulled her pants up as the now naked Celine and Cara shook out their clothes. "Can you imagine how out of place we'd look walking down the street with dripping hair this time of year? We'd have to pretend to shiver."

"Uh, I hate pretending to shiver," Celine said as her black shirt made its way over her head.

Arlana, Celine and Cara turned their focus to me, still gently waving my tail to keep afloat. I figured if I lagged a little, Arlana would want to leave me behind in an effort to stay on schedule. I needed to stay long enough to try to explain away what had just happened to David.

"Are you coming?" Arlana asked, already headed toward the dock to grab her shoes, socks, and cell phone. Out of all my sisters, Arlana's reactions stayed consistent to her main priority: order.

"I still need to get that book from the library," I answered, trying to sound more relaxed than I felt.

"Oh, you haven't done that yet?" Arlana slipped her shoes on. "What about your wet clothes? You can't go to the library like that."

Celine and Cara stood dressed, waiting between the dock and the bush.

"I have a set of dry clothes in my bag. Along with my library card." I flashed a smile to show how well I'd planned.

"That's weird, but okay," Celine said.

Celine and Cara jumped onto a fir tree branch above the hedge of bushes.

"But don't take too long," Arlana added. "We have to leave right after the sun sets to do our hunting before intersecting Vanessa." Arlana joined our other two sisters in the tree.

"Bye!" Cara said behind her as the three leaped from the branch and out of sight.

I waited until I knew they weren't coming back—until their car engine revved to life—before I allowed scales to melt from my shoulders and started to change the rest of me back to skin and legs.

"Stop. Don't." David's stern voice echoed across the water and smashed into me.

Without looking, I knew he stood beside his rock, staring right at me, probably watching my tail wave back and forth under the clear blue water. My black tail. But, I couldn't turn around and face him. I couldn't give up my secret, even though I knew it was no longer a secret.

"Allura," he called to me. But my voice refused to work, refused to answer.

The sound of a loud splash resonated off the rocks and evergreens. The water shifted with movement as he swam toward me. I shivered at the thought of what would happen next. His hand touched my tail for a half-second before sharply pulling away. I still refused to turn and face him. His fingers tapped my tail again, only this time they didn't pull away. I wished they would.

I'd never felt the urge to bolt as intensely as I did in that moment.

But I didn't. I waited.

With balled hands and clenched teeth, I fought the urge.

Seconds later my fingers loosened to allow water to touch my palms again. My jaw slackened. The strong, gentle pressure of his skin against my scales brought a tingly sensation.

His hand glided up to the small of my back.

His head emerged from the water.

His breath lingered on my shoulder.

His fingers slid up along my back and changed direction to caress down along my right arm.

His chest brushed against me.

"You shiver when I rub your right arm." His words were careful, slow, thought out.

I sighed. "Rubbing the right arm is a very affectionate act of my kind."

Not his kind.

My kind.

I'd voiced my truth, put words to the secret I'd been clinging to since my aunts first allowed me around humans, since I was little. And it felt like...nothing.

I only felt his presence, screaming at me. Though, I couldn't decipher what exactly it screamed. Or maybe I didn't want to. Maybe it scared me too much, the possibility of his rejection.

His scent, his breath, his voice, they all commanded me to turn and face him, but I held fast. I couldn't handle seeing disgust painted across his expression. Not when I felt so vulnerable, on display before a human in my truest form.

"Can you not feel this because of the scales?" His left hand found mine and traveled from my hand up to my elbow.

"No, I can feel it the same as with my skin," I answered. "It's just uncomfortable for someone to rub up. The scales grow down, so..."

His hand stopped, but didn't drop from my arm. "I'm sorry, did I hurt you?"

"Don't worry," I assured him. "You can't really hurt me. At least not physically."

I steeled myself to face him, dreading the fear or lust I'd been warned I would see in his eyes. How could have I let him find out about me like this? Such an idiot. As I turned, he reached to touch my face, so very gently. Only acceptance lived in his expression, on the slight smile playing along his mouth. He leaned in ever so sweetly and placed his lips on mine. And I was just fine with that.

After a few seconds of enjoyment, I pulled away, enough to look at him. "You're not supposed to know about us."

"Your kind?" He peered down at my tail. "Mermaids?"

I braced myself for the sharp prick of anger, the bristle I'd felt every time I'd heard a person talk about mermaids, as though we were one in the same, as though sirens hadn't outsmarted and outlived mermaids. But the deep annoyance never came. A sigh of relief escaped my mouth.

"No," I answered, deciding how much I would share with him.

"Enlighten me." We sat on the pebbles, submerged in the water.

"We're not mermaids." I peered down at the shallow water. "Same species, but totally different culture." I couldn't believe we were actually discussing this. I didn't have a lot of experience explaining to someone that I was meant to be his predator and he was kind of supposed to be my prey. Especially when I was clearly starting to crush on that someone.

"Okay, so how much do you know about mythology?"

"Only what I learned in fifth grade. And maybe a little more, from movies," he added.

"Notice how in mythology sometimes mermaids are synonymous with sirens? And sometimes they're not?" I watched his expression of curiosity and continued. "Because at one point in our history, mermaids were made out to be the good sisters and sirens were considered the bad sisters. Though, honestly, they're extinct and we're not. We're the practical ones and the mermaids were naïve. We used to be the same. Scales. Tails, Breathed under water. All that. We were all Femina Mari—it means water women. But the foremothers of the sirens and mermaids disagreed about how to live. Mermaids insisted humans were trustworthy and the sirens insisted they weren't. Eventually they went their separate ways." I allowed a pebble to ease onto the backside of my submerged hand and I rolled it across from side to side as I spoke. I peered up at David.

His brow arched. "And?"

"You sure you want to know?"

David nodded. I felt exposed, allowing David to see me this way, tail and all, while I bared pieces of my heart—of who I was. I pushed away my hesitance and answered his question. "Think of sirens as the mermaids' evil sisters."

"Evil how?" He shook his head.

I gave an awkward laugh. "Over the years, sirens have had to change

129

the way we lived in order to survive among humans. When human males rose to power above all others, and the humans began demonizing anyone not like themselves, that's when the Femina Mari split ways. The mermaids' ancestors thought our kind should ride it out, keep our faith in the humans' that once deified our kind, faith that their goodness would return. My siren ancestors disagreed. They began fighting back. Their willingness to kill their foes made them stronger, so they stuck with it." On purpose, I kept from stating exactly how my foremothers fought back, how they killed. "The mermaids' trust in the humans is what wiped-out their kind. When humans got more advanced, we changed again, stopped fighting back and started living undercover, among them."

"Most wildlife and even some people have had to adapt over time," David said, completely taking my news in stride. "There's nothing wrong with natural evolution. But I think I know where you're going with this, in relation to sirens."

"It'd be hard to miss," I said. His eyes watched me and I wondered if this was the part where he ran away.

I imagined what he could be thinking. Me, grabbing him by the ankle like I had earlier, pulling him down to the depths. Allowing his lungs to fill with water. Taking his life. A small twinge sprang through my body. My stomach growled and I pushed back images of how differently this meeting could end.

"Sirens ate people, didn't they?"

I scooped up another handful of pebbles. "No, not people—men."

"Why just men?" he asked.

"They have that special mix of testosterone and adrenaline—"

David's next question cut my answer short. "Do you still eat...men?"

I shifted my weight in the water. "No, we stopped that stuff centuries ago. It became too risky. Humans traded swords and pitch-forks for guns and GPS tracking, so the siren leaders decided it'd be best if we went into hiding." The truth weighed heavy on my heart. He already knew what I was, should I finish revealing the depth of the differences between us?

No, I refused to offer up my secret about Skater Boy. Plus, biting wasn't necessarily eating.

I chucked the little stones across the lake smacking them against the rock David had been hiding behind only a little while earlier. Tiny shards from the large stone broke from the side and slid down into the water.

I could see he wanted to understand, to know me, but I couldn't just show him one side of the three-dimensional puzzle of myself. I couldn't just show him the pretty, sparkly black tail and glistening scales fitted to my body. And why would I want to? Men had been lusting after my kind, or the thought of my kind, since the first man laid eyes on a Femina Mari. And the men stupid enough to taunt, or seduce, or even try to take advantage of a siren, had usually paid with their lives. At its core, that's what separated the mermaids from the sirens. The sirens were ready and willing to devour any man thoughtless enough to try to sexualize or hurt them.

I pushed myself deeper into the water, away from him. "No, we don't still eat men," I answered with guilt gnawing the edges of my mind. "I've never eaten a man." A piece of truth wouldn't hurt. Maybe it'd even erase my guilt, a little. "But," I added for the sake of half-truths, "It's not because I find it grotesque. My sisters do, but I don't."

I scanned his body language, his facial expression. Nothing. So I continued. "Sirens eat raw animals, raw plants and raw fish, and sometimes when we're working as a team we can take down a bear, or a big shark. At some point though, when we reach adulthood, something inside clicks. And although it's not allowed, in varying degrees, we hunger for man. It's who we are. It's who *I* am."

I refused to watch the slow stream of pictures now flickering in my head, and tried to focus solely on David's face, not the men being torn to shreds in my mind.

David shifted his weight and pushed himself deeper into the water. The shifting liquid brushed the top of his shoulders. "So you come from a long line of finned maidens?" he said with a semi-joking smile.

"Yeah, but the tail isn't what makes me what I am. What I am creates the tail." I arched my back and slammed my tail into the water. "And we have our own legends about where the scales came from."

"So how does it work?"

"The legend?"

"No, your tail." David looked to be inspecting my lower half so I brought my thick, strong tail up from the water, and flashed my bottom fin.

"I don't have bones like you, they aren't dense and heavy. They're light and pliable like a fish's bones, no matter what form I take, for both resilient strength and speed." I waved my fin at him. "My tail can move up and down, or side to side. Whichever is needed for the hunt." I unfolded my bottom fin completely in a taut, rigid fan with what looked like rods pulling the webbing tight. "With a whip of my fin in this position I can slice the head from my prey." My bottom fin folded into itself from both sides until it looked like a closed fan, a straight line of black. "I can out-swim most any creature in the ocean, and because the pure power in my tail is the same embodied in my legs, I can outrun most things on land."

I cast my body into the water, making a U-turn and swam toward David who still sat, watching, in the submerged bank of the lake. My arms held me up, straddling his legs. My scale-covered breasts hovered above his knees. His eyes bounced from my chest to my face.

I opened my mouth and licked my teeth. The rumbling from my stomach returned in full force. I dropped down beside him with a "humph", thankful that for some reason, being near David kept the acid surge at bay.

I exhaled. "Are you going to ignore my texts now?" I asked in a quiet voice.

"I really appreciate your honesty."

Not the answer I was looking for.

He smiled and put his hand on mine. "It's a lot to process," he said. "I knew there was some incredible thing you were hiding from me, though. I just didn't know your amazingness was the stuff of legends."

"Haha," I pretended to laugh. "What about the eating men thing?" My eyes found his.

"You can't help what your ancestors did. And even if that piece of them is still in you, that doesn't mean it *is* you." He touched my face and gently eased my chin up so my eyes gazed into his. "I'm going to show you that I'm one of those decent guys out there, worthy of living." His smile disappeared. "Hopefully, even worthy of you." He bent his face in and gently placed his lips upon mine.

"This does help me understand why we need our relationship to be a secret, though," he said with a loud sigh when our kiss ended.

"Completely secret," I urged.

"Should we find a new meeting place, then? Your sisters seem to have claimed this one."

"No. They're the reason we have to stay a secret, them and my aunts. I won't let them take this place away from us too. It's too perfect." I leaned into him and kissed his cheek. "We'll just be careful, and anyway, I don't think they'll come here once their moms get home. Our leash is usually much shorter with my aunts around."

"When should they be back? How much longer do I get to enjoy your freedom from caregivers?" He combed his fingers through his thick dark hair, shiny with wetness.

"They're at a Council meeting discussing something they refuse to talk about. I don't know when they'll be back, but probably not much longer after Vanessa leaves." My eyes widened. "Crud, I forgot, I have to get home. Vanessa's coming in tonight."

"Vanessa?" he asked, one brow lifted.

"She belongs to a different clan."

"Clan? As in Irish families?"

I laughed and thought of the kelpie twins. "No, we're not an Irish family. Though, my ancestors may have picked up that word from them. It's what we call our siren groups. But, Vanessa's visiting so I need to get home before dark, that's when we're going to hunt and then meet up with her." I willed my black and emerald green scales to melt into my tan skin.

I stopped and peered up at David. Skin covered my face, neck, shoulders, and the top portions of my breasts.

"Oops. It's habit." My hand dropped and I reached to grab my damp jeans and white t-shirt. "I'll go change down there." I motioned to the bottom of the lake.

"No, you should put your dry clothes on. The ones you told your sisters you'd brought. I'll go back to my rightful place." He pretended to hang his head. "Behind the rock."

David pushed himself from the tiny pebbles and walked seven steps into the water before diving under the crystal blue surface. I watched him swim to the opposite side of the lake, and pull himself up from the liquid to walk behind the gigantic rock. His Henley looked glued to him, as were my eyes.

"Okay, you can change now!" he shouted from behind his rock.

I stopped to listen to the woods to make sure not a soul was near. I sensed the scales melting into my skin like a feather dusting from my breasts down to my legs. The transformation felt like millions of goose bumps prickling along my body, leaving in their wake a wave of pleasure.

My scales diminished and the bottom of my tail turned into calves. I watched as the rods that held the webbing of my bottom fin taut folded in on themselves and retracted enough to form ten toes. I wiggled them and then scurried to my backpack and pulled on the dry clothes.

"I'm done!" I shouted to David.

He showed himself from behind the rock.

"Meet you at the dock," I said, pointing to the old wooden slats hovering above the water. Without holding back, without hiding who I truly was, I sprinted to the dock before David had gotten far from the rock's shadow.

"Wow! You weren't kidding." He walked toward me. His eyes glimmered with fascination. "Strong or not, I'm still holding those bush branches apart for you to climb through."

A smile leaked into my voice, "I think I can handle that."

CHAPTER SIXTEEN

)(

I returned home before dark and the evening went as planned. After hunting cod and trout—which is always less of a hunt and more of an order-up, fast-food type of meal—my sisters and I rounded the Sound to meet up with Vanessa and help her navigate the twists and turns that converted it into a maze. The water was deep and dark, nothing like the clear, blue lake I had splashed around in with David hours earlier.

We had never met Vanessa before, but there were no such thing as strangers among sirens. The moment we swam near the beach of Deadman Island and spotted her snacking on a bundle of green seaweed, we waved and called out to her. She sat as she munched, the top of her head barely grazing the surface of the water. Bright red scales covered Vanessa's dark brown skin, and as her head jerked away from her meal and into our direction. Her many jet black braids smacked her face in slow motion. A grin pulled at her full lips as she dropped the few strands of plant and swam toward us.

Introductions were made with hugs and the five of us immediately fell into light-hearted discussions about her trip and her opinion of our neck of the sea. All positive, of course. Demeaning another siren's territory would be rude.

"I wasn't sure if I should meet you on land or not, but I figured staying under the water would be safest." Vanessa looked toward the beach and back at us. "It's been years since this island was the stomping ground of our kind and who knows what's changed since then."

"Not much," Arlana answered. "But either way is fine. Unless you prefer to hunt up there."

"No, I'm good. I ate on the way," Vanessa said.

Arlana, Celine, Cara, Vanessa, and I chatted non-stop all the way home. But while my lips moved every so often to comment, my mind stayed occupied on David. I wanted him to know the real me, and in a way I had shown him, but did he really understand that my dark tail and the dark waters I hunted every night matched the darkness lurking within me? There was no way he could fully get that and still want to be with me.

This very thought led me to another. An answer to a question I hadn't known, until now, rolled around in my head. Or was it my heart it occupied? What about David did I like so much? Kaven had hinted his affection for me now and again. And I did nothing to reciprocate. How was David different? The answer rooted itself in my heart and grew through my mind.

I was drawn to David's humanity. Since day one David seemed to embody the attributes I appreciated in humans and none of the unfortunate qualities I'd come to despise. When I'd exposed my reality to him, he responded with questions—an inquisitive human desire to know more. At no point did he express fear in the unknown—a human tendency to blanket-judge.

But if I admired his humanity, did I then dislike my lack of it?

Up until this point, I'd always been perfectly accepting and content with the shadows of my foremothers living within my DNA, intertwining their pasts with my present and future. The fact sirens still existed today proved my ancestors were fierce and strong. That they, at any cost, ensured their legacy lived on. That sirens wouldn't die out and become extinct like the mermaids. They gave my generation a chance to exist. Who was I to question their methods of survival?

Only, now that this new hunger grew inside of me—the hunger my foremothers accepted gladly—I kind of did question their choices. Hunger for the hunt and an insatiable appetite to procure our prey was merely survival. But knowing that they also hunted men for increased strength—and now this desire grew within me—made me a little scornful of their dark practices. Yes, I had attacked Skater Boy. But, I also allowed Kaven to stop me before things got out of hand. Before I killed him. I fought that darkness inside that they so gladly obeyed.

I didn't want to hurt David—not physically or emotionally. And as my black scale-covered body glided through the darkened water, I decided I wouldn't. He wasn't like the men my foremothers had hunted and killed; he had nothing in common with them. If I could just get my body to believe that, I wouldn't have to feel so torn when I was with him. I wouldn't have to feel as though I was somehow disgracing my mother, grandmother and great-grandmother by wanting him to look at me with adoration. Although, the lack of acid swirling in my mouth when I'd been around him lately told me my body already halfway knew he wasn't like the others.

Arlana popped her head from the surface first to make sure we were alone on our part of the beach. She waved her arm in the water to signal it was clear.

Vanessa's deep red scales melted into her dark skin as her braids brushed against her shoulder blades. "Wow, the cliffs are pretty angry looking around here. Different." She studied the beach as she walked from the water.

Celine handed her the extra set of clothes we'd brought from the drybag we'd left on the rocky shore. "Yeah, it's no wonder why our mothers chose an island to raise us on. The "angry cliffs", as they call them, keep the water access pretty private."

"Plus, the rain is clean and pure, not to mention an almost daily part of life here," Arlana added as she buttoned her jeans.

"That makes sense." Vanessa pulled a white cotton tee over her head.

"I'm still hungry." Cara pretended to clutch her stomach as she looked in my direction.

"There's sushi in the fridge," I said in a get-over-it tone.

"Gross." Cara raised both hands in the air as though she were weighing two invisible somethings, one in each hand. "Sushi? Or shark? Dead, day old fish or fresh flesh? Hmm. Shark, please."

"You've ruined her," Arlana complained. "Nothing will ever compare for her again." Arlana shrugged and threw the backpack over her shoulder. The other girls grabbed their things and we started walking to the house.

"Wow! Seriously? How often do you all eat shark?" Vanessa asked as we made our way up the hillside path.

"Since Allura started hunting them, pretty often," Arlana said.

Vanessa's brown eyes were wide as she watched me rather than where she walked. "Not on your own. Your mother helped, right?"

"My mother's dead," I replied, looking ahead at the house, somewhat surprised at how easily the words slipped from my mouth.

"Yeah, she does it all on her own." Cara spoke like she was my own personal cheerleader. "We watch from a distance and then once she has it disabled, we help to finish it off. It's pretty amazing! She stalks like a pro."

"So then *you're* the next Provider in your clan?" Vanessa nodded her head with a gleam in her eyes and a smile on her lips.

"What do you mean? That's impossible. The Providers died out a long time ago. When humans were taken off the menu," Arlana half-asked, half-told.

Vanessa's eyes stayed glued on me as we climbed the trail up the side of the cliff. The rushing wind worked at cutting into our bodies. "They didn't just lead the man-hunt. Nowadays clans work together to take down their bigger prey, but back in the day that responsibility rested on the Provider, to help keep her skills sharp." Vanessa's eyes changed from staring to searching, still looking at me. "The Provider's main purpose was to hunt men for the celebrations."

"Yeah, but now that the *main purpose* is against the rules, there's no need for a Provider," Celine said, turning the knob on the back door to our house, leading into the kitchen.

Vanessa pulled out a chair at the kitchen table and sat down. "That's what we thought, but the Council seems to have other ideas. New ideas."

"Such as?" Arlana perked up and sat across from Vanessa.

"I called home while I was in Seattle the other day and talked to my mom. She said the Council had visited our clan recently, asking about me." She scanned my sisters' faces before continuing. "Asking about my hunting abilities—if I stood out from my sisters in that department."

"Why?" Celine asked.

"Because I'm of age and pledging to a clan."

Arlana nodded her head.

"Except, I don't fit the guidelines," Vanessa continued. "I don't hunt better than my clan mates. And guys don't fall all over me more so than my sisters. The only guideline I fit is that I'm pledging. You can't be a Provider until you've pledged your life to a clan."

"So what did your mom tell them?" Cara asked.

"She answered their questions. She told me that it was obvious to them I'm not what they're looking for, and they left. Plus, neither my mother nor my grandmother had shown Provider tendencies, and it's known to be a hereditary thing. I just wonder why they're even looking for a Provider." Vanessa shifted in her seat and gazed at me. "Either way, it's an honorable position within the clan."

"I'm not what they're looking for either," I said in defense, as though my aunts were around to hear they've chosen the wrong siren. "I'm not old enough to pledge, and I don't have guys flocking to me." Paranoia swept through me. I wondered if they all secretly knew what I'd done to the skater boy, and the ultimatum Kaven presented to my aunts.

I wasn't thirsty or hungry, but I wanted to drink water, or snack on something to keep my hands and mouth busy. I grabbed a glass from the cupboard and filled it with the water cooler's purified water. I assumed my aunts were, in that moment, discussing my recent slip-ups with the Council. I hoped they denied my aunts' request to make me Provider on the grounds I hadn't pledged yet.

"So," Arlana thought out loud. "If the Council is in search of a Provider, they must have something up their sleeves. Probably the same thing our moms are meeting to discuss."

I remembered a few choice words said to me during my scolding for saving the woman, and spoke up. "Aunt Dawn told me the night that woman almost drowned, that the Council was in the area. She said I was lucky they didn't catch me."

Vanessa's eyebrow rose in question, but neither my sisters nor I would share the incriminating information of what really happened that night with the woman. Not when the revelation could paint our clan in a bad light.

"So, back to the Provider issue," Celine said. "Back in the day, when it was normal for each clan to have a Provider, the Provider hunted the larger game for regular meals and she also hunted their human victims?"

"Yes," Vanessa answered. "Some celebrations and man-hunting were on land, and some were at sea. It depended on the celebration. But the monthly ones were at sea. Our foremothers celebrated the changing of the tides with the new moon—it's darkest during a new moon. A few clans in the area would get together and have something like a party. Then they'd follow the Provider to search for a ship. That's when the Provider picked a man, usually a sailor, and lured him to the edge of the boat. Some Providers had a great voice, so they'd sing. Others could speak beautifully tantalizing words. Either way, she hunted and attacked him and that's when the other sirens would come out from hiding to help her finish the job." Vanessa's eyes locked on mine. "Just like you did with the shark."

I shook my head at her dramatics and took a sip of water. I had to get out of this Provider thing. The more we discussed it, the more I believed I was too young to throw my future into learning to hunt innocent men. Especially considering I had feelings for one.

"The Provider's real job, the one where she had to do more than lure a lonely man to the side of his boat, was for the Legacy of Life celebrations." She scanned my sisters' faces.

All three of my sisters now sat in chairs around the table, their mouths slightly open—no doubt eating up her words. The kitchen table was much smaller than the one in the dining room, and had only five chairs, which put me at the end in the odd chair. I clutched my now half-empty glass of water and wished my sisters would stop egging her on so she'd shut up. Her assumptions of me were just that; assumptions. My particular skillset hadn't come by way of genetic influence, but rather a bloody show from a suicidal human. Of-course, Vanessa would never know that.

Every clan has their secrets.

"You've heard of it right?" Vanessa asked. "The Legacy of Life celebration?"

"Yes," Celine said, "but only in stories told to little sirens."

"I think I read about it, or my mom mentioned it when I was younger, but I don't remember her saying it was a celebration," Arlana answered.

"Well, that's because it isn't celebrated anymore," Vanessa said. "The elders and the Council decided a long time ago that the festivity brought unwanted attention to us, making it too risky."

"Because of a big party?" Arlana looked confused.

"That and the deaths of local men on the same exact night." Vanessa smirked.

"Oh, you have to explain that one." Celine scooted to the edge of her seat.

"So, you know that the Legacy of Life is when the younger members of the clan return from their sabbatical and pledge themselves to living with their clan and continuing the legacy of our kind."

"That's what you're going to do. Congratulations, by the way," Cara interrupted.

"Yes I am. My clan is pretty excited about it too, thanks." She flashed Cara a grin and turned to look back at Arlana. "But, the only ones celebrating my return will be my own clan and dead men will not be part of the equation." Vanessa crossed her arms and leaned back in the chair. "Okay, so you've heard how they used to pledge, how all the local clans would celebrate it together?"

My sisters nodded. I just watched.

"Unlike the tide change celebrations, this one was on land, usually an island, a cliff or the forest where they wouldn't be interrupted. So, say a member was coming home to pledge, the Provider's role was to provide the meal and the entertainment." She chuckled. "They're one in the same aren't they?"

"And by entertainment and meal, you mean dead men?" The corners of Celine's mouth rose.

"See?" I said in exasperation, holding back from shaking my head at my sister's delight. "If anyone has an ounce of Provider blood, it's Celine."

"Don't hate, sister," Celine joked with a laugh. "It's in our DNA."

Vanessa smiled.

How? How could they take killing innocents so lightly?

Arlana took no part in the joking and laughing. She rested her chin on her upturned palms as she leaned her elbows on the table. "So, explain the entertainment portion of the celebration. I'm sure we were taught this, but for the life of me, I can't remember." So Arlana's lack of lightheartedness about this all had nothing to do with discomfort over the topic and everything to do with her search for facts.

"The Provider is the only clan member who has the array of gifts needed to gather the men and lead them to the island or forest of their own free will, alive and well." Vanessa's eyes peered up at me and my sisters' eyes followed. "We all have the ability to lure men, and kill them too, but the Provider can do it so much better. She has a finesse about her that causes her to not only lure them with her looks, but her personality as well. She can not only make a guy lust after her, but she can make him fall in love with her, make him do anything for her, including follow her to an unknown location despite the pit in his stomach that warns him it's dangerous."

Vanessa paused to study me. I did my best not to squirm under her gaze. I pushed David from my thoughts. He had no business swimming around my mind during a discussion like this. What he and I had was real. Right?

She went on as if she didn't notice my unease. "The Provider doesn't simply grab a couple men at the local hang-out and promise them a good time. No, she handpicks them, sometimes months in advance. Then she gets to know them, works on them, learns everything about them, and shows them pieces of her own soul until they see a future with her."

My stomach sank, a heaviness swirling at the edges of it. I knew about the proclivities of my ancestors, but I'd never heard it in such detail. And never after getting to know a human male. We'd always kept away, maintained a safe distance, refused to let them in. But now, these stories weren't just about creatures, humans, different from us, separate from us. The victims of these stories were living, breathing people...with families.

"How does she pick them?" The moment Cara asked the question my stomach twisted tighter. I had heard enough already. I had been sure I wasn't even close to being a Provider, but the more Vanessa explained, the more I doubted my resolve. No. No, I couldn't be a Provider.

I stepped away from the table, set the empty glass on the counter and started walking to the stairs. I needed to seek refuge in my room. I needed to text David, to read his words and be reminded that he wasn't my prey—the male I slowly and carefully lured into the web of a trap. But it wasn't like that. I refused to believe it was. He was my boyfriend.

"Wait," Vanessa called from the table. "You'll want to hear this."

No, I really don't. But I couldn't let them know how heavily her words weighed on me. I slowly walked back toward the four of them. I stopped at the counter and waited.

"She was somehow drawn to the guys who wouldn't be missed much; and not the delinquent kind, either. I guess now, in our society today, she'd be attracted to the guys with no family nearby who live on their own. Or the ones who grew up in the foster care system—

guys like that." When Vanessa finished, Arlana nodded as though she now fully understood.

My tongue stuck to the roof of my mouth; I needed water. I grabbed my glass. Empty. I wanted to go fill it up, but knew my guest and sisters would think my urgency odd. Unsure, I froze where I stood.

"That's so smart. I would've never thought of doing that," Arlana said, still in thought. "And it makes sense why they'd take the sailors for the monthly parties—to keep their edge."

"Okay," Celine spoke up with eagerness. "Tell us what our roles would have been back then. What would we have gotten to do with the men?"

"Ah, this is the best part." Vanessa flashed me a smile, showing me that if I would have been the Provider back then, I would have been the lucky one, by her standards at least. "We would get to do kind of what you did with the shark, only much more fun. Sometimes the men thought they were invited to the party, sometimes they started to figure it out shortly after they arrived. It all depended on which personalities she brought. But she usually wouldn't pick the stupid ones, so at some point the men began to realize they weren't there as her date or close friend. That's when they would run."

Vanessa's eyes clouded as though she were in a far off place. "Can you imagine it? Watching men, so full of themselves and their own strength and power over women, slowly turn from that egotistical mindset to one completely engulfed in fear of women? I would give my left fin to see that."

"Not all men are like that," I added without thinking. My head pounded against my temples. I leaned on the counter for support.

"Well," Vanessa turned to me as though I'd interrupted her train of thought. "Of course, they'd target the drudges of society. Predators wiping out predators."

"Two birds with one stone," Arlana muttered, as though she were placing each piece of information in its correct slot in her mind.

"What happened when the guys ran?" Celine asked; her voice dripped with longing.

Vanessa's eyes cleared. "If we lived back then and were at the cele- bration, we would get to hunt them, chase them, surround them, and once the Provider gave us the signal, we'd take them down one bite at a time. They'd be powerless to hurt another person, and we'd be strong and satisfied."

I didn't need water anymore, my mouth wasn't dry. Acid dripped from my razor-ridged teeth. I had to swallow before the liquid substance seeped from my mouth. Images of men running for their lives flashed through my mind. I could almost smell the fear seeping through their sweat and beckoning me. The adrenaline pumping. I thought of the woman in the water, how lovely the blood looked as though it wrapped her in a red ribbon, and then pictured the same ribbons trailing from the running men who got their jollies preying on others.

My stomach growled, begging for more sustenance than merely fish could give. The darkness of my foremothers swirled within me, goading me on, giving me permission to imagine it, to picture luring unsuspecting men to their deaths in a way they'd never see coming. Teaching them the last lesson of their lives: to fear women, but more so, to fear sirens, the creatures they had hunted to near-extinction.

My eyes smiled while I licked the acid from my lips again.

"Look at her." Vanessa's words broke through my blood-red trance.

I blinked, being pulled from my fantasy with what felt like a harsh rope that I really didn't want to hang on to. All four sirens stared at me, their lips tilted in devious smiles.

"She's licking her lips. Yup, she's a Provider." Vanessa pushed her chair away from the table, stood, and walked over to me. She placed her hand on my right arm, but did not rub it. We hadn't known each other long enough for that.

I wanted to shove her hand from my arm, but I refused to give my audience any more of a performance than I already had. "I'm not a Provider. You're wrong."

Arlana stood, but hovered near the table.

"Okay." Vanessa dropped her hand and shrugged her shoulders. "Maybe I am wrong. I didn't mean to upset you."

"You didn't," I half-lied. Vanessa herself didn't upset me. Her words, however, did.

My aunts were wrong. Vanessa was wrong. She still didn't know how I came to this state—the hunting, the bloody fantasies. My newly graphic images had nothing to do with my family line and everything to do with a freak accident.

"Even if she's not the Provider, she can still hunt for us, right?" Cara asked.

"Allura, you'd better just go hunt down a tiger shark before Cara's begging starts to get irritating." Arlana shook her head.

"It's not already irritating?" Celine said before the kitchen exploded in laughter.

Celine and Cara made their way over to Vanessa and me. It looked like they were trying to move the conversation to the living room. But I could tell they were aiming to diffuse the situation—protect their sister from doing something she ought not. Protect me from losing my shit on Vanessa.

"But doesn't one of your mothers do most of the shark-hunting?" Vanessa asked with a half chuckle.

"No, well, together they can take one down, but it doesn't happen very often," Arlana answered as she too started walking toward the living room to the more comfortable couches.

Vanessa stopped. "That doesn't make sense, though. I heard your clan had a member with amazing hunting abilities; one of your mothers." The laughter in Vanessa's voice came to an immediate halt and her face jerked toward me. "Oh, it was *your* mother."

The kitchen fell silent. Stillness engrossed us as a thickness surrounded us. I saw the widening shock in my sisters' eyes. Did my own mirror theirs? I didn't know what to say. What to think. I opened my mouth but nothing came out. If my mother had been the main hunter in our clan, why hadn't I known? Why would she kill herself with a new baby who needed her *and* a clan who had relied on her? My heart grew heavy and raced at the same time.

"That's it." Vanessa's eyes sparkled as though she'd just solved a puzzle. "It all adds up. I thought the Council called a meeting because elder Liana just became the new Council leader, but now I think I may have been wrong." Her hand pressed my right shoulder. "You're the reason the Council is meeting right now."

CHAPTER SEVENTEEN

)(

I awoke the next morning and automatically looked to see if Cara still slept in her bed. She had followed me to our room after the whole Provider discussion. Cara assumed by the bloody pictures Vanessa had painted with her words that my head had been swimming with hunger and decided if anyone knew hunger it was her. My sister stayed up with me and chatted on and on about every subject except food. It took a while, but my tense muscles had gradually unwound until I had been calm enough to sleep.

As I scanned the room I expected to see Cara still sleeping in the bed opposite mine, but I was alone. Of course I also wished Cara was with me so I could stay hidden in our room for longer, rather than be subjected to Vanessa's searching eyes and rueful smile.

I sauntered down the stairs to see my sisters and Vanessa in the living room watching television. Pillow-muffled greetings floated my way as I fell onto the couch beside them.

"Sleep much?" Celine chided without turning her gaze from the T.V..

Cara eyed me for a second and then turned back to the movie they'd been watching. "It's a lazy day." She sighed and pushed herself back into the couch cushions as she stretched her arms.

Arlana shot Vanessa a smile and explained, "It kind of has to be." She paused the movie. "We live in a small town on an island. So when our moms tell the school that we'll be gone today and possibly tomorrow on a family mini-trip, we remain scarce until dark. Thus, movie day."

Vanessa nodded. "Forethought, I like it."

Celine's cell phone buzzed, rattling in a little circle on the coffee table as a snippet of a rock song about girl-power filled the room. She silenced the music with the touch of her finger before holding the phone to her face.

"Hi Mom. Yes, she's here and we're all doing fine." Celine nodded and smiled at Vanessa. "Okay, I'll let them know. No, she's leaving tomorrow night, after she's rested a while. Okay, we will. Love you, too. Bye." She set the phone on the coffee table. "My mother said they're leaving tomorrow night so they'll be home in two days." She regarded Vanessa again. "She said they're sorry to miss you, but they're sure they'll see you again sometime soon and to have a safe trip home. Oh, and that they're very proud of you and happy for your clan."

"Did she tell you how the Council meeting went?" Vanessa scooted forward on the couch.

"No, if they tell us anything, it'll be after they get home, when we can all discuss it as a clan." Celine sat back on the green and white couch, stretching her legs in front of her.

Arlana pressed "play" on the remote control. They all stared at the television again as though they were never interrupted. I tried to shut my mind off long enough to watch with them, but I thought I heard a buzzing upstairs and hoped it was coming from my phone.

As I made my way to the stairs, I walked passed the kitchen and noticed the blue numbers on the microwave. Three o'clock. School was out. *David must be texting.* I stopped myself from running to my phone and instead skipped up the stairs. When I got to my room, I shut the door behind me and ran to my bed. Flinging my pillow up to expose my hidden phone, I stopped to listen. No one was coming. I picked the phone up and saw David's name flashing. *Yes.* I opened the message.

Missed you today.

I replied, Miss you too.

Your aunts still gone?

Yes.

Can you meet me at the lake?

No. Can't leave.

Can I call you?

No. Sisters will hear me talking.

When can I see you? David asked.

Day after tomorrow. After school.

Okay. He responded.

When I heard footsteps on the stairs I slid my phone back into its hiding place under my pillow. I'd never had to hide my phone before, but now that David texted me, I couldn't risk having one of my sisters see his name on the screen. I made a quick mental note to change his contact name into something less obvious, and maybe even look into an app that'd keep our texts more private.

Cara cracked the door open and poked her head in. "Everything okay? You still thinking about last night?"

"I'm just tired," I said.

"Now's the time to rest. It'll be dark in a few hours and it looks like your fans are requesting an encore." She slipped her body through the crack she'd made between the door and the doorjam before shutting it behind her.

"Encore?" I asked, pulling my legs up from the ground to recline on my bed.

"Vanessa wants to see you hunt."

My eyebrows lifted.

"To be honest, we all want to. It's fun to watch. Exciting."

I moved my legs over closer to the wall and she sat on my bed.

"What about what your mothers' said?" I asked. Irritation climbed up my back and into my skull. Vanessa held onto this Provider thing a little too tightly. She needed to just let it go. Plus, my sisters should have noticed my discomfort last night and steered Vanessa's mind and words away from me.

Cara smoothed the comforter around her. "We talked about it, and—"

I interrupted her, my own frustration getting the better of me, "You mean Arlana and Celine talked about it?"

She scowled. "No, this was a group decision. I don't always follow what they say, I think for myself, too. It's just that I agree with them most of the time."

Her defensiveness fizzled out my irritation. "I just don't like seeing them boss you around." I placed my hand on hers and she stopped smoothing the comforter.

She looked up at me. "They don't boss me around. I choose not to speak up." She slowly pulled her hand from beneath mine. "I'm competent, I just don't have to wave it around like a flag and be pushy about it."

"I'm sorry, Cara. I didn't mean it like that. I didn't say you were incompetent. I just think you're more sensitive, and I don't know, a piece of me wants to protect you I guess. You're my sister."

"Protect me because you're the Provider? I'm not weak, Allura."

"I never said you were. Where is this coming from? And why are you calling me that?" I raised my hands in the air. Her body language and tone of voice confused me. I'd never heard her talk to anyone like this before.

Cara sat rigidly on my bed, her back as straight as my headboard. "I've just been thinking a lot lately since Vanessa told us that stuff last night and especially when she talked about your mom being the Provider."

A pit in my stomach started to form. I didn't want to talk about last night. "She doesn't know anything about my mom. Providers died out a long time ago. It isn't possible." It was one thing to tentatively agree to step into the traditional siren role to keep the kelpies from waging war, but this whole "chosen one" thing didn't sit well with me. Plus, it seemed the kelpies split town after Kaven visited my home. No one had seen or heard from them since. So maybe I didn't even need to follow through with their demands.

Cara shook her head, dismissing my comment, and continued. "It got me wondering what my role in our clan is. The whole legacy thing. If every member in a clan has a role to play, what's mine?" She paused, and glanced over at her bed and the framed picture of her mother holding her as a baby on the night stand. "If you're the Provider like your mother, and Celine is confident like her mother, what about me and Arlana?"

"What do you mean? Since when did we have to fit into clan roles? We're just who we are."

"Arlana is nothing like her mother, personality wise. And in some ways I'm not like mine either. My mother is more like Aunt Dawn, the take charge type; the get things done and don't ask questions type. And if Celine and Arlana fit those roles in the clans, there's only one role left; Aunt Rebecca. She's always in the background, all quiet and not making any clan decisions."

I adjusted myself on the bed, pushing my arm behind me for support. "I think I see your point, but I disagree. Even if we did have set roles, Aunt Rebecca is probably the most important of us all—she's our healer."

"Yes important, but not respected. Have you seen how her own daughter treats her? Arlana barely listens to her mother. I don't want that to be my role." She let out a heavy breath of air and finally slumped back against the wall.

"I still don't think this is about roles, though, Cara. If you think you should have more input then you should try it, maybe you'll get the respect you feel like you're lacking. But I'd hate to see you completely change yourself for some stupid supposed role. You shouldn't have to try to fit into a mold."

I wondered if my words should be pointed at me, too. The mold I had been born into required a lifestyle free of romance and devoid of any human relationships, but was that really what *I* wanted? "They should accept and love and respect you for who you are right now, not who they want you to be!" I raised my voice before widening my eyes in disbelief that I had just basically yelled at myself.

"You might be right," Cara said.

"Just try it."

Cara gave a heavy grin and pulled me close for a hug. "Oh, but to get back to what I was saying earlier." She spoke into my ear as we embraced. "What do you think about going for a hunt?"

"It depends." I pulled away and my hands cupped her shoulders. "Do *you* want me to do it?"

"I could always use a good meaty shark dinner." She shook her head. "No, wait, our mothers said no shark hunting, so that's out of the question." Cara stood to pace the floor from one end of my bed to the other. "What if we swim out to the ocean where there's more of a selection and find something other than shark? Then we'd still be technically obeying by not hunting shark."

Cara needed to call the shots for once. "I think that's a great idea." I reached over and caught her right arm. She stopped walking long enough for me to run my hand along the length of her skin from her shoulder to her hand.

I wondered, as my favorite sister's smile beamed brightness through what had been a cloud of hopelessness moments earlier... I'd already had to keep secrets from her, secrets about the skater boy and my aunts' decision for my future. If I obeyed my aunts and learned to hunt men, what else would come between the two of us? What else would wedge us apart?

And would it eventually break us?

CHAPTER EIGHTEEN

)(

"Allura," Aunt Anise called for me.

I tried to prance down the stairs as though the world wasn't crashing down around me. Shortly after Vanessa left to rejoin her clan in California, my aunts returned home. While they'd been in a great mood, I was waiting for the other shoe to drop.

Aunt Dawn's full-bodied auburn hair fell down around her shoulders as she nodded her head. She sat with her sisters on the green and white striped couch, giving me a bout of *déjà vu*. "Allura, we've had plenty of time to discuss you with the Council over the last few days."

I nodded, fighting my hands from wringing. So I had been the topic of discussion. Vanessa had been right.

What if the Council hadn't vetoed me, an underage siren, becoming a Provider? I closed my eyes and exhaled what little hope I'd had left.

"Now, in the past a siren wouldn't begin to exhibit Provider tendencies until she was a few years older than you, so the rules surrounding your role are geared for the older member; one who's already pledged to her clan. That being said, we know this particular situation is special and should be dealt with accordingly."

If I hadn't helped the bleeding woman in the water would I have avoided all this? Would I still be dealing with Provider tendencies? I nodded my head that I understood, although, at the moment, I wished I were clueless in everything Provider. My fingers inched free to play with a wrinkle on the thigh area of my jeans.

"So, for now we've been given permission to waive the rule stating that you have to be pledged to a clan before filling the role of Provider. I mean, honestly, we already know you're loyal and it's more important that you uphold the rule of not pledging until you've reached adulthood, than having you pledge early." She turned to acknowledge both my aunts nodding beside her.

"How does that sound to you, Allura?" Aunt Anise, Cara's mom, asked with a smile.

I wanted to tell them I deserved to have a choice, not to have to comply with some passive form of shoving me into a role I wasn't sure I even understood enough to want. I didn't, though. The idea of telling them "no" sounded less appealing as I thought about the punishment my response would inflict: fireweed times a hundred. And if I refused to do it, would they still threaten to force Cara into the role? I couldn't bring her further into a mess I'd made.

"I'll do what I have to," I said solemnly. The only way I'd knowingly hurt an innocent human was to save the life of a siren, of my own kind. I saw this agreement as saving Cara's life, or at least her life as she knows it.

I concentrated on distinguishing the full meaning of my aunts' words. Reading between their lines. Was this about me supplying the clan's food? They were talking about food, right? Why, after barely mentioning the Providers of old, was that title being thrown around so much lately? Did it have anything to do with what Vanessa had said about the newest elder leader, Liana?

"Lovely." Aunt Dawn's smile dropped from her face. "Now, about your new shark-hunting abilities." She stood from the couch to kneel in front of me, placing her hands on mine. "Do you feel drawn to attack them? In a way you can't explain?" she asked, peering into my eyes.

Thanks to Vanessa, I knew why she asked these things. Though, a part of me wished I didn't.

I assumed these were questions the Council had prodded her to find the answers to. I wanted to say no, but that'd be an obvious lie. "Yes, but—"

"And some powerful instinct inside leads the attack?" Aunt Anise interrupted.

"It does," I muttered, giving up any explanations I'd hoped to share or even get from them. I felt like they were locking me in a box with metal bars. I could see out, but every time Aunt Dawn spoke, the bars got thicker and pressed in on me. The box they were placing me in shrunk with each passing moment.

Aunt Dawn's hands were heavy on my own, and my fingers begged to do something...anything.

"Lovely." Aunt Dawn squeezed my hands. "Just go with it. Allow your body to lead the way. Practice is vital to your growth in this area." Her gray eyes sparkled with excitement as they stared into mine. "Remember, you're special with special abilities, and a special role; you're owed special considerations, too." A piece of light shined on Aunt Dawn's words, on the hidden meaning between the words. *Special considerations.*

I wanted to cry, scream out that this wasn't for me. I didn't want special considerations, not when the cost behind those considerations had to be astronomically high. Not that I completely knew the price. But I knew it would change my life in ways they were keeping to themselves. They were too excited for this to be a meaningless role they were placing me in.

Aunt Rebecca's quiet sigh caught my attention and I looked up over Aunt Dawn's shoulder to see Aunt Rebecca's head down, gazing at her feet.

"Now, with everything we do, there are limitations in an effort to uphold our secret," Aunt Anise piped up. "That stunt you pulled with the drowning woman was a dire mistake and must never be repeated."

"Yes," Aunt Dawn agreed. "You're very fortunate that woman hadn't come to with you nearby. It was ridiculously stupid."

"Not to mention the penalty for revealing our kind. The Council's punishments are swift and brutal." Aunt Anise stuck her bottom lip out as though she were pouting. "How do you think it would make us feel having to rip you to shreds?" Spikey imaginary fingers crawled up my spine at her uncharacteristically gruesome words. "Your sisters would be devastated if they were forced to do such a thing." She shook her head.

I swallowed hard and tried to muscle through the conversation in search for trinkets of facts, tried to pretend they hadn't just threatened to have my own sisters kill me. "Can I ask a question?" I regarded Aunt Dawn, as I worked to read her expression for some sort of indicator as to where the line between me being inquisitive and me being disrespectful was currently drawn.

"Sure," she answered.

"I guess I just don't understand—why now? I know we've got the whole kelpie thing to deal with, but they left. No one has heard from them. Maybe we can hold off a while."

"You let us worry about the timing." Aunt Dawn's smile tightened as she inched away from me.

My frustration of getting nothing from them clouded my judgment and before I realized I had successfully leaped over the previously drawn line into the incredibly disrespectful region, the words I had meant to only think, became audible. "But, I just—"

"Allura." Aunt Dawn stood in a flash and towered over me where I sat. Her tense voice matched her lips. "That's enough. We are still the leaders of this clan. A clan that you have not yet pledged to. One that you are not yet entitled to take part in the decision-making of, let alone know the reasons behind those clan decisions. We've told you what you need to know. All you need to do now...is *obey*. We want what's best for the clan. Don't you?"

I nodded and hung my head in submission.

"Well then." I stared at her bare feet as she spoke. "I'm glad you're on board." She made her way to the couch. "Now, you'd better get to bed. You only have a few hours left before it's time to get up for school and with your new urges and strengths, you'll be needing more sleep than usual."

With my head still low, I hurried away, fear of fire weed and much more pricking at my skin, drowning out the uncertainties churning within my mind. As I bound the steps two-by-two, my aunts' hushed tones nagged at my thoughts, reminding me who really held the control. And if they continued to tighten their grip on me, they'd observe every faucet of my life.

David was only a quick revelation away.

I stood at my bedroom door to slow my breathing before turning the knob.

When I opened the door, the lights were out and Cara lay on her bed facing the wall. I could tell she wasn't really sleeping because her foot stirred under the sheet. When we sleep we are completely still and silent. Thankful that she pretended to doze, I played along by silently shutting the door behind me and creeping to my bed. My head hit the pillow and I already knew I'd be pretending right along with Cara. Tonight would be a sleepless night.

CHAPTER NINETEEN

)(

The next morning I popped out of bed and got ready in a hurry, pulling on my jeans, a long sleeve cotton shirt and a corduroy jacket. After stuffing my homework binder and textbooks into my backpack and slipping my flats on, I waited impatiently beside the door for my sisters.

I realized in the car, during the silent, and awkward drive to school, that I'd forgotten to brush my hair. I ran my fingers through my tresses and by the time we arrived at school I looked less disheveled. The tension filling the small space shifted as I moved in place. My sisters had questions. Lots. And they all refrained from asking anything, which made me that much more anxious. I carried a burden for my clan, without being able to share my inner thoughts with even my sisters. As soon as Arlana pulled the parking break, I shot from the car.

I marched straight for the library as soon as my flats hit the parking lot pavement and waited in the hidden back corner where the reference books collected dust. I heard David's slow and even breathing from a few rows over and that sound, mixed with his scent, unwound a few knots in my back. As he walked toward me, his grin parted just enough to reveal his top white row of teeth. His eyes grinned too. The first button on his Henley hung open to show a triangle of tanned skin and that little indentation where his chest met his neck. His thick, black hair looked smooth and wet. He carried his black motorcycle helmet at his side.

"So, I got your text," he said as he wrapped his free arm around my waist.

I could only imagine the blank expression painted across my face. While I had spent the night wondering what my aunts' new interest in me meant for David and my relationship, I hadn't actually determined how much I would tell him or even in what way.

He put his helmet on a bookshelf before kissing the top of my head. "I've been thinking about you a lot, since I haven't been able to see you in days."

"And?" I leaned my head into that nook right above his chest muscle, but below his shoulder.

"And I have some questions about you. About your kind, I should say."

I tilted my head up to look into his eyes.

"No, I'm not rethinking this. Don't look at me like that," David said with a light chuckle. "I *want* to be with you."

My fingers traced where his artery ran down the inside of his arm, although he wore long sleeves. The blood pumping on his super-highway of veins pulsed beneath my fingertips.

He smiled and tilted his head, before he peered down at my wandering fingers. "Hungry?"

"What? No!" I jerked my hand down to my side. "I just like the way it feels. So much strength coursing through you."

"Don't stop. I was just joking." When I kept my hands at my side, he changed the subject. "Can I pretend I didn't say that and ask a normal dating question?" He reached out again to reestablish a line of physical contact, and I allowed his arm to wrap around my lower back. "Like, what's your favorite food?"

I shuddered inside wondering if human would soon become my favorite food. "Shark," I answered. "How about you?"

"Pizza with anchovies. My family thinks it's disgusting, but I love the salty taste. One of those strange things I probably inherited from my birth parents."

"That's not bad in terms of human meals." I smiled, only inches from his face. "I missed you." It felt good to smile, to think of something other than possibilities of impending doom.

To feel normal.

He leaned in to kiss me again. "I missed you, too."

I nestled back into that little dip on his chest where his collarbone met his shoulder when a blanket of guilt crept over me. It was time. I had to tell him. I searched for the exact terms. The perfect meanings. Nothing.

"What are you thinking about?" he asked, as though he knew.

"I saved a woman from drowning that day I met you and I absorbed her blood which flipped some switch inside me and now my aunts are saying I'm a Provider and that they discussed me at the meeting they attended, which means they have more planned for me than merely hunting sharks for dinner." The words poured from my mouth. Whether they were the right words or not, they were out there and exposed. I finally exhaled. "Crap."

"Okay, I think I got about half of that, but what's a Provider?" I knew without looking at him that his eyes were wide, or his eyebrow rose, or something along those lines.

"Crap. Crap. Shit." I shook my head. "I've been wracking my brain all night and this morning for the perfect way to explain the mess I got myself into, and this is the best I can do?" I removed myself from the comfort of David's chest and stood on tiptoes to look him in the eyes. "There's something going on in my sphere of life right now and I think I may be at the center of it, or at least I will be soon."

"As the Provider? Whatever that is." A hint of frustration flickered in his eyes. Did he hate being on the outside of my personal life?

Hell, I hated being on the outside of my personal life.

"I shouldn't have said that title...or most of what I just spewed at you." A weighty groan escaped my mouth. "But honestly, if I explain all this siren history to you, a human, it would be as if I'd just signed your death notice…with my own blood."

His chestnut eyes closed. He sighed and then slowly opened them again. "If I can't ask how this affects you, can I at least know where I come in?"

I wished I could tell him to forget everything I'd just said. That I'd handle this and not to worry. But I couldn't be sure how much would be the truth and how much would be lies. "I don't even think this has anything to do with you, but I want to be as honest as possible and give you a heads up that I feel the tide shifting, and I'm not sure in which direction the waves will hurl."

I eyed the clock opposite us high on a wall. "We'd better get to class." I frowned and slowly reached up to kiss his cheek, not sure if he felt particularly affectionate at that exact moment.

He didn't respond, so I took that as my cue to leave. Except, his arms refused to let go of me.

"I think I love you," he whispered.

My head jerked to peer at him. I sprang from his embrace.

"Don't freak out." His body shifted, leaning from one foot to the other. "I freaked you out didn't I?"

"No," I blurted and then nodded my head. "Well, kinda." He had no way of grasping the severity of his words. Not that he couldn't understand love, but love between a siren and a human was impossible.

He dropped his backpack and closed the gap between us. His hands cupped my cheeks as he tilted my chin upward, my eyes meeting his soft gaze. "I understand. We've gotten real close real fast. And if you can't tell me everything, that's fine. I get it. But don't pull away from me. I love you, and if that means I have to wait for you to be one hundred percent mine, or deal with some family drama, then I'll wait. As long as I know it's you I'm getting in the end."

"I wish it were that easy." A tear pricked my eye, but I forced it away, unwilling to completely release my emotions. Someone actually wanted to make me his number one, and because of the rules and expectations my aunts had placed upon me, I couldn't allow him to love me. One person. I wasn't allowed to have even one person.

Except for Cara, I reminded myself. But this was different. Wasn't it?

"I wish you would try, instead of brushing me off by telling me how useless it is to hope," he said. He grabbed his backpack and started walking past me to leave the library.

I reached out for his hand. "Can we talk more about this later?" I couldn't have him mad at me on top of everything else going on.

"Sure." David landed a kiss on my head. "I'll see you later, then."

"Good."

We left the library separately.

I quickly headed through the empty hall to my first period class, late again. Deep purple lockers streamed past me as I walked at a humanly pace.

"Allura, wait," Cara's whisper drifted to me.

I turned as she approached.

"I wanted to tell you something. I thought about it all night, and I feel like I need to say it." Cara eyed me seriously.

I just stared at her, knowing full well the bell would ring any moment.

"I don't think my mom and our aunts want us talking about the Provider thing right now, but I can't let you feel alone in all this. I need to tell you my thoughts and then I'll drop it."

I nodded.

"You should embrace this, Allura. This is the answer to your questions. You don't have to fight it anymore, you can embrace it, and you should."

I started to argue, but she cut me off.

"I'm not done. As the Provider you'll be able to lead the clan one day; even though Aunt Dawn says she's not the leader, we all know better. But after my mom and our aunts leave, it'll be us four, and you'll be the leader. And our clan, it'll be the strongest clan around."

"It's not that easy," I whispered, glad Arlana's and Celine's classes weren't nearby. I'd just told David the same thing. None of this was easy. Not for me.

"Why? Your body wants to kill and eat. The Provider kills and eats. Win-win."

"My body wants to devour men. But my head still says it's wrong. If I give in to one, I'm torturing the other." I shifted my bag when the first period bell rang.

"You're late, ladies." I swung around to see Jason, the jock jerk, walking toward us.

I turned back to Cara. "What's with this guy interrupting our locker conversations?"

"Ignore him," she suggested.

I hugged Cara and thanked her for her honest thoughts.

Suddenly, something groped my butt.

I swung on my heel to see Jason's outstretched arm, nodding head, and stupid smirk.

My muscles didn't have time to clench or my stomach time to tighten.

I lunged at the dickwad, shoved him into the lockers and pinned him there. "You seriously grabbed the wrong butt," I seethed. I really didn't need this shit right now.

"I don't know, it felt pretty right to me," he responded with a laugh.

"Not for long." I didn't want to bite Jason to death. I wanted to beat him within an inch of his life *and then* bite him to death. I pulled my arm back, my fist clenched tightly.

"Stop, Allura!" Cara yelled as she grabbed at my back, pulling me from the jerk.

I gulped down a trickle of acid.

I let Cara ease me away until he was just within arm's reach. I swung my arm. My fist crashed into cheekbone, the slamming sound replaced by a crunch.

He yelped out loud and then fought back tears. But he didn't scream or shoot me the death glare I half expected. It suddenly occurred to me that I might have gone too far. If he pressed charges, I would get expelled. At the moment, I didn't care. Let him, and my aunts, choke on that.

"You like my hands on you?" I asked Jason before I hooked my arm in Cara's and walked away. I turned to acknowledge the still-stunned jerk with tears in his eyes. "Try that shit again and my sister won't be able to stop me."

"Wow," Cara clutched my arm. "Was it hard not to bite him?"

"Yes." I smiled with an ounce a pride. I had controlled myself. "It was hard as hell."

CHAPTER TWENTY

)(

After another kelpie-free lunch period with my sisters, I headed toward math class and found a desk available in the back of the room.

"Excuse me," a male voice said, uncomfortably close to my ear.

I turned to see who dared to talk to me. Jason, the full-of-himself jerk who apparently enjoyed my beating the first time so much he'd come back for more. He took the only other seat beside mine and pulled his book and a pencil from his backpack.

I eyed him a moment more before facing forward in my chair.

"I don't think I've introduced myself," Jason spoke again. I didn't answer. "Allura right? My name's Jason."

I sighed and turned my head to see Jason's hand outstretched toward me. "What do you want, a knee to your junk or a fist in your face?" Irritation saturated my voice. I did not have the emotional bandwidth to deal with him today.

"I wanted to say, hello." He held his hand out for a moment more and then rested it on his desk, fiddling with his pencil. "You were unbelievable earlier. Who taught you to hit like that? Amazing. I've never had someone fight back. I kinda dig it." He rubbed his purple and blue cheek. Maybe that crunch I'd heard was the locker and not his face. He was lucky I'd withheld my strength and a bad bruise was all he got.

His big brown eyes reminded me of a needy puppy begging for attention, if for only a nod and a glance. His lowlighted blond hair fell from his head in a way that most girls would probably call perfectly tousled. I called it high-maintenance.

As a baseball player on the varsity team, girls swooned over him. He had plenty of admirers to choose from, a new girl on his arm every two weeks. Each girl ended up as nothing more than a conquest to be laughed about with his buddies. Kaven and Sean had told me plenty of stories about Jason. Disgusting. Not to mention his overly-friendly dickwad hands.

I glared at him, scrutinizing his expression. His regular cocky sneer and eyebrow raise were non-existent. Now his brows knitted together and his lips sagged. He pulled his dark purple and gold letterman's jacket from his arms and hung it on the back of his chair, watching me while he moved.

"Listen Jason," I leveled. "Let's be honest. You don't care about getting to know me almost as much as I don't care about your...existence." The words crept from my mouth in a way to accentuate their meaning. Normally the icy exterior my sisters and I exuded worked well at keeping horny boys at bay. I thought David was the exception, but now I wondered if I was losing my finesse.

I turned back toward the front of the classroom as the teacher wrote something on the whiteboard. Her long, brown skirt swayed as she reached up to start the math equation at the top of the board and worked her way down, spilling red numbers and symbols onto the stark white.

"I understand." Jason's throat caught with a heavy sigh. "It's just that, I think I really like you."

"What?" I whispered, brows furrowed and eyes narrowed.

"I've always thought you were hot, but today, the way you handled yourself, the more I think about it the more I realize...I love you." He picked up his pencil again, nervously twiddling it with his fingers.

Sick. He liked the way I *handled* him. "Don't talk to me. You're crazy." I turned away from him again and plastered my eyes on the whiteboard.

"Crazy about you," Jason whispered.

I ignored him, but could still hear his pencil twirling. *Weirdo.* For the rest of the period I tried to focus on the teacher's lecture while Jason's sighs and deep breaths grated on my nerves every few minutes. I watched the clock. Stuffing my binder and book into my backpack, I prepared to jump up and bolt out of the class before Jason found another reason to get my attention.

Right as the bell rang, before Jason could so much as whimper in my direction, I fled from the class and down the hall, until I reached my locker. I opened it and leaned my face inside, wishing the silent darkness would surround more than my head. My temples ached and my fingers fidgeted. I did not need this.

David knew to keep his distance in public, to act as though my icy, pretend-arrogance worked on him just as it had always worked on others in the past. Jason, on the other hand, was going to make a spectacle out of me whether he realized it or not. And then what would happen? Would others in the school notice my new approachable status and decide to take a shot? And there was the whole sisters-and-aunts-finding-out issue. No. I had to deal with Jason. But in one swift, powerful swoop of cruel siren aggression? Or cold indifference? Something told me the latter wouldn't work.

CHAPTER TWENTY-ONE

)(

My clan swam through the Puget Sound, nibbling on starfish, cracking open mussels, and picking off small fish from their schools. Aunt Dawn swam up alongside me. Her tailfin announced her approach as she neared. Black, white, and crimson scales intermingled over her tail and body, but her tailfin boasted a vibrant deep-red color that sometimes—in the right light—appeared to be dripping with fresh blood. When she needed to hide underwater, she had to fold her fin in tightly to conceal as much of the scarlet as possible. I had always thought her tail and auburn hair mirrored her fiery personality. Now, I knew there were deeper, darker depths to that personality than I'd ever imagined.

"Hungry?" she asked, eyeing the now empty mussel shell I released from my grasp as it floated down beneath my ebony and emerald tail.

"Yes." I hovered near a rock and picked the biggest, plumpest starfish I saw. Its rough, raised texture helped me grip it better as I wrenched the animal from its safe perch. The pink leathery star fought me, clinging to the rock when my aunt spoke again.

"You had a visitor while you were napping after school today," she said, as though she were merely commenting on the ridges in the stone my weak prey worked to cleave at.

David. I told him to stay away from my house, from my sisters and aunts. My fingers released the starfish and I turned to read my aunt's face. "Who?" I asked innocently.

"Some boy named Jason." Her lips curled into a smile and her gray eyes widened slightly. "He looked like a lost soul tracking down his owner, as though his life depended on it."

I sighed, thankful it hadn't been David. And then another alarm went off. Jason. Well, there went handling him in a discreet way.

Despite her smile, I needed to explain that I'd hadn't broken any rules. "He just started talking to me in school today, out of the blue." Except for that time I had pinned him up against a locker.

"I understand. These things happen."

"Not to me," I blurted.

"They do happen to the Provider." She smiled as warmly as Aunt Dawn could without looking like she was masterminding a devious plan in her head. "I have to ask though, just to make sure; you don't have any feelings for this Jason boy do you? You're not attracted to him?" She appeared uncomfortable discussing a boy with me, talking about a subject we usually had no reason to discuss.

"Ick, no. He disgusts me." I shook my head and scowled at the thought of being attracted to the womanizing jerk.

"Good." She peered down and smoothed her hands over her red, black, and white, scaly hips. "I spoke to the Council this afternoon, and they wanted me to double check." Her eyes returned to mine. "And what about that other boy following you around?"

I gave her a blank stare. There was no other boy following me around school.

"What's his name?" Her fingers tapped against her scales as her palm rested on her hip. "Daniel?"

My heart went from zero to sixty in less than a second. I knew my blank stare morphed into full recognition as I shook my head. *Who told her? How did she know? How long has she known? David* never *follows me around school!* She could keep guessing too, because I refused to give up his name.

"That's his name, David," she said too easily and uninterested. "The boy who stayed with us a night."

The muscle in my hand twitched; it wanted to ball up, clench tightly, and fight against the anger swelling within me from hearing *his* name pass through *her* lips.

"You aren't drawn to him either, are you? In any other way than you're drawn to a shark, or this starfish here?" Her auburn eyebrow rose as she studied me.

I gulped. I had to protect David the only way I knew how. I had to pretend he, basically, didn't exist to me. That her sources—whoever they were—had gotten it all wrong. "No." I tried to fake the same disdain I'd had for Jason, but it wouldn't come. "And he doesn't follow me around school. I barely know him."

"I'm glad to hear that," she quipped, completely ignoring my attempt to clear his name. She peered down at my free hand. I quickly unclenched my fingers. "If a Provider developed feelings for a human she'd have more to worry about than boys following her."

Her tone lightened as she chuckled. "Oh, Allura, this must be such a confusing time for you." She shook her head and feigned a sympathetic expression.

Her roller-coaster vibes were giving me whiplash.

"Don't worry. Everything will be cleared up very soon." She smiled.

"How so?" I peered down at the starfish, although the conversation was making my stomach churn.

"The Council is coming. Actually," she said with a hint of happiness in her voice, "they're already on their way." She watched for my reaction.

I had to do something, something normal that showed this topic was like any other, and in no way upset me.

I ran my fingers over my potential meal as it regained its attachment to its rock. It tightened under my touch and I wondered if my Aunt Dawn could sense me tightening under her questions. I held my face upright, and met her gaze.

A lonely, gray fish swam underneath her blood-red fin, only slightly bumping her fan-like body part. With blurring speed, she reached down, snatched the fish, and broke its body between her vice-grip fingers. "Are you ready to train for your new role in our clan as Provider?" She bit into the side of the fish as she eyed me, awaiting my reply.

I thought for a moment, but not too long to make her question my answer. "Yes, I'd like to know all that it entails." This time I wasn't technically lying. Cara might be right. I might be able to control things better if I played along and took the powerful position. And, if David had anything to do with my role, it was crucial I find out so I could somehow change the direction of their plans or influence their course of thinking.

"I bet you would." She tore the limp fish open and stripped its meat from its scales, tossing bite-size pieces into her mouth. Threads of blood wafted from her lips. "Being the Provider is a big responsibility, one that our kind doesn't take lightly."

Again with the skirting-around-the-answer responses.

"Why can't *you* explain it all to me?" I asked, trying to bolster her ego. I hoped she wouldn't take my inquiry as me questioning her authority. "Why do I need to wait for the Council?"

She finished stripping the fish of its meat before tossing the carcass aside. She leaned her right arm against the rock I hovered near and ogled the starfish before meeting my gaze. Her face inched toward mine and her smile dropped as anger flashed through her eyes.

My heart pounded in my chest as I kept completely still, frozen, waiting for the tongue lashing. I muddled through my racing mind to fix my mistake, to somehow backtrack or change the subject. But, before my speeding mind could slow enough to work properly, my aunt almost hissed an answer.

"We would love to teach you the Provider ways." Her lips tightened as she spoke. "But, the Council doesn't exactly agree with our methods." She paused. "And upsetting them right now would not be beneficial for our clan."

Aunt Dawn pulled away from me, but kept her hand pressed to the rock. "They've made us promise to allow them to deal with you in all Provider matters. They don't want us making the same mistake twice." She turned her gaze on my starfish and ran her fingers down the center of it. All I could do was watch as she eyed my food.

"Mistake?" I asked. Her body language and tone of voice invited me into the conversation rather than warned me to tread lightly.

She looked around and her eyes rested back on me. "Apparently that too is not my explanation to share."

Her fingers left the pink starfish and rested for a moment on my shoulder before she swam off. The starfish and I were left alone to finish what we had started. What I had started.

Finally being able to breathe, I exhaled and an explosion of fury and tension rippled through my arms and tail. *Crap. Crap. Shit.* I was literally stuck—out of options, except to wait for the Council of elders to explain what the hell was going on. My shaky fingers dug between the coarse stone and the five-pointed sea-being clinging to life. My nails ripped the starfish from its perch along the rock. I wrapped my fingers around its arms, two of its triangular extremities in each of my hands, and the fifth pointed up at my face. It wriggled slowly for a short while as I zoned out, only half-watching it try to free itself from my grip and the other half of my mind frantically spitting rebellious words at Aunt Dawn. My focus rested back on the creature. Was that me? Squirming in my aunts' grasp with the unrealistic hope of over-coming whatever future they had planned for me? No. I wouldn't allow it. I placed the animal back on its rock, where it clung to life once again, and slowly moved away from me. I envied it. I didn't have the option of changing my scenery, of putting distance between me and the siren set on ripping my heart in two.

CHAPTER TWENTY-TWO

)(

"We have to talk." I wrapped my hand around David's wrist and led him outside the school.

"Now? We have class." Right as he said the words, the bell for first period rang across the parking lot. "Wait. You just talked to me in front of people. You touched me too."

"You rode today, right?" I asked, scanning the parking lot for his motorcycle.

"Yeah, it's right over here." He pointed to the street. His dark blue motorcycle with white pin striping and lots of shiny chrome sat against the curb. We didn't talk again 'til we reached the two-wheeled vehicle. "Where are we going?" he asked. His gray Henley stretched tightly over his chest as he grabbed the extra black helmet he kept latched to his bike and handed it to me.

After I strapped the helmet ties under my chin, I answered, competing with the sound of the engine roaring to life, "To our lake."

As we rode, I relished in the absence of words. I sat behind David, squeezing him tight against me. The rumbling of the engine drowned out my thoughts. I needed to sit near him and cling to him. I knew the moment I revealed the truth—at least some of it—there would be a huge possibility that he'd question my intentions, that a piece of him wouldn't trust me and would always wonder if my Provider guiles were luring him in and working him over.

Goddess knew, I wondered the same thing.

The broad bike leaned in one direction and then the other with each turn. I spotted David's tinted visor pulled up exposing his face in the reflection of the side mirror. The rumbling effects of the engine lost their magic and my heart and mind took turns ruling my thoughts. How much should I reveal to him? Telling him would help him be prepared and decide for himself whether or not he still wanted to be involved with me. Fear chipped away at my nerves. What if he didn't think I was worth the trouble?

He must have spotted me trying to peek at his facial expression through the mirrors because he turned his head toward me enough to meet my gaze in the reflection and winked before returning his attention to the road. My heart thudded in my chest. *He has to know. He has to protect himself.*

David pulled the motorcycle off the road and onto the pine needle-covered dirt beneath a cluster of fir trees lining the property. He started removing his helmet, and I knew next he'd get off the bike and turn to help me. But I couldn't wait for his chivalry, not today. I swung my leg over the sissy bar on the back of the seat and jumped down onto the ground. I grasped at the straps under my chin. I flung the black helmet onto the motorcycle seat and began trudging through the mud as drops of water fell onto my head. I didn't know why I wanted to get to the lake so badly. Maybe part of me wanted it over with, wanted to stop wondering how he'd react when I told him more than just bits and pieces of my siren reality. But there was this other part that wished the lake would never come, that hoped we could walk together for days and never reach the place where I'd have to draw the line.

He quickly caught up to me and held my hand as our feet moved in step. Pinecones crunched beneath us as trees swayed above us. The air smelled different than moments before, fresher, wetter. A storm was coming. The weather mirrored the way I felt: sad, dark, commanding, and impulsive.

I arrived first at the tall bush separating us from the lake, and shoved my hand into the tightly wound branches, pushing them apart, forming an opening. As we neared the dock I dropped David's hand from mine and hurried forward.

"Are we swimming?" he asked, traces of confusion in his voice.

My eyes locked onto the lake. My heart ached. I wanted so badly to pull him into the water with me, to watch his legs fuse together as scales cascaded over his body. To swim away with him. Far enough away to shed my supposed responsibility as Provider; man-hunter.

A shrill of fear mixed with pain and hunger rang through my body. I knew it. Somewhere inside, I'd known it for a while—since Vanessa painted it all in a very clear and vivid picture for me. It was part of the reason her words struck me so deeply, angered me. Aunt Dawn confirmed it last night in the ocean, and now I had to tell David.

This was happening. Her plan would move forward.

I had to explain the blood. The hunger and thirst. The acid that dripped from my teeth just picturing these things.

"Allura!" David called. He had stopped halfway to the dock. I neared the edge.

I halted mid-step and swung around to face him. "What?" I shouted, anger rising up my body. How dare he make me feel this way! Why did I have to fall for him? Why did he have to bring me to this crossroads where I'd have to choose to reveal everything to him and possibly cause hardship for my clan and me, or keep it all a secret and risk his life? The decision tore me in two like the near-fate of the starfish I had let go. No matter what side I took, no matter what choice I made, I'd have to neglect part of me so much so that I'd never be whole again.

"What are you doing? You said you wanted to talk." Concern replaced confusion on his face.

"I don't know what I want, David. I want you, but I want you to be like me, so then do I really want you?" I took a step back. My heels hung over the side of the dock. "When I first met you, I wanted you to leave me alone, but your...your comedic confidence made me like you somehow. Your humanity hooked me at the exact moment I began losing my own." My voice lowered, "Then I wanted to kill you...to devour you. Did you know that?" Suddenly, I knew my decision. I knew how much I was going to tell him. I had to protect him. My body, my mouth, maybe even my heart had decided for me.

He stopped shaking his head and stared in stunned silence.

"Yes, David! Apparently, I'm a Provider. It's what I do!"

He still didn't move or make a sound. The words hurt to say. The confession I had made out of love sounded like such a venomous, hateful statement.

A sheen of tears covered his russet eyes and snuffed out their warmth.

I took a step toward him and lowered my head. "That first day in the woods I thought you were going to be my meal. I *hoped* you were going to be my meal." I wanted to reassess his expression, but I couldn't bear to see the hurt in his eyes, because I wasn't done yet. "I felt drawn to you and when I didn't kill you that day in the woods, I shocked myself. So I let you be around me." My throat caught.

He exhaled deeply and my head jerked up. One single tear slid down his cheek.

Without thinking, I quickly started toward him but stopped abruptly when he flinched at my movement. Oily tears trickled down my face as the two of us stood five feet apart, staring at one another like two forlorn statues destined to be set apart from each other for the rest of their existence.

"Please, David." My tears flowed freely now as I gulped back the words. Tenderness grew inside, a brokenness that shattered a little more with every tear shed. "I was wrong. I thought I was drawn to you to devour you, but I was wrong. I'm supposed to be with you. Siren or not, I need to be with you."

Another tear released from his eye and wound its way down his face.

"Damn it, David! Please, say something." My cries turned into whimpers. "I need to know that you still love me. I can't live without you."

"I..." He cleared his throat and tried to speak again. "I don't know what I think; you just dropped this on me. Obviously you've had time to process this, I'm only hearing about it right now."

"Can I come to you?" I asked in desperation. I needed to touch him, to feel some sort of connection.

"Yes." He shook his head. "No, I don't know. Damn it, why do you confuse me so much? I told you, I can't read hieroglyphs."

"I'm sorry." I closed my eyes for a long moment, wishing this could be over and I could be in his arms again. "This is all new to me."

"I know you're sorry." He threw up his hands. "I also know that you can't help what you are." He started pacing the width of the dock. "I need to know more about you being the Provider. What exactly does that mean?"

I peered down at the wooden slats beneath me. "A long time ago the Provider would lure men so that her sisters and sirens from other clans could eat them. It gave them strength. And the Provider had that responsibility on her shoulders. To keep our kind thriving."

"And your kind isn't thriving right now?" he asked.

"Not according to my aunts. And you should know…" I wanted to shut my mouth, but I had to be honest. This was, after all, honesty hour. "I've bitten someone. But I stopped from going any further."

"Wait, you've bitten a guy?"

I didn't answer. Shame washed over me as I stared at the water passing beneath the slats of wood I stood upon.

David made a grunting noise and asked another question. "This ability, to kill and eat humans, is in you?"

"Yes." I waited for the next question. My fingers fidgeted.

"How does the Provider lure the men?"

Shocked that he wasn't pressing the me-biting-a-guy matter, I looked up to meet his gaze. "There's something about her that draws men in, and they'd give anything for her, follow her anywhere." I dropped my eyes back down. "Plus, she has these natural hunting tactics she uses."

"Do you think I'm being lured by you? That I don't really love you?" His eyes burned into me. There was the question I had been waiting for, the one I had been asking myself.

"Yes, sometimes," I whispered to the slats of wood and the lake water sliding by beneath.

"Look at me, Allura." The seriousness of his voice commanded me, "Look at me."

I raised my now-heavy chin and stared him square in the eyes.

"I don't follow you around because I want something from you. I don't pine after you. I don't lust after you like that." He sighed and his eyes softened. "I love you because you're you. You're strong. You know what you want, and I even like that pushy, mean streak you have that shows me you're not faking what you're feeling. You're real, more so than any other person I've met."

My chin dropped to my chest as slick tears poured from my eyes. How could he love someone who had wanted to kill him at first? I was a siren—his predator. No, not his predator, never his, no matter what my aunts or the Council did or said. My chest heaved; my body couldn't absorb oxygen quick enough and I opened my mouth to gasp for air.

Acceptance surrounded me, embraced me, and caressed me. His arms wrapped around my shoulders, clothing me in love. His affection made my chest heave harder. The tears poured fiercely.

"Shh." He rocked me safely between his arms. "It took a lot of guts to open up like that. Thank you."

"You're welcome," I managed to spit out in between sobs. "But..." I tried to take another gulp of air. "But, that's not all. Now that I brought you into all of this, my aunts know about you." I looked up at him. "You need to stay away from them, from all of them. They think you're my prey, and they're planning something."

"Planning what?"

I buried my face into his chest and the words came out slightly muffled. "They won't tell me, but it's not hard to guess. The siren leaders, they're our elders and we call them the Council, are on their way. I think they're coming to evaluate me or something, and I can only assume why they're in such a rush to start using me as the official Provider." Another sob racked my chest as my fears became real enough to say out loud. "I think they're going to start the ceremonies again."

When David didn't react I pulled my chin from his chest and tipped it up to look at his face. His gaze went to a far off place as he mentally pieced things together. I gave him a minute before I continued voicing my own thoughts.

"And Vanessa told me that she thinks my mother was a Provider. Then one of my aunts mentioned yesterday that the Council wouldn't let my aunts have anything to do with me learning what a Provider is all about because they didn't want the same mistake repeated." I stared directly into his contemplative eyes. "If Providers are rare oddities and my mother was one, and my aunts made a mistake having to do with a Provider in the past, did that mistake have anything to do with my mother?"

I closed my eyes and breathed in David's scent, trying to let it soothe me. The falling rain accentuated his natural fragrance and I absorbed it in through my pores.

"So you think they plan to start those ceremonies back up again? Like, human hunting?" His gaze shifted and his chestnut brown eyes focused on mine.

"Yes." I sighed. "My aunts want our clan to have the ear of the Council and be more influential. I assume having a Provider in the clan will help. And it seems the Council just wants the whole race of sirens to be more powerful. My aunts have always complained about how weak we've become and how we'll one day be so weak that the humans will have no problem picking us off until we're extinct, like the mermaids. Not to mention the other species out there. I always just thought they were being overly dramatic and doomsdayish. Now I'm thinking that's actually a real threat and the Council is taking action."

"Do you think you're heading toward extinction?" he asked.

"I can't be sure. Humans don't even know we exist."

"Then why can't you tell them no? I mean, go to the ceremony, because if you rebel completely they won't respect you enough to care about whatever stand you make. But don't do what they tell you to do if it ends up being something like killing a person."

"Disobedience is a big deal to us, especially in front of the Council. What if it ends up being a kill or be killed situation?"

"I don't know." David shook his head.

"I'm scared for you," I said. "What if they punish my disobedience by hurting you?" The thought of them killing David felt like a fist to my gut. "I won't let them touch you." I reached my fingers up and ran them through his thick, wavy hair. "Promise that you'll stay away from me, at least until this is over."

"I don't know," David protested.

"Most of this Provider stuff is pretty foreign to me. What if I go into a trance and sing some sort of song, or put off a scent that attracts you to me and that's how the Provider ultimately lures men? I mean, I've never heard exactly how they attract the men. Just that they do. We can't risk it. It's safer if you just stay away." My fingers trickled from David's hair to his cheekbone and down to his jaw. "I'll call you when it's safe."

His mouth fell on mine as his hands worked their way to the small of my back and pulled me closer. His heavy breathing and the pounding of his heart created one of my favorite melodies. My hands met behind his neck and wove together, forming a chain bonding us. I cared for him. I cared for him so much.

"I won't let them hurt you," I breathed, my voice thick and throaty. "Even if it kills me."

CHAPTER TWENTY-THREE

)(

We were to meet the Council—my whole clan—on the beach of Deadman Island. As we swam toward shore our scales melted into naked skin in preparation. My aunts reminded my sisters and me not to speak in front of the Council unless asked a question. We were to maintain all rules in the highest regard and basically keep our mouths shut.

"They won't have much to do with you girls." Aunt Dawn gestured to my sisters. "But you, Allura, you will be their focus. Don't forget, they are the descendants of past siren leaders, show them the utmost respect. Everything you say will be heard. Everything you do will be watched." She swam closer to me, laying her hand on my right arm. "To be a clan with a Provider makes us a powerful clan. I know you will represent us well."

I responded with a half-smile and a nod of my head. My aunts had only prepared us for the Council's visit by telling us what and what not to do, by explaining our roles, but never really shedding any light on the Council's full reason for coming. I exchanged looks with my sisters, whose eyes were filled with unspoken questions.

My aunts walked from the ocean and then my sisters and me followed. As the water moved down their bodies, they spoke in hushed tones amongst themselves. I glanced at Cara who bit her lip. I raised my eyebrow but she only shrugged her shoulders. I looked at Celine, but she was too busy staring ahead to notice me. Her eyes were wide and a slight smile played on her lips. Arlana watched my aunts convene, watched her mother, Aunt Rebecca, hover on the outskirts of my aunts' discussion. Arlana's eyes narrowed as Aunt Rebecca gave her a nervous glance.

"They're coming." Celine gasped before clamping her mouth shut.

Five sirens appeared from the tree line, stepping from the covering of branches to the pebbled beach. All were older women. All beamed with a sense of entitlement from their high-tilted chins, to their graceful movements. I'd never seen sirens like these, adorned with brilliantly silver locks. Age creased the skin around their vibrant eyes.

My aunts stood in a line in front of my sisters and me.

Aunt Dawn spoke first. "Welcome," she said as she bowed her head.

My other aunts bowed their heads too and whispered, "Welcome."

One silver-haired woman with a cropped hairstyle stepped forward, leaving two Council members flanking each side of her. I assumed she was the new Council leader, Liana. "Many thanks for the warm welcome," she said.

As she spoke, more sirens appeared from the trees. I recognized Vanessa leading the group. She caught my eye and winked before pulling back to form a line with her clan behind the Council.

This all seemed so unnecessarily formal to me.

In watching Vanessa, I caught a glimpse of something dark orange running through the trees behind her: A flicker of fire within the evergreens. It disappeared behind a thick tree trunk. Despite my impeccable vision, I had to squint to get a better look. A dead, half-eaten silver fox dropped from a tree limb and landed in the dirt with a thud.

"Allow us to introduce Miyu," one of the Council members said.

The blaze of fire reappeared, perched upon a branch above the Council. I blinked and jumped back. Celine, standing rigidly tall beside me, smacked my backside, making me quickly find my board-straight posture again. My wide eyes stayed locked on the choker necklace of fire-orange stones clinging to the long, delicate neck of a siren. The woman crouched, and dropped to the ground.

She landed in silence directly in front of the line of Council members. Eyeing her surrounds, she pulled herself up. Her black, almond shaped eyes scanned my aunts from one side of the line to the other before looking past them and scanning the line my sisters and I made. Her gaze rested upon my face as her blood-smeared lips turned upward.

"Miyu is the Provider we've located and chosen for the clans on the other side of the Pacific Ocean," one of the Council women stated. "While we can instruct your new Provider in her history and her practices in theory, Miyu can teach her more completely."

The wind ceased for a moment and Miyu's thick black hair settled, framing her face. Her high cheekbones led into a set of intensely bright, narrow eyes which sat under perfectly arched, black eyebrows.

"Per our request, Miyu has swum all the way from Kamakura, Kanagawa, Japan, to train your young Provider." After the Council member spoke, she returned to her line of silver-haired women and nodded to Miyu.

Miyu grinned. Her eyes stayed locked on mine as she licked blood from her lips. Without regarding my aunts, she walked around my three clan leaders, in front of my row, and stopped directly before me. Her left hand lifted and she gently placed it on my right shoulder.

"It's a pleasure to meet you," she said with absolute confidence.

"Thank you, but the pleasure's mine," I uttered, almost fumbling over my words.

What little pride I had in the Council calling me a Provider multiplied as Miyu touched me. Her hand felt strong, deliberate and yet gentle, her presence extreme and distinct. A gamey scent of blood swirled around her and I lifted my nose for more.

"Miyu?" a Council member called.

Miyu turned to look at who beckoned her.

"Let us get a look at her."

She nodded and escorted me, with her hand on the small of my back, to the center. Her hand placement made David pop into my mind, but I quickly pushed him out. I couldn't think about him right now. I had to pay attention, learn exactly why they had come, and what they expected of me.

Miyu and I waited between four rows, two before us and two behind us.

The five Council women strode to Miyu and me, creating a half circle in front of us. A shorthaired woman ran her fingers through my dark brown hair and lightly squeezed my arm.

"She's strong," the shorthaired woman said.

Miyu smiled warmly as she watched the leaders inspect me.

Liana, the woman who looked to be in charge, turned to Vanessa's clan. "It appears we will go ahead with the celebration as planned."

"Wonderful!" A woman, who looked a lot like Vanessa, nodded her head with a grin from one ear to the other.

The Council broke their half circle around Miyu and me, and in seeing that the business portion of the meeting was done for now, the other sirens exited their rows to greet each other with a relaxed welcome.

"Come," Miyu spoke under her breath to me. "We begin."

As the words left her mouth, she marched away from my clan toward Vanessa's clan and then past them. I followed, glancing back before entering the forest. My sisters' excited eyes locked on me until they were out of my line of sight.

I followed Miyu to one of the short cliffs along the side of Deadman Island. Without a word, scales the color of fire trailed down her neck. I joined in, and as the scales multiplied over our backs, we jumped from the cliff and plunged into the sea.

Miyu swam the Pacific Ocean as though she knew her way around. My heart thudded in my chest. Her confidence was both intimidating, and alluring. I wanted to have that kind of confidence, needed to have it. I had no idea who this woman was, what she had planned to teach me, and yet I trailed her like a duckling.

She stopped outside a natural underwater cave. "You've taken down sharks, I hear?" she asked, her no-nonsense gaze pointed directly at me.

"Yes." I eyed the opening to the dark cavern. Of course caves didn't scare me and darkness meant nothing to me, but still an ominous feeling washed over my body, prickling my skin.

"Good. So, you know how to kill prey who use tails and teeth to fight. You will learn how to attack and kill every type. Any you choose to devour will be yours. As Provider, it is your right to take whatever and whomever you wish as long as they are not siren." She followed the direction of my gaze and one side her mouth raised. "Yes, in there is your lesson."

I wanted to hang back and ask a few question first—arguing types of questions—but the steel in her eyes combined with the half-sneer on her lips, squelched the desire to ever disagree with her. In any way.

Deciding I had no other option, I slowly began to creep into the darkness that lay inside the huge, underwater hollowed-out rock when she gripped my bicep. "Remember. You want him. He *is* yours. You will not settle for anything less than his blood and flesh." She released my arm and waved me to go ahead.

I crept into the cave, allowing the darkness to engulf me. As I moved, I worked at deciphering the taste of the water around me—its exact movement and any sounds. Nothing. Complete stillness. I wondered exactly what Miyu had in mind for me to attack in this cave. Obviously not a human, but seeing as she was teaching me to assault and end the life of a creature without a tail, I could only assume she would use this creature, whatever it was, to work my way to men.

My muscles flexed for a quick second as though an electrical current shot through me. Work my way to men. Sadness and desire swam like Ying and Yang in my thoughts until I shook my head, flinging any ideas—other than ones that would help me in my current situation—away and out of my mind.

I need to concentrate and get this over with.

I drifted perfectly still in the blackness. Microscopic life floated like tiny dots all around me. I had to erase all thoughts of my existence outside of this moment. I filed through my favorite fantasies, and mentally landed on the one I'd had the hardest time pushing away in the last few weeks; me, on the shore, hovering over the man I'd just taken down. The hunger of the hunt ached within my gut. Thoughts of dousing my pores and mouth with the scarlet liquid-velvet intensified until the yearning in my stomach graduated from a pleading desire and churned with painful demands.

"Uh." The sigh escaped my lips before I could shove it back into my mouth, and swallow it into my cramping abdomen.

A light current of water from deeper inside the cave pushed at my scales. I absorbed what I could before it passed, but the taste seemed foreign. I wanted to swim toward whatever caused the movement, but I couldn't be sure how far back the cave reached. To place myself beside another predator—who happened to be my prey—without a way out, would be a deadly tactical decision.

Pressing my body against the slimy cavern wall, I inched my way toward where the movement originated and scanned the water for any visuals, silently thanking my eyes for being able to see in the dark. Twenty-five feet ahead of me, along the bottom edge of the cave wall, a thick vine-like thing sprang up, curled into itself and pulled back toward the sea floor. This time its shifting pushed a stronger current of water into me and its scent almost bowled me over.

A giant Pacific octopus. How could I have missed it before? I shook my head. I needed to throw myself into this, or I wouldn't get out alive. The scent alone was a dead giveaway—not quite fishy, but salty and briny and definitely male. I couldn't remember ever eating one of these. So, I had no clue what it would taste like.

It flung another huge tentacle and allowed it to settle to the bottom.

I watched the octopus move slowly along the sea floor, tightly winding up into itself. Its large, round body eased up the rocky wall of the underwater grotto. I fanned my tailfin out taut and in one hard stroke of my tail, closed the gap between us. At about ten feet away from the creature, I stopped to reassess the situation. It seemed to catch my scent because one thick tentacle sprang up from its body, reached out in my direction and unfurled less than a foot in front of me. Billowing puffs of sediment rose up to meet my tail. Tiny fragments of rock pricked my scales. It could almost reach me from ten feet away?

Miyu picked a big boy!

It pulled its tentacle back and coiled again while slinking to the opposite side of the cave. I wished I were seeing red, the way I had while hunting sharks. But, despite the hunger and knots in my stomach, the weight of who waited outside the cave, of who waited at home, and of who waited at the school for me, hung heavy across my shoulders.

I tried to center myself again. *You're here to kill. Kill or be killed. You're not leaving 'til you finish the job!* I hovered in the water and allowed my body to sway with the rhythm of the movement around me. *Time to go to work.*

As it slinked across the rocky wall, I sprang onto it, grabbed a tentacle in each hand and pulled, thrusting the pink vines away from one another, working to tear them from its body. I wouldn't have a chance to reach its body and deliver the fatal bite while the creature still had eight arms grasping and flinging at me. Tearing the rubbery tentacles from their base proved harder than I'd imagined. As I pried one tentacle from my scales enough to give me some wiggle room, another three wrapped around me—one on each arm and one around my waist.

"No you don't!" I said as I sunk my teeth into the viney limb wrapped around my right arm. It held tight, the suction cups gripping my skin.

My jaw tingled and my muscles quivered. I pushed my mouth to the tentacle and took a bite. Then another. And another. I tore the rough skin to shreds with my razor-like teeth. Bits of flesh and blood broke away from its body and swirled down my throat. Acid released into my mouth. *Finally.*

Thoughts of sampling the octopus for pleasure rather than necessity swept over my taste buds. My heart beat wildly, thudding in my ears.

The bloody tentacle on my right arm went flaccid and released from my skin. The tentacle wrapped around my left arm gripped tighter, as though it were trying to crush my bones under its pressure. I snarled as I gnawed intermittently on the muscular extremity, chewing off circular suctions cups, drinking in the blood that swirled around my lips. Another tentacle reached up in response, greedily grasping my right arm.

"You just don't give up do you?" I seethed as I worked at shredding the unrelenting skin.

Its enormous, oval body and splaying arms blurred in my vision, but I didn't need my sight anymore. My instincts took over. The predator in me scratched at the animal, tearing at it with my nails and teeth.

As tasty as octopus shreds of skin were, fighting with its many arms was getting me nowhere. I decided to switch tactics. My instincts screamed at me to go in for the kill and not allow the beast to put up a fight any longer. I yanked my arms outward, causing the two limbs encasing my elbows to spread out and pull tight. I swung my hands under and around the tentacles and grabbed two more. My fingers struggled to enclose the two thick flailing vines in each hand. One tentacle still swung loose, but I disregarded it, and pushed myself, head first into the oval body.

I rammed the top of my head against it and leaned my chin back, opening my mouth to bite deeply. But instead of skin, a thick cloud of black ink filled my mouth and the water around me. I couldn't help but breathe it in, absorb it through my pores. Unlike the water, this blackness I couldn't see through. I needed to feel around to find its body so I could land the killing bite, but I couldn't risk letting go of its tentacles that now writhed in my hands.

Suddenly, I couldn't taste its presence. The ink impaired my palate.

"You play dirty," I scolded, waiting for the water to clear while trying to keep ahold of its hostile arms.

But before the water cleared, the octopus started wrenching my arms, as though it were trying to pull them from my body the same way I had.

I jerked the four tentacles hard and fast. Then I shoved my mouth into where I thought its body would be amidst all the cloudy darkness. As my lips searched for skin to break under my teeth, something sunk into my neck. I struggled and tried to pull away, but it refused to let go.

It's biting me!

With every ounce of strength I could muster, I flung my tail back and forth to break free from its death grip. My ab muscles contracted and expanded, shoved and tugged my body. Strands of my hair tangled around the rubbery appendages, and each time it heaved, my head jerked and hair tore from its roots. As its rigid, pointed beak clamped into my neck and shoulder muscle, its barbed tongue began scraping my scales.

What felt like a thick, wire brush bore deeper and deeper into my neck until I screamed out in agonizing pain.

Its tentacles tightened again, and pulled my lower body closer. I tried to fight, but its saliva, now flowing into my veins, weakened me. It was as though it were turning my blood to liquid metal. My body felt heavy, and my heart beat slower.

Strength withered away with every heartbeat. My arms only stroked the animal now, rather than push it away. It squeezed tighter. I didn't want to give up. I couldn't give up—it was mine—but what choice did I have? It'd beaten me.

At least if I were gone, my aunts' plan would fail and David would be safe. The Provider—me—would be gone.

My neck went slack, and my arms gave in.

"Allura!"

With scorching pain, I barely raised my head. The cloudy water had cleared somewhat, and her body hovered in the opening of the cave. Miyu. Another Provider—no doubt more deadly than me—would be their back-up choice. I couldn't let this eight-armed beast take me. I had to protect David. And my clan, my sisters, they needed me.

"Allura, your tail, it's not over yet! Your tail!" she shouted.

Yes.

I curled my tail behind my back. My fin stretched to a fan. My head swam with pain and disorientation. I tried to ball my fists, but my arms refused to tighten. I pushed every last bit of energy, of anger, of pain, into the lower half of my body. I thrust my tail, propelling myself toward the center of the octopus' body. I shoved my razor sharp tail fin into the thick, circular body of my foe and tugged downward. Clouds of red replaced the fading ink as its arms fell limp and the two separate pieces of it tumbled to the sea floor with a muted thud.

I couldn't hover or even hold myself up. Shortly after the two pieces of dead animal fell, so did I.

CHAPTER TWENTY-FOUR

)(

It felt like a muffled dream—someone held me as they raced through the water. We passed the blurred plants and sea animals. I couldn't feel my tail, my arms, nothing actually—just scorching pain. A burning, searing agony pulsated on the left side of my neck. Fireweed had nothing on this.

I tried to see whose arms held me, but my heavy eyes closed against my will.

Did I rest in David's arms? Was it all over? Had the Council left already? My heart lifted for a second until I realized streams of water rushed past me. No, David could never carry me in the water like this. He couldn't urgently force the two of us through the liquid with only a pair of legs. A slick tear wound its way to freedom.

*M*y eyelids strained to be released from one another before slits of light entered my vision.

"Ow." I winced, reflexively rubbing my temple.

"You're awake, good." The tender voice belonged to Aunt Rebecca.

"Don't worry about your headache, it should only last another day or so. You're lucky to be alive."

"What happened?" I asked, squinting, barely able to see my clan's healer.

"A training accident." Her voice echoed traces of contempt. I struggled to make out her expression, but the light radiating through the window behind her made it impossible. She sat beside my bed, looking more like a shadow than a person.

"Oh, the octopus." I winced again. Dull pain reverberated through my lower neck.

I reached up in slow motion to rub the pain and assess the damage. Aunt Rebecca blocked my hand and placed it back onto the bed.

"No, you don't want to re-open that wound. It's been hard enough keeping the thing closed long enough to begin healing. Those octopus bites are nasty. Their saliva is a bit like ours, it has a compound to break down its opponent's tissue. Not to mention the fact that its ink and saliva combined causes disorientation and weakness. I don't know why they ever agreed to allow you to go up against such a thing." She *tsked*. "And without proper instruction first."

"She was training me," I managed to say through a dry throat. "Yes, Miyu's stunt that she deemed training, could have killed me. But I also felt a loyalty, a connection to her—one my head was too fuzzy to process or explain.

"I know, I know. I just can't say I approve much."

I prodded her a little with my words, hoping she'd give more of an explanation. "She said I need to know how to hunt and kill creatures without tails." I waited for her response. She probably had more information of where my training was headed than I did.

After an uncomfortable stent of silence she lowered her voice. "Yes, I suppose you killing creatures with tails isn't exactly the end goal for them." She rubbed her hand gently up and down my arm as I lay on the bed. "I just don't like it."

"Like what, Aunt Rebecca?" I yearned for her to come out with it already, to tell me what I wanted so badly to hear. "What don't you like?" To confirm my suspicions.

"No, if I have a problem with this, I need to be taking it up with my sisters and the Council, not some young siren who has no say in the decisions her elders make." She patted my hand.

"But I'm confused. I have no clue what they expect me to do and I'm afraid of how far they'll want me to go." I tried to remain general in my statement. I still wasn't sure how much she disagreed with the choices being made and I didn't want her to know that I already had assumptions of my own.

"Is this about David?" Her reprimanding, sharp whisper broke through my resolve.

"Why would you think it's about him?" I tried to make the word "him" sound as though it disgusted me.

Her hand gently rested on my head as she began stroking my hair. "You are more like your mother than you will ever know."

I could see her clearly now as my vision adjusted to the brightness surrounding her brown hair. Dark, heavy bags hung below her hazel eyes.

"Let me give you some advice that I wish someone would have given her." She lightly tapped my head. "If you use this," her hand moved and then she tapped my upper chest, "and this, and you use them together to make decisions, you will choose wisely." She pulled her hand away and looked me in the eyes. "But if you use one or the other, and not both together, it's likely you'll make the wrong decision."

"Who's making decisions?" Miyu's authoritative voice sprang through the whispers as my bedroom door opened. She didn't look the same without her scales. Her fiery blaze of a tail seemed to match her personality far better than a set of legs. An orange choker necklace wrapped around her thin neck, a reminder of her inner fire.

"Allura is." Aunt Rebecca stood from her chair and gathered a couple zip-lock bags from the ground, placing them in the box clutched under her arm.

I blinked at her as though she'd just exposed me to Miyu. Aunt Rebecca smiled back at me before turning to my trainer. "She needs to be the one to decide if she's ready to get up and push forward or stay in bed and rest."

"And what have you decided?" Miyu asked, standing at the foot of my bed. Her onyx eyes challenged me to stand, to finish what we had started.

"It depends, how long have I been asleep?" I wondered, still a little disorientated as far as what day it was.

"Two and a half days," Aunt Rebecca answered, standing beside Miyu at the foot of my bed. They both stared down at me, their eyes bouncing from my neck to my arms.

"What?" I asked, peering down awkwardly with my chin to my chest. "Oh." Round, red hickies plagued my arms. "That looks gross."

"Be proud of them, they're your battle scars," Miyu said matter-of-factly, as if thinking of the unsightly blemishes any other way would be ridiculous.

"They'll go away in a week or so. An octopus' suction cup is a pretty powerful thing." Aunt Rebecca made her way to my bedroom door, left open by Miyu. "The ceremony is tomorrow night. You need to get your rest." She walked out of my room, her tin box in tow, and closed the door behind her.

Miyu came to the side of the bed and sat down on the chair beside me. Wincing, I slowly sat up and turned to face her. My feet dangled along the edge of the bed. My head pounded and my bite wound pulsated.

"A Provider pushes past the pain," Miyu said, watching me close my eyes and slowly open them as I worked to twist my body into position. "You did very well the other night."

"I was almost killed. I lost. The octopus won. That doesn't sound like doing well to me." A flood of flashbacks played through my mind: tearing at his arms, fighting for life rather than mere success.

"Every Provider is almost killed during training. If I doubted your ability, I wouldn't have sent you in that cave."

I gave her a puzzled and slightly offended look. She'd never seen me before the day she urged me into a cave with an octopus. How would she know what I could and couldn't handle?

She laughed. "If I can't watch you perform in your weakness, in an unfamiliar situation, how can I know what to help you improve on?"

I could have died, so she could see me in an unfamiliar situation?

"Have you trained many other Providers?" I asked. The fact that she encouraged me to continue fighting rather than killing the octopus showed at least some of the skill and patience of an instructor.

"None." She shook her head. "Our kind has faded into human existence. We are only now rising up from under their heel to reclaim our power." She shifted in her seat and crossed her legs. "I am the Provider of my region, and you will be the Provider of yours—all of the North American Pacific Ocean Region."

"Will be?" I asked.

"Normally you have to pledge to your clan first, but that won't be for another year and a half, so for you, they made an exception. Your region has been without a Provider for almost sixteen years. And even then, the Providers were nothing more than animal hunters, never respected for their linage and traditional role." She dropped her head a little and I thought I knew why. She was referring to my mother.

I had been under the impression sirens hadn't had Providers for a lot longer. But I had a bigger question more insistent on being asked. "Why don't they just wait until I pledge, though? What's the rush if we've gone this long?"

Her head rose and her full lips turned into a smile. "Because our new Council leader has decided that living as the humans live has become detrimental to our kind. The growing weakness of each generation and the decreasing numbers of Providers is proof. Other creatures will soon challenge us for our territories. We are at risk of fading into memory much like the mermaids. The Council has given the order that we are to begin slowly phasing back into our old ways." Her eyes sparkled and her grin widened. "The first and most important step is the pledging ceremony: Vanessa's tomorrow night, which you will be Provider for because she is from your region. This will unite the local clans and grow support for the decision, as well as the new leader."

My mind whirled with fogginess and I fought to concentrate enough to ask about the ceremony—what I'd be doing, and would they expect me to kill more than animals? I winced at the thought of ending the life of an actual living, breathing person, and then a smile threatened to reveal my delight in the image it concocted. Which made me want to vomit.

"Have you ever been the Provider for one?" I knew she had just told me sirens hadn't done these types of ceremonies in years, but her confidence and strength made me think the question was worth asking, that the answer could possibly be yes.

"No. In that I envy you. Vanessa is the first siren to pledge since the Council made their announcement. There will be quite a showing at this one. It's the first region-wide pledging ceremony for our kind in centuries." She stood from the chair and paced the floor of my bedroom, walking in and out of the light streaming through the window. "But I *have* killed a man since becoming a Provider." She shot a look at me full of excitement and...fire.

"When?" I asked. "Why? Is that allowed? Killing men outside of ceremonies?" From the way Vanessa had explained the Provider's role, taking the lives of men was to fit securely inside the confines of our pre-arranged events. Even our monstrous side had limits, right?

"No, it's not allowed, but it's almost expected at least once from a new Provider." She stopped pacing and sat down beside me again, sliding silently into the wooden chair as her excited eyes met mine. "You have me to guide you, to train you. I had no one. My mother is not a Provider. My grandmother was, but she had left by the time I began showing signs of the ability. My mother tried to explain all she knew of the role and the traits attached to such a gift, but we Providers are unique. We're different than other sirens. I'm sure you've noticed that."

"Yes, but how?" I knew the obvious difference—the strength, intensified hunting prowess and the stronger luring ability. But, how much of that strength had come from my skater mistake and how much was just a part of what I was?

Why were we different from our sisters? And how deep did that difference go?

"You lure men, but sometimes that goes both ways. Something about the men lures you back. It's a give and take relationship. I think you would call it a love, hate. They feel as though they need you for life, that they couldn't go on without you."

I nodded my head in agreement before I even realized I'd agreed. My back straightened as I soaked her words into my understanding. It explained Jason. In fact, it sounded a lot like something he had said. But to what end did I lure them? I didn't want to consider it.

"But, you are not completely immune to them, either. They have something you want too—something you feel as though you cannot live without. Your sisters will never experience such a pull. Part of you hates the males for being weak enough to be lured, but sometimes part of you is thankful and cannot stand the thought of them leaving, the thought of them not being drawn to you." She lowered her head while still staring into my eyes. A glint of fierceness flashed in her black irises. "My mother never prepared me for that. A young man in a neighboring town caught my eye one day at the fish market. I caught his too because he approached me. He offered to walk me home. I think he planned to introduce himself to my father, but he never made it to my town."

My eyes widened. I wanted to hear more. I needed to know that in some way, in some obscure circle of life, I was normal. My back felt like steel, straight and tight, unmoving.

"His scent alone caused me to taste acid on my tongue, and not the normal amount we secrete while eating. It filled my mouth with the sweet venom. As we traveled, he asked questions about me. It felt like the walk to my town took days. I restrained myself for so long. I wanted to go home and ask my mother what was happening to me, but when he touched my hand I could not contain my need any longer." One side of her lips pulled upward. "He never saw it coming."

David flashed in my mind. He never saw it coming, either. I thought of the woods and how I had him pinned against the tree. Where no one would hear his screams. How badly I had wanted him.

How I could have devoured him right then and there. My stomach tightened. If I'd killed him then, I'd never have gotten to know him. Never have fallen for him. Miyu was right. I did need David, but not in the way she explained. I needed him for him—for his companionship, not his death. When I thought of him, I didn't think of food. I thought of how amazing he was, how much I cared for him. He didn't cause acid to fill my mouth. A smile inched across my lips. Something inside had stopped me from devouring him that day in the woods.

"I hear you have not yet lost control with a male. Is that true?" she asked pointedly.

"I accidently bit one, but that's it. I haven't lost control and killed anyone." I shook my head, gladness rushing through me.

"But, you do have a male begging for your affection." It wasn't a question. She had been talking to my aunts. Or the Council.

"Yes." I dropped my head and tried to remind myself that David was in no danger. I had already warned him. He wouldn't be lured to me. I had made sure of that. I couldn't say the same for Jason. I didn't like the guy, but I didn't wish him dead either. What would I say, though? *Oh, by the way, Miyu, I know you're bigger and badder than me, but I won't let you hurt Jason.*

"Good. Then everything is set." Miyu stood again as though she lacked the ability to sit still for long. "Now, as far as your tactics go, you do well on stalking your prey and the initial attack. I did see though, that you're too impulsive, too quick." She reached her hand out to me. "Stand."

I grasped her hand and used it to pull me out of bed. A sharp pain shot through my waist and I grimaced, but still worked to be upright. Once I was on my feet, she backed away.

"You did not truly believe the octopus was yours."

"I did," I argued, a light dizziness making my head swim.

"No, if you knew it was yours, you would have been patient. If inside, you believe that your prey belongs to you, waiting is not a difficulty. You trust in the end they will be dead and you won't." She walked over to my dresser and picked up a bracelet from the little wooden plate I kept my jewelry on. She dangled the glass-beaded string from her fingers. "If I took this and told you I would return it to you by the end of the day, would you fight me to take it back, or would you simply wait for the day to be over?"

"I'd wait. No sense in potentially hurting myself or my bracelet."

"Exactly. Because you know it belongs to you, and ultimately it will come back to you," Miyu said.

"I see."

"The octopus was yours. But, you refused to wait for the ink to clear. You risked your safety to procure a creature that already belonged to you." She shook her head. "Unwise." Miyu eyed the piece of jewelry and placed the bracelet on the wooden plate.

My dizziness grew and mixed with a headache. The carpet seemed to sway like waves of the ocean. "I understand now." I took a step toward her and tripped over my foot.

Miyu caught my arm and held it tightly. She led me back to the bed. After she helped me lower my body onto the comfort of the mattress she turned and slid the wooden chair away from the bed and against the wall.

"I'll let you rest now. It looks as though the plant your aunt placed on you has begun to work at relaxing your muscles." She motioned to my stomach. I lifted my shirt to see a thin strip of light green stretched in a line above my navel. My body ached so badly, I hadn't even felt the plant.

"Wait, we need to train though," I tried to say as my tongue slurred the words.

"No, you are ready." She placed her hand on the doorknob but didn't turn it. "You slayed a creature with eight arms, each reaching ten feet. I'm confident you can handle a creature with half the extremities." She opened the door and left, closing it behind her.

David. I had to text him—remind him to not come to me under any circumstance. I twisted my body enough to push my hands beneath my pillow in search of my cell phone. A muscle pulled at my side in protest, but I refused to give in. *Where is it?* I pushed my pillow aside, throwing it to the ground. *I left it right here!* When I'd exhausted exploring the upper part of my mattress, I reached my hands along the front side of my bed, jamming them between my bed and the headboard. Nothing. The dizziness made my head swim as my eyelids heaved shut.

A thought lingered through my mind like a dream I had no control over. *They took my phone before I could change David's contact information. They took my cell phone.*

CHAPTER TWENTY-FIVE

)(

When I awoke, the setting sun filled my room with yellow and pink hues. Everything it touched, glowed. The pounding in my head had dulled and the pain in my lower neck had downgraded to only an ache. I reached my arm into the air to examine the marks left by the octopus' suction cups. The redness had faded to purple circular spots. I slowly lifted my head and shoulders from the pillow, using the strength from my abs to do all the work. Pushing the sheet off me, I pulled my shirt up to examine my stomach. The plant had been removed and the purple bruises were lightening, some even turning yellowish-green.

Carefully, I swung my feet to hang from the side of the bed and used my hands to push against the mattress until I stood. In bare feet, I padded over to the mirror and rested my weight against the dresser. Grabbing the collar of my t-shirt, I stretched it out to expose my lower neck and inspected it carefully. Aunt Rebecca had done a masterful job. It didn't look infected at all. A dark pink half circle covered my skin where my neck met my shoulder muscle. I gently trailed my fingers across it. Small bumps where the octopus' beak had broken through the surface rose from my skin.

The soft sound of someone's feet gliding up the stairs made me turn to my door right as Miyu opened it. "I thought I heard you. How do you feel?" She walked through the door, but didn't close it behind her. The fearful, questioning of me wanted to be like Miyu, embody her confidence and strength in who she was. I bet she didn't carry within her heart, a twisted knot of shame and reverence for our ancestors. When I looked at her, I felt like I was gazing into the distant past, beholding the greatness of siren-kind. But I also knew a monster lurked behind her sharp teeth and quick mind.

"Much better, just groggy mostly," I answered, turning back to the mirror.

"Your aunt gave you something to keep you asleep. A plant. She knew it would help you heal faster." Miyu reached around me to grab the glass-beaded bracelet on the little wooden plate atop my dresser. "Here, you should wear this today."

I eyed the clear beads reflecting the yellow hue filling my room, but the smell Miyu brought with her floated past me when she moved, commanding my attention. My stomach twisted with hunger.

"You smell amazing," I said, absorbing the air around her. Saltwater and brine.

"You must be starving," she answered with laugh. "You have not eaten in days. Here." She dropped the bracelet in my palm. "I have prepared a meal fit for a Provider."

I hoped she meant fish. Yeah, the brine and saltwater had to be fish.

I followed her downstairs. Silence filled the empty house. "Where is everybody?"

"Today is the day; you have been sleeping a long time. They are out preparing for the celebration," she said as she looked ahead.

We pushed through the kitchen door and my eyes searched the room until I locked upon my meal. I counted more than ten fish swimming in a saltwater tank that was about the size and width of the island counter it sat upon.

"I can't go swimming?" The fish looked appetizing, but nothing compared to catching them myself.

"No, it is almost time to begin the ceremony. You are healed. Now you need to eat for strength. To hunt could weaken you before you have replenished your energy." She waved her hand toward the full tank of unsuspecting fish.

I watched a big brownish-gray halibut with anticipation. When it turned to swim to the other side of the tank, I shot my hand into the water, sank my fingers into its side, and pulled it out. The halibut wriggled back and forth, fighting for life. I brought its flinging body to my mouth, one hand on the tail and the other gripping the head. As I sunk my famished teeth into its scales, my hands flexed, breaking its bones, killing it instantly. After I finished, I flung its skeleton into the trashcan nearby and reached for another.

As I emptied the tank, I noticed Miyu wasn't eating.

"Have some," I encouraged, my mouth full of raw, delicious fish.

"No, I already ate and you need it. You are doing most of the work tonight."

I used the opportunity. "What kind of work?" I asked.

"Don't worry," she answered. "You will be pleased."

Miyu neared the kitchen table and wrapped her fingers around a piece of clothing draped over the wooden top. She raised her arms high enough for a dark green and black sleeveless dress to hang seamlessly in front of me. The cloth looked light-weight and flowy. I finished the last fish in the tank, threw its remains into the trashcan and reached to touch the almost shiny fabric. How did they get it to gleam without sequins?

"It reminds me of my scales," I said in awe, pushing away the urge to demand she tell me what I'd be expected to do tonight.

"Yes, in these ceremonies we do not hide who we are. We embrace every aspect of our kind." She passed the dress to me. "Put this on. Then we will go."

Miyu turned and grabbed an orangish-red and black dress from the back of another chair and put it on. The flowing garment mirrored my own in every way but color. After undressing, I placed my outfit above my head and slid my arms into the holes. The dress glided down my body and fell perfectly in place. It felt like satin. No, more like liquid as it melded against my curves and hung in all the right places.

Miyu reached her hands toward me. Her black, thick hair cascaded in waves down her fire-covered shoulders, while her bright onyx eyes shined even brighter against the orange. Her full lips were painted red and her black arched eyebrows framed her face with the prefect finishing touch. I took her hands as we faced one another, looking each other over.

"Are you ready?" she asked, her voice soaked in delight.

No. "Yes." I failed at making my voice sound as enthusiastic as hers.

She gave my hands a quick squeeze. "It's normal to be nervous. It's a big night for you and many sirens have come to witness this ceremony."

I inhaled sharply. I wished I could go hide in the dead octopus' empty cave. The seconds ticked by, shoving me toward a fate I had no power to change. A fate I was expected to accept for the good of my clan.

"Just remember," she said with a smile, "he is yours. You are entitled to him. Like the bracelet you wear now, he belongs to you."

I wished she hadn't said that. Her words incited a new anxious need to turn and run the other way, but my instincts warned against fleeing. Miyu lived for the chase. I had to be smart about this. Had to outthink rather than outrun.

She released one of my hands and continued to hold onto the other. Miyu led me out the back kitchen door, through the dew-damp grass, down the steep hill and onto the pebbles lining the beach. She released my hand as we ambled to the water. The full moon looked like someone had torn a perfectly round hole in the navy blue sky. Yellow moonbeams frolicked across the liquid.

Her dress rose as she moved deeper into the sea; the tangerine fabric danced on lapping waves. I thought it weird we weren't disrobing before entering the water, but it wasn't as though I'd never swum fully clothed before.

David entered my mind, and our time at our lake. I hoped he was sitting securely in his home, and nowhere near the Puget Sound and the man-eating women who swam under the waves.

We sank under the water as scales crept down our bodies, blurring our skin with color. My black and emerald dress clung to my scales as the water welcomed me, surrounding me with relaxing comfort. I absorbed the sweet, salty liquid.

"I needed that," I said to Miyu when she peered back at me with a raised eyebrow.

When I saw that I had her attention I asked, "Where are we going?"

"The ceremony will be held on Deadman Island. Fitting name, I think." She darted away, toward our destination.

Deadman Island. Weakness bit at my mind and begged me to turn around, not to do this. But where would I go? A siren without her clan is as good as dead. And I had Cara to consider.

Soon the jutted rocks that sprang from under the surface of the island's cliffs were in view. My stomach lurched.

David is safe. He's at home. I'll see him in a couple days when this is all over and everyone has left.

When my head had persuaded my heart that he would be fine, Jason's face popped into my mind. Impending dread brought logic in its wake. They were going to have me kill a male. My nightmare was coming to fruition. How would I keep him from being killed? I was ninety-nine percent sure he'd be the one I lured to the island. So I needed a plan. Just in case.

The two far sides of Deadman Island were different from one another. One had sharp cliffs stretching out high above the water, and the other boasted sandy beaches. I thought we would swim to the sandy beach side, but Miyu went straight for the base of the rocky cliffs. We reached the stony wall with its pointy edges only slightly smoothed by the crashing waves.

"You ready?" Miyu asked. Before I answered, she dug her fingers into the rock and pulled her weight up the wall.

Among the demanding rush of the waves, numerous sirens shouted joyfully as they awaited us at the top of the cliff. Their scent, energy, and excitement pulsed through the air. I was ready to do what

I had to do. I felt it in my bones. It was time to provide for my clan and the others, even if I wasn't quite sure how to do that without ending anyone's life in the process.

I clung to the edge of the cliff, pushing my body against the slick, wet blackness. Green plants grew from the cracks and wound their way upward as though they too were trying to climb to the top. My feet dug into stony divots, pushing my body upwards as my hands pulled me. Like two graceful, deadly spiders, Miyu and I scurried up the treacherous side of the rocky cliff. Wind whipped our hair in every direction as we hoisted ourselves over the edge of the cliff and to the top.

I stood from my crouched position and stared into the countless eyes watching me. A roar of cheers rang out at our arrival as another wave crashed against the cliff. Each siren wore dresses similar to Miyu and me, the colors mirroring the scales decorating their bodies.

The High Council woman, Liana, stepped forward, her dress a vibrant bright blue. "Welcome Providers," she beamed. She turned to address the assembly of sirens behind her. "Tonight marks a momentous occasion. Tonight we return to the ways of our foremothers, practicing the ceremonies that once enriched the lives of those who thrived before us. Ceremonies that once gave them strength and power beyond our comprehension." She took a step backward toward Miyu and me. "Tonight we take back what is rightfully ours on the same island our foremothers celebrated upon."

The crowd shouted in agreement.

My emotions swam through me like piranhas, biting at the edges of my resolve. This is what I never knew I had been craving. The acceptance my aunts couldn't give me. The unity I'd always thought I'd missed out on without my mother in my life. Here they were, for my taking. The cost? I didn't want to think about the cost.

"Vanessa will you please step forward?" Liana called out.

Vanessa emerged from the crowd, her mother's arm looped through her own. Vanessa's dress sparkled a magnificent deep red against her dark skin, the loose hem fluttering in the breeze. Her thin braids, black entwined with streaks of red, flowed down her shoulders and rested on her chest. She was absolutely striking. Her mother walked with her part way to the Council woman, but stopped and watched her daughter close the gap on her own.

Liana addressed the crowd, "Vanessa has come of age and now chooses to sever the umbilical cord to her clan that only existed by way of her mother. She wishes to create a new tie for herself."

The Council woman reached to Vanessa and the two stood side-by-side, holding hands.

"Do you Vanessa, being of the earth and the seas, forever bind yourself to this clan, promising to live as they do for the good of our kind?"

"Yes, I do," Vanessa said through a grin.

"And do you swear to forever act as one with your clan, putting the needs of your clan before your own, and even before your own life?"

"I do."

Liana raised her hand in the air, causing Vanessa's hand to follow. "Then as High Council woman, I declare you now a pledged member of your clan!"

The huge cluster of sirens roared to life, shouting and yipping in response. Miyu and I clapped and shouted along. A deep sense of pride welled up within me and bubbled over. My kind stood before me in all their glory. Faces mirrored my own despite the many different colors and shapes, representations of who I was and who my mother had been. Here lay the beauty of who we were. But, I knew that as I watched them, they in turn watched me, waiting for my performance as Provider.

My muscles clenched, tightening in my legs, twitching in my jaw. I knew what they wanted of me. I remembered the way I stalked the sharks, how I had hunted and devoured my prey.

The Provider was a part of me.

I couldn't deny it any longer.

I also knew what I had to do if I wanted to continue being accepted in the siren community. That's one thing David failed to fathom. Humans had the ability to escape, meet new humans and create new bonds. Not so with sirens. We were all connected, and if one betrayed her clan, all would turn their backs on her. I had to admit I didn't exactly feel connected and loved by my aunts, but I had my sisters to think about. What would Cara do without me?

Just picturing the task the cheering sirens anticipated for me sped my pulse. What would David say? A trickle of guilt ran through my mind. I knew what he'd say. If something is wrong, the circumstances surrounding it do not have the power to make it right. Nothing and no one has the power to make something wrong, right. David's humanity entranced me, drew me to him...and demanded that I take heed if I had any hope of holding onto my own sliver of humanity.

Jason, as disgusting as he was, had to be somewhere on this island. And somehow, someway, I was going to get him off this chunk of land. Alive. My acceptance was not worth his life.

"Vanessa," Liana's bellowing voice broke through my strategizing. "In honor of your great commitment to the protection and advancement of our kind, your region's Provider, Allura, will entrap and present you with your first meal as an adult clan member."

"I thank you," Vanessa said.

My eyes bounced to the tree-line in search of Jason. The dense forest blocked my view of the beach beyond the woods. Maybe he was at the beach.

When my gaze bounced back, Vanessa turned to acknowledge me. "I would be honored to partake in your provision and glad to share it with my sisters...within my clan and otherwise."

The crowd thundered again, cheering at her first words as a true member of siren society.

Liana quieted the multitude before she spoke. "Then, may I present to you," she waved her hand toward the center of the crowd and the cluster began to open down the middle, "your ceremonial meal."

Sirens shuffled from the center of the circle they had formed earlier, the colorful dresses reflecting the moon light. Acid dripped from the roof of my mouth, and I swallowed the substance down before it lingered on my tongue, before I could taste the pre-meal liquid. I fought back the excitement to completely fall into my role, to

214

hunt and kill my human prey. My heartbeat pounded in my ears as my eyes narrowed, waiting, surveying. Did they have Jason here already? Behind them?

One straight, empty line shot down the middle of what once was a cluster of sirens and as the Council women and Vanessa stepped to the side, out of my line of sight, I peered through the opening.

Arms bound behind his back, David stood glaring straight at me.

CHAPTER TWENTY-SIX

)(

Air stabbed at my throat. I gasped. *No. No! Why is he here? He shouldn't be here!*

Aunt Dawn's lips turned upward as she stood behind David, clasping his tied wrists. The wind disheveled his hair and sweat lined his furrowed brow. His damp Henley clung to his broad shoulders and arms. His chest rose and fell as he took quick, shallow breaths.

I scanned the expectant faces around him. Wildness danced in their eyes. They watched me with hopeful gazes.

Miyu's hand pressed against the small of my back and gave a nudge. It was my turn to perform.

I walked slowly, trying to make each step meaningful and concise as though I were sizing up my prey. His eyes locked on mine and worry filled his expression as his gaze bounced to the wound on my neck and the marks on my arms. I yearned to run to him, to cover him with kisses for his devotion to me, to return his love. But I couldn't. The countless eyes that watched me expected nothing less than a Provider's show and I had no choice but to give it to them. If I didn't, I was certain they'd kill him.

"Why is he tied up?" my throat caught as I spoke. I stammered, trying to regain an authoritative voice, "What fun is it to hunt a caged prey?"

As I neared David, my aunt Dawn stepped aside. She watched me closely and almost expectantly.

The pinhole stars did little to light the sky as the moon cast shadows upon the ground through a thick layer of fog rolling in. I wondered how well David could see in this darkness. How well could he run to escape?

I sauntered over as though I owned him and thrust my hand up to his face, barely missing his nose as I ran my outstretched fingers through his hair. For a moment his scent entangled my emotions and I ached to wrap my arms around his waist and feel his breath on my forehead. But I couldn't do that now; it was not an option. For his sake and for mine.

I stood on tiptoes and brushed my mouth across his ear, pretending to tease him. As my lips touched his earlobe I faintly whispered, "Close your eyes."

When he obeyed, I traced my fingers down his neck and onto his shoulder. I walked a full circle around him, allowing my fingers to trail over the top of his shoulder, across his back, to his other shoulder, across his chest, and land on their starting point.

I glanced at the hungry eyes watching me in anticipation, tense smiles hiding sharp teeth just waiting for a chance at David. My David.

I leaned in again toward his ear and dragged my tongue from the top of his shoulder to his ear. With his eyes closed, his chin turned toward my face and rubbed against my cheek.

"Why are you here? Did they bring you?" I asked under my breath so my fellow sirens couldn't hear my voice among the crashing sea and tense shouts of excitement.

"You texted me, said to meet you here." His lips moved against my cheek as he spoke.

I'd figured they'd taken my phone. I just didn't think they'd sink to this level.

"It wasn't me," I hissed. "It was them."

This was all my aunts' idea. A set up. My aunts had their daughters. My sisters had their mothers. I had no one until David came along. David was *my* person. I refused to give them what they wanted, to give them my person. But seeing as the Council and the other sirens weren't in on this, they wouldn't understand my blatant disregard for their ceremony and their rules if I were to just let David free.

No, my aunts started this game and I had to finish it. If I didn't, both David and I would lose. I had a sinking suspicion that if I defied them, they would kill me too. I had to keep my pawn one step ahead of theirs.

I pulled away from David and swung around to address the Council women. "This is no fun and certainly not a show worthy of such an occasion."

My Aunt Dawn's gray eyes glared at me and turned to focus on Liana, awaiting the leader's reply.

The High Council woman looked to the other Council members. The crowd of sirens also changed their focal point to the small group of gray-haired women.

With their attention temporarily diverted, I whispered again to David. "You brought a boat?"

He gave a quick, short nod.

"When I untie you I want you to run as fast as you can to that boat and get off this island. Do not stop until you're home."

"What about you?" he mouthed, his head cocked down, hiding his lips.

"I'll figure something out." I turned to listen to Liana as she addressed the crowd, and pointed her words at me.

"You may release him," she said curtly, as though not every Council member agreed.

I nodded and turned back to reach my arms around David as I stood in front of him. I pretended to nibble on his neck as I spoke into his ear. "I love you." My fingers worked the rope around his wrists until it came loose. "Now *go.*"

He stumbled back away from me and turned to head for the

cluster of fir trees in the middle of the island. The crowd gave shouts of elation as I raised my voice for all to hear.

"Because I enjoy the hunt, I'll give you to the count of twenty to run, but make no mistake...You. Are. Mine!" My voice roared through the wind. Those around me shivered with anticipation.

Every eye watched David longingly as he pushed his way past the tree line and disappeared. I led the count, the crowd of sirens signing the numbers with me as though they were waiting for the New Year's ball to drop. Slowly, I yelled out, "ten, eleven, twelve..." Before I could say, "thirteen," a face peeked out from behind a tree trunk.

His fingers grasped at the bark his arms were wrapped around.

"Jason?" I almost screeched in shock.

Jason stepped forward, leaving the covering of the tree-line. "Something told me you'd be here tonight." He looked around at the ladies who stood behind and beside me. "I just assumed you'd be here alone."

"What do you want, Jason?" I asked, running different scenarios through my mind of how to end this.

"You," he said, exuding more confidence than any one person should possess.

Laughter sprang from the women.

I beckoned the only other Provider I knew. "Miyu?"

"Yes?" She stepped toward me and leaned in.

I lowered my voice to a whisper. "You chase Jason. I'll take the other one." I hoped she understood that chase didn't mean eat.

Her chin jetted up and her sharp eyes shot to the blond boy clutching the tree. "This is not my celebration. I have no right to take him down."

"I'm not suggesting you take him down." I let out a huff and thought for a moment.

If I could get Miyu to lead the chase of Jason, then half the sirens would follow her. That meant the other half would follow me. Protecting David from other sirens would be difficult, but the lower the numbers the better the odds. I hadn't trained in fighting my own kind. I just knew if it was between Miyu and me, I'd lose. She'd been a

Provider longer, and I was sure killing and devouring a male had given her way more strength than my one bite. I had to keep her away from David.

"Keep an eye on him. Keep him occupied." I shifted my weight from one side to the other. Was I asking her to break the rules? Would she question my request?

A tight smile lengthened across her face. "I'd be honored." She gave a short bow.

My anxious muscles slackened. "Great. You chase him. I'll take down the other guy before he escapes. I'll be back to finish this one off."

Miyu's gaze rested on me. She swept her hand up my arm. "Enjoy your meal." As her fingers left my skin, her body twisted away from me, toward the tree line.

Miyu shrieked as she progressed into a run. Sirens followed her, chortling and screeching behind and beside, egging her on.

Jason's self-assured smile dropped from his face. He quickly spun around and ran back into the trees.

I pivoted on my heel and bounded toward the beach. A handful of sirens followed me, screeching into the night. Thankfully, I was stronger and faster than the ones who followed me. Because of my taste of male flesh, or the fact that I was Provider, or probably both, I widened the gap between the following sirens and myself.

Every time my bare foot pressed into the ground, the movement catapulted my legs, pushing me harder. I didn't hold back. I couldn't hold back. I had to lose my hungry followers.

I reached the line of trees separating the rocky beach from the forest and stopped to scan the view. Two sirens had kept up. They paused to catch their breath.

I couldn't locate David or his boat. If he had already gotten off the island he was faster than I'd thought. I shot back toward the cliff I'd climbed earlier without giving the two panting sirens even a hint that I'd decided to change directions. The view from that part of the island would give me a better shot at locating him.

As I ran, I listened for breathing, absorbed the air for the sirens' scent. Nothing, other than a faint trace of seaweed. No one followed me now. I dodged the thick tree trunks scattered in my path and ran right through small bushes. I freed myself from the forest and ran harder, stretching my leg muscles with each stride. My feet smacked upon the smooth rock until I flung myself off the side of the cliff, scanning the horizon for my male.

Only, the sight I caught was another male, his kelp green face watching me from below. Kaven.

My body flew through the air. Scales climbed down me, multiplying over my waist and spreading across my hips, swiping along my skin with the feel of an invisible feather. My legs came together and melded into a tail as scales covered me in shades of green and black. I forced my arms out in front of me and dove into the waves, swimming hard and fast. I landed where the kelpie had been moments earlier, but he was nowhere to be seen. My tailfin fanned and shoved water out of my way, ripping through the liquid. I couldn't get distracted. Kaven wasn't the one who needed saving.

I scanned for any sign of David or the boat he had used.

Where is he?

I swam up near the surface of the choppy water as waves pushed toward the shore of San Juan Island and then shoved me back out to sea. As I fought the ocean, I searched the surface for the bottom of a boat. Nothing.

I popped my head above the white-capped waves and looked around. "David!" I shouted, barely audible above the roaring sea. Rain drops pelted my face. "David!" I called again.

I looked back toward Deadman Island. Would my hungry followers know I'd left the island and come after me? I turned toward the shore of San Juan Island and spotted movement. David worked to row the small boat through the waves, plunging the oars into the water and forcing the wooden planks through the liquid.

I ducked under the sea and raced toward him. When I reached his boat, I grabbed an oar and yanked it down until he let go. He stopped rowing and looked over the side of the boat with the beam of a flashlight pointed at me. My head burst out of the water and I flung the oar into the boat.

David jumped back and his fist swung forward. "What the—?" He regained his legs and peered back over the side of the boat. "Your eyes." He flashed the light in my eyes a split second before lowering the beam. "They reflect a green, shiny color. Like a cat's eyes."

"It's a part of the whole seeing in the dark thing," I answered quickly, not wanting to discuss something as trivial as my body parts at this very moment. "Throw the other oar in. I'll push you to shore. We have to hurry." He tossed the second oar into the boat with a thud. I moved to the back of the vessel and propelled my body through the water.

It didn't take me long to swim the distance, even pushing a boat. As we approached the shore, David jumped out from the side. I shoved the boat onto land, leaving a stripe in the sand until it careened to a halt. David bent down and wrapped his arms around my waist, lifting me from the water in a hug until my scale-covered hips were no longer hidden by the waves. He smoothed my hair from my face and kissed my forehead and cheeks.

"Are you all right?" He kissed me again. "I was so worried about you. I hated leaving you there."

"I'm glad you did, but David, I can't do this right now."

"I don't want to let you go." He squeezed me tighter.

"You have to. I have to help Jason."

He pulled his face away from mine and looked me in the eyes. "Jason?"

I gave an urgent nod and looked back toward Deadman Island.

"As in Rapist Jason?" he asked.

"Huh?" I caught his eyes.

"Yeah, some girl brought up charges against him last year, I heard. His uncle has some pull, I guess, and the charges were mysteriously dropped."

"I didn't know," I said quickly. "Still, I need to get back." We weren't judges who got to decide what crimes are punishable by death.

"Allura, wait. I need to say this, before you leave. I don't know when I'll see you again." David paused for half a second. "Did you mean what you said back there? Do you really feel that way about me?" Rain dripped down his eyebrows, but he didn't even blink as he waited for my answer.

"I love you." As I said the words my heart tightened and slick tears trickled from my eyes.

His lips leaned in to mine and he placed his hand behind my head, tilting my chin up toward his.

"I don't care what my aunts say. I won't be who they want me to be. I want to be myself, be with you," I assured him and myself.

Thoughts of my mother flooded me. Is this how she died? Did she follow my aunts until she lost all sense of who she was, and ultimately ended her life? Did they drown her in their lies and manipulation until she no longer recognized the spark that made her uniquely her? Did they snuff out her soul?

I turned my head to look out at the sea, toward Deadman Island. "They know. They know how I feel about you. Why else would they have told you to come? If you were lured, you would have come on your own like Jason. But they knew that what you and I have has nothing to do with me being the Provider. They wanted you out of the picture and what better way than to pretend you were my prey in front of a crowd of hungry sirens?"

How dare they use David against me. They made him stand in the middle of a deadly siren circle, hands bound behind his back. My fists balled and my heartbeat thudded through my body. "I'll kill them."

"Wait, don't do anything impulsive, Allura. You've always been afraid of them, and now you think you can take them on?"

"I'm the Provider. I'm stronger than they are." Fury rang in my ears. "I'm tired of them pushing me around, making decisions for me. But trying to have you killed—they just took it to a whole new level." I turned back toward him.

I wanted blood. Their blood. How dare they? They weren't only controlling and secretive, they tricked me, manipulated me! I knew they didn't love me like they loved my sisters, but I thought they at least loved me a little. And they told me I was special, when in reality they were using me to annihilate their only opposition, the only person I would possibly choose over their orders: David.

He smoothed his hand over my hair. "They're the mothers of your sisters. You know what it feels like to not have a mother. Don't force that experience on them, too."

I thought of my sisters. They were innocent in all of this. I couldn't steal their mothers from them the way mine had been stolen from me, even if it was ultimately her choice.

"You're right." I took a deep breath to calm my racing heart. "What should I do then?"

"Be the Provider. Provide a new way. If they are as rare and powerful as you say, your aunts will want to hold on to you. That means you have the upper hand. You're an asset to them, not the other way around." His lips moved toward mine, hovering above my face. "Go give them hell, baby." His kiss pushed urgently against my mouth.

He released me into the water and kissed the top of my head. "I love you, Allura."

I gazed into his deep eyes. "I love you, too. Now get out of the water and on to that motorcycle of yours so I don't have to fight off hoards of sirens who literally want a bite of my man."

David stood to turn and jog up the hill. When his bike roared to life, I flung myself backwards into the water and swam to Deadman Island.

CHAPTER TWENTY-SEVEN

)(

Once my tail separated into legs, I walked out of the water onto the beach side of the island. Sirens laughed and sang, celebrating, in the distance.

Kaven stood, his skin green, covered in strips of kelp originating from the top of his head. I knew him by his eyes and the way he stood, proud and tall. He waited for me on the sand.

I had to get back to the others and save Jason.

I shot Kaven a look. "Where have you been this whole time?" I asked, marching past him. "I needed you."

"Looks like you did just fine on your own," he responded with a clipped voice, not moving to follow me.

I shook my head and trudged forward.

"I came to tell you that as long as you're training to use your hunger correctly, the kelpies will stay away," Kaven said, his tone void of any friendliness he once had. "But the same doesn't go for the others. We'll be watching to make sure they stay in their lanes."

I paused and turned to question him. Watching us? Stay in their lanes? Who did the kelpies think they were, trying to govern us? But what I found was an empty beach, with only my footprints and the tracks of another. Kaven had left, but now I knew he'd never be too far away. I shrugged and turned back toward the trees. I had more pressing matters than kelpie betrayal.

I made my way through the cluster of woods.

Jason's scent lingered in the dirt, on the pine needles and in the breeze. A shiver ran up my spine as a drop of acid released into my mouth. I hurried from the woods to remove myself from the trees and Jason's luring scent, until I reached the clearing near the cliff. Sirens danced and screamed into the night, there arms held high. One woman waved a flag above her head, the fabric flapping in the wind. Wait. I peered closer at her celebratory item. It wasn't a flag. It was Jason's letterman jacket.

Suddenly another scent collided into me. Blood. Flesh. Deliciousness. I shook with want.

"What have you done?" I shouted as I ran to the woman and snatched the coat from her hands.

She gave me a quizzical look and eyed the tight circle of sirens nearby. I threw Jason's jacket down and shoved my way into the circle. The smell of fresh flesh swirled through the air. Blood stained hands patted my skin as I bore into the center of the group. My pores greedily accepted their offerings. I tried to wipe the red goodness from my skin, but it was too late. Acid filled my mouth and a loud growl escaped my lips. It was as though they were each holding a syringe full of the drug I craved most. The drug offering more strength and addiction than a thousand vials of steroids.

Five crouched sirens jumped back from their meal in surprise. And that's all Jason looked like. A meal. The women dancing must have already had their turn with him, and what I stared at now was...leftovers.

My fists clenched into balls in an effort to keep me from either grabbing their meal for my own or ringing their necks for killing an innocent human. I couldn't be sure.

"What have you done?" I yelled, canvasing the group. "Where's Miyu? Where's Miyu?"

A bloody finger pointed to the other Provider, glowing in her orange dress splattered with red, dancing in a single moonbeam peeking through the clouds. I trudged over to her, feeding off of anger rather than turning to feed off what was left of Jason.

"What the hell is that, Miyu?" I motioned to where Jason's body lay. The group gathered around his remains returned to enjoying their meal.

Miyu stopped dancing. She regarded me with a smile. Blood streaked across the lower half of her face. "I couldn't help myself. You understand." She lifted her arms. "I saved you some." She brought her wet hands down and smeared me with Jason's blood, from my neck to my fingers.

I usually feared Miyu, but with the acid exploding in my mouth and the blood surging in my veins, I was beyond any understanding of fear. "Shit, Miyu! I told you to watch him, not kill him!" I glanced back at the kneeling circle of women.

"I am a Provider. I *do not* watch! I *do* kill," Miyu reminded harshly.

"But you *said* you'd watch!" I shouted and shoved her. "He wasn't yours to kill, remember? This isn't your ceremony!"

"You were stupid to leave me with him!" She shoved me back.

"You were stupid to take down the prey of another Provider!" I flung my fist toward her face, but she ducked and the punch missed.

She crouched and kicked. Her foot slammed my stomach. I fell back a few steps, but quickly regained my footing.

"Why are you so upset?" Miyu asked, positioning to hit me again. "You lured two men. You got one to yourself, we shared the other."

She spoke of David and Jason as though they were nameless nothings. Anger and hunger boiled within me. I lunged forward and wrapped my fingers around her neck. I squeezed as she clawed at my arms and face.

"Providers!" Liana yelled. "Enough!"

The crowd quieted.

I dropped my hands to my side and Miyu backed away from me. The council leader had spoken and everything in me commanded that I listen.

Liana daintily wiped red from the corner of her mouth and my stomach flipped with want and frustration. She stood between Miyu and me. And announced to the sirens watching, "Our Providers, are they not fierce?" She grasped one hand from each of us and brought them above our heads. The crowd roared with acceptance and reverence.

Liana shot us both a reprimanding eye before stretching a smile across her face and addressing the onlookers. "It seems, though, the trainer still seeks to teach her trainee."

Light-hearted laughter rang through the night air. They were proud of their Providers. Their deadly, fighting Providers.

"I believe, though, our reinstatement of the traditional Legacy of Life ceremony has gone quite well. Don't you?" The women answered in screeches. "We still have hours of celebration left before the island clean-up is to begin. What do you say, my siren sisters?" She dropped our hands and kept her arms in the air. "Shall we go for a swim?" She ran for the trees and the group followed her.

The hoard of shimmery dresses headed for the beach, my sisters following, throwing off their fake scales and donning their real ones in the process. I almost grabbed Miyu's arm to finish what we'd started, but my Aunt Dawn's steel gaze cut through the moving bodies and froze me. Jason was gone. No amount of fighting would bring him back. But with my aunts, I had business to attend to.

Miyu gave me a sharp smile and nodded. When I didn't return the gesture, she turned and followed our leaders to the water.

As the women ran through the trees, my aunts and I stayed put. We eyed one another. Aunt Dawn commanded my sisters to join the others. Soon my three aunts and I stood alone in the clearing on the cliff.

The wind blew our hair and rain pelted down. My aunts formed a line and began walking toward me, but by the time they reached me, Aunt Dawn was in the front, with Aunt Anise and Aunt Rebecca flanking her.

"How dare you let that boy go," Aunt Dawn spit her words at me. "His broken flesh should be swimming in your mouth!"

The siren child in me wanted to cower down, to accept the scolding and punishment of my clan leaders. But, the Provider in me stood firm, and confident. They needed me. It was no longer the other way around.

My words started out weak, but grew in strength. "How dare you bring him here."

"You will not take that tone with me! You will submit to my authority." Aunt Dawn stepped toward me. Her gray eyes flashed as her red hair whipped around her face.

I didn't answer. I wanted to, but I fought with the words eager to be said. I wasn't used to standing up to her and my mind tried to go blank, tried to erase each statement before I had time to say it.

"Do you realize what you've done?" she spoke down to me. "If you don't fix your mistake by tomorrow morning—"

"Fix what mistake? Yours? David wasn't lured by me!"

"No, but that boy stands in the way of our future! Of your clan's future and that of your kind!" Aunt Dawn said.

"You want to revert back to the old ways so badly that you're willing to break the same rules that govern them?" I asked, shaking my head.

"Council woman Liana has tried to enact these changes for years. Finally, she's secured the head position and has the power to make decisions for our kind. We have waited too long for some ridiculous puppy love to get in the way." Aunt Dawn's eyes burned with resentment. "If you do not take care of that boy immediately, the Council will hear about how you went against the orders of your clan leaders."

A new strength filled me with confidence. My focus became clear without the familiar fear of my aunt jumbling my thoughts. "Go ahead, tell the Council that you stole my phone, pretended to be me and told him to come to the island. That you tried to lure and kill a man who would be missed and looked for. David didn't have issues like prior arrests and drug use. If any part of him showed up, human authorities wouldn't assume he'd gotten himself into trouble again. They'd investigate a homicide. Tell the council that you brought someone who was not lured by me. That *you* broke the rules." My eyes jumped to my Aunt Anise. "What is the punishment for breaking the ancient ceremonial laws? Death, right? You want our clan to be stronger than the others, right? How will it do that without leaders?"

Aunt Anise fidgeted with her dress and looked down at the ground.

"I thought so," I said, glaring back at Aunt Dawn. I remembered the words spoken to me about breaking rules and I returned them to my aunts. "I'd hate to have to kill you. To help my sisters tear their own mothers apart."

Aunt Dawn gasped.

Aunt Rebecca stared at her feet, her lips barely smiling.

"So here's how this is going to work." I took a step toward Aunt Dawn and held my head up high. Fire burned in her eyes, but she knew just as well as I did that there was nothing she could do. As the clan leaders, their punishments for disobeying would be much harsher than my own. "You won't breathe a word of this to the Council. We'll pretend like this little meeting never happened. I will continue seeing David, and *you* are going to be okay with that."

"But what will we tell your sisters? They'll wonder why we're letting you," Aunt Anise interrupted. "They'll know you didn't kill your prey."

"You figure it out. You're good at lying and manipulating." My focus flashed back to Aunt Dawn. "You will not so much as think about hurting David. And your days of controlling me are over."

My eyes bounced to each aunt. None of them responded.

"Have I made my demands clear?"

Aunt Rebecca nodded, as did Aunt Anise, but Aunt Dawn only started at me.

"Fine," I spun on the ball of my foot and headed toward the trees. "I'll go have a chat with the elders of the Council."

"No, no. Wait." Aunt Dawn held out her hand. "I won't stop you from seeing him."

I swiveled on my foot to face her. "And?"

"And, I won't hurt him." The words sounded as though she fought to push them out.

"Smart." I gave her one nod, turned, and ran for the trees to catch up with my fellow sirens.

"*I* can't believe they just gave in so easily." David ran his fingers along my own as my hand rested on his thigh.

We were perched on top of the huge boulder that lined our lake. We sat looking out at the water, my back leaning against his chest as mist covered the glassy liquid and crawled up our dark rock. Evergreens surrounded us, keeping our presence perfectly private as a light breeze rustled through the deep green trees. His chest rose and fell, and I relished the fact that I didn't have to pretend to breathe normally if I didn't want to.

"They didn't really have a choice, and I doubt it was easy." I smiled picturing their faces, especially Aunt Dawn's stunned expression.

"I would have loved to see that, my Allura asserting herself to someone other than me." He laughed and kissed the top of my head. "Oh, I forgot to tell you the other night, when you swam up to the side of my boat and stole my oar, I thought you were one of them and I almost hit you over the head with the other oar."

I laughed and looked at him, shaking my head.

"Then, in that split second when your beautiful face came out of the water, and your dark hair framed those green eyes, I thought that must be what you'd look like to a sailor, when you're doing the Provider thing. And even knowing what I know, I still think I'd follow you into the water if I were a sailor." His tone changed, as though he tried to joke and be serious at the same time. "Not that you're ever going to do the Provider thing again."

I lightly smacked his hand. "I know. I'm being a good girl. No more biting men for me, sharks, and..." I sighed and peered back toward the water. This was going to be hard, fighting the Provider in me every day for the rest of my life.

"We can joke about it," I said more seriously now. "But it's like an addiction, to something that makes you feel whole and full and strong."

"I'll help you. Whatever it takes, I can be strong for you." David's touch soothed my fears and uneasiness.

"Just know how rough this is going to be. To fight this and to be on the outs with my aunts, and potentially with my whole clan."

"Do your sisters know what your aunts did?" he asked, rubbing his fingers up and down my right arm, sending shivers through my body.

"No. I don't want them to know. I don't want them to feel like they have to choose sides." I leaned in to kiss him. This little slice of perfection wouldn't last forever. There would come a day when my sisters found out and lines would be drawn. As it was, I knew somehow I had to get to the bottom of my mother's suicide. And if my aunts had a hand in her death, our clan would be torn apart from limb to tail. My sisters would be forced to pick sides.

And Kaven made it painfully clear my siren kind were under surveillance, no longer friends of the kelpies.

But, as I sat with David, free to love him and to be loved, I pushed the future trials from my mind and concentrated on the present triumphs.

"Your aunts will come up with some excuse why you're still seeing me, but what if your sisters catch on and ask you to tell them what's really going on?" His eyebrows lifted.

"I'll just tell them the truth." I leaned back, my spine against his thigh, and cupped my hands around his face, pulling his mouth down toward mine. "You lured the Provider in me, and I love you for it." I giggled as my mouth hovered over his. "I guess I can tell them the predator learned she couldn't live without her prey."

SOME KIND OF PURE OBSESSION

SOME KIND of PURE OBSESSION
(Siren Sisters 2)

EXCERPT

)(

The torturous binding squeezed my rib cage and strained my ability to pull air in past my lips. Thankfully, I didn't have to rely solely on my mouth to extract oxygen from the air and into my body. I squirmed where I sat beside David on a boulder, and adjusted the straps on my bikini top.

The notion that mermaids and sirens adorned their breasts with shells or whatever else was completely wrong. Most of us refused to wear bras even.

Naked = good.

Clothing = bad.

"Why are these things so popular?" I muttered to myself.

July sunlight warmed the lake with its peak heat of the day. At least that's the way David put it. Hot or cold, I couldn't tell the difference.

"Then take it off," David suggested with a laugh.

He stretched out on the huge rock we shared beside our lake, soaking up the rays. As though he hoped I'd heed his advice, he removed the towel from covering his face and suddenly sat up to peer at me,.

"Even if I went topless, I could cover my chest with scales," I said, deflating David's hope with one sentence.

He kissed my back, right above the irritating bikini strap, and returned to sunbathing. "Then do that."

I stopped fidgeting and lay beside him, determined to get used to the torturous contraption. I had my heart set on a particular goal by the end of the summer; spend the day at a public beach with my boyfriend, like most couples do. Relationship goals for the win. David didn't care one way or the other, but I'd decided that despite all the crazy I'd brought into his life, and the fact that he could share none of it with his friends, he deserved at least a little piece of normal.

I turned on my side to gaze at his smooth, tan skin, growing darker by the minute. He looked as though he literally soaked up the sun. Arms resting under his head, his torso stretched enough to accentuate the muscles beneath his skin. I appreciated the unobstructed view of his pecs and the nearly-there six-pack that defined itself more each time he shifted his body.

"I want my first public beach outing to be somewhere more... public," I said. "I can't wear my scales in public—thus this stupid bathing suit."

The towel muffled his answer. "I've never known you to take baby steps."

"I was thinking Alki Beach in Seattle," I went on, ignoring his comment. He was right, baby steps weren't typically my thing. But I cared about him, and if learning to cover my scale-less body in the water helped give him a more normal dating experience, then I'd do it.

David rolled to his side, flexing those abs of his in the process, and stared at me as the towel fell from his face and onto the stony surface.

My gaze bounced from his abs to his dark brown eyes.

"You sure that's a good idea?" he asked, concern filling his voice.

"Yeah. What's the worst that could happen?"

"Well, I don't know. Accidently unleashing your siren, for starters. Killing innocent people. Turning the Puget Sound red with their blood. Outing all sirens. Being taken into custody for testing." He reached to touch my hand.

I pulled away.

"Just." I swallowed the tiny stream of acid his words had caused to flow through my mouth. "Let me." I closed my eyes and tried to remove the image of blood-filled water from my mind, replace it with fish...no that didn't help. Dogs. Puppies. Yes, puppies. I'd never fantasized about eating puppies. "Okay." I took a deep breath and clasped David's hand.

"I'm sorry." His voiced lowered. "I shouldn't have said that. It was insensitive."

"No, it's fine. Pussyfooting won't help. Just like this damn bikini, I need to build up a tolerance by being subjected to the things that set me off. Swimming here with you has helped. I don't automatically go into hunting mode when I'm in the water anymore. So there's that."

I paused, deciding to say the thing I'd been privately practicing for days. "I think it's time to take it to the next level." My statement rang through me with more than one meaning, and all kinds of emotions— fear, excitement, lust. I reached out to run a finger down David's chest.

His eyes darkened and I swallowed down any remaining acid, just in case the kiss I saw coming was of the open-mouth persuasion.

He scooted nearer, 'til our bodies touched, and leaned in for a long kiss. I ran my free hand up and down his exposed side. His fingers wove through my hair. He pulled away, just enough to speak, before I had the opportunity to give into my urge enough to rip off my bikini top and bare my scale-less chest.

"My next day off just happens to fall right on the eighth month anniversary from when we met," he said. "How about we go to Seattle to celebrate? And if you feel up to it, we'll visit Alki Beach."

I landed a quick kiss on his lips. "Sounds perfect. And I promise that if I'm feeling tempted in any way, we won't swim around humans." I wouldn't want to ruin our anniversary date. "There's enough rumors flying through the clans about mysterious rouge sirens. I don't want to be counted among them."

"Yeah, I've heard a couple around the shop." David commented, as though he'd told me this a hundred times. Which, until now, he hadn't mentioned once.

My protective instincts perked up, called to attention. I had a huge bone to pick with my aunts, and I felt a sort of segregation from my sisters, but still, at the root of my being, the desire to protect them roared with discontentment. "The motorcycle shop?"

David had gotten a summer job at a motorcycle repair shop, although I suspected it'd last longer than the one summer month we had left. He was a natural when it came to everything motorcycle.

"I could have sworn I already told you," he said, trailing a finger over my knee.

I gave a blank look that spoke volumes. No. He hadn't.

"It's not much," he explained. Just that there are a few locals who think the disappearance of Jason wasn't an isolated incident. They don't believe the whole drowned and eaten by sea life explanation."

"Why?" I asked. "Why are they questioning it now? What's changed?"

Miyu's betrayal, her monstrous decision to end Jason's life on Dead Man Island while I left to save David, still gnawed at me. Not that she cared.

"Because, the newest disappearances of guys on the mainland," he answered.

I sighed. "Shit."

David's expression softened and reached to touch my arm. "The guys at work were teasing the locals who think these cases are connected. Called them conspiracy theorists. Said these are the same people who believe our government is controlled by reptilian over-loads. It's nothing, just a joke to them."

"It's a huge something. Because they're right." I massaged my temples and contemplated all the different ways to break the news to my aunts—none of which would actually work out for me. "My aunts are going to want to get involved."

"You lost me. Get involved with what?" A flicker of understanding flashed through his eyes. "Wait. Does this have anything to do with these clan rumors you keep mentioning, but fail to ever explain?"

"It's siren business. I didn't want to worry you." I leaned in to touch David's forearm, now my turn to comfort him. Admittedly, I couldn't keep my hands off him. The sentiment went both ways.

The reality of our newest siren secret already had Cara on edge, had her questioning not only her role within our clan, but the role of sirens within nature. And Cara had grown up hearing stories of our siren foremothers. I had no idea how David would react.

"You worry me when you hide shit." David's chocolate eyes bored into mine, searching for clues. "Makes me question if I can trust you."

That one stung. I swallowed down my pride and took a cleansing breath.

I studied his eyes for a reaction as I lifted yet another veil of secrecy. "I'm scared that you'll think if my siren cousins aren't able to control their hunger after the ceremony on Dead Man's Island, then I can't completely control mine either."

"Wait." David pulled away and stood. He stared at me like I was suddenly a caged lion on display. "So those disappearances on the mainland, all up and down the west coast, those are connected?"

"Yes." I didn't stand or reach for David. I only watched him pace the small walking space of the boulder we were on and shake his head.

"People are dying," he offered.

"I know."

He paused and shot a look at me. "Why aren't you doing anything about it?"

His question caught me off-guard. "Me?"

"Yeah, you're the provider. Why aren't you stopping them?"

Now he was sounding like my aunts who had a knack for volunteering me for the worst of jobs. More like voluntold. "It's not that easy," I retorted. "There's clan politics to consider."

This was the exact argument Arlana brought to the table the night our clan discussed the most recent killing three days ago. And she had been right. These rogue sirens, however many there were, each belonged to a clan. We would know how many went rogue if their clans reported them missing, but clan roots and loyalties run deep. They protect their own. Which to me, meant that if I pursued them without elder approval it would be a blind hunt ending with clans turning on each other to keep their members safe. Or turning on me. Killing a human male was not necessarily against our rules. Killing another siren without direct orders from the elders was very much against the rules, even in self-defense.

"But Allura, people are dying. Innocent people." David reached down and I accepted his hands as he raised me to stand.

My siren side and humanity side were constantly at war with one another. Lately, my humanity had been claiming more battles. I had David to thank for that. On this, though, I wasn't going to budge. Having the battle brought to me was one thing. But I didn't make it a habit to go out chasing them.

"The situation is being monitored," I stated in a leave-it-alone kind of way.

David pulled me close to him. His heartbeat thudded under my ear. I had a heartbeat too, but not like his. A siren's head and heart hold a certain disconnect. I suspected it was necessary when they split ways with their mermaid sisters in an effort to stay alive. It's a survival instinct, separating one's head and heart. David's was fully connected. His thoughts affected his feelings which affected his thoughts. He cared. About life. About the lives of strangers.

"Monitored?" he pushed further. "Sounds like a science experiment or something."

I hadn't thought of that, but he was right. I wondered if the elders were staying back to see how this all unfolded. In a way, it lined up with their agenda to return sirens to our glory days of hunting men. What if these rogue sirens represented the elders' end goal for our kind? Once they collected their data, though, if they were allowing these sirens to hunt men for such a purpose, what would become of the rogue sirens?

"They're on the mainland, though," I reminded. "If I step in, that means I'll be gone for who knows how long. We won't see each other."

David rested a gentle kiss on my forehead. "So, we won't see each other for what, a week or more? The girlfriends and families of the sirens' victims will never see their men again."

"Okay." I reached up and kissed David's lips. "I'll agree *if* the elders ask me to intervene. But until then, there's not much I can do. I'm sure there's a lot more going on behind the scenes with the elders than I'm aware of. But I'll do what I can when I can. That's all I can promise."

"I understand there's red tape. Everything has red tape. That's all I'm asking, though. What you can, when you can." He kissed me again, deeper this time.

His hands clung to my back and pulled me harder into him. I wove my fingers through his hair before trailing them down his spine. When his lips moved south and rested on the top peak of my right breast, I dug my fingers into his skin. I moved to untie my bikini top, but he brushed my hands away and did the honors himself. I leaned my head back, fully immersed in a pleasure stronger than the hunt.

I worked at untying the string holding his swimming trunks onto his body, when my phone shattered our moment with a blaring ring. David paused and pulled away.

"No, it's okay," I assured him. "I'll ignore that."

"It's Cara." Ugh. He'd memorized the ring tones I had for my different clan members. I always answered Cara's calls. He grabbed my phone, still ringing, and handed it to me.

I gave him a "seriously?" look and answered the phone. "Yes?" I asked in a deep, throaty tone.

"Interrupt something?" my sister asked.

"Yes, thank you very much," I said, clearing my throat. "What's up? So I can get back to what I was doing."

"More like get back to who you were doing," Cara said with a chuckle.

"Yeah, that." I shook my head, but let a smile slip through. I'd promised my aunts to keep David a secret from my sisters, but nothing got past Cara. Over the last few months, David had been the unspoken knowing between my roommate and me.

"Hey, I'm calling to tell you to come home. We've got a visitor who isn't welcome, but won't leave 'til he talks to you."

I rested the phone between my cheek and shoulder as I retied my bikini top with utter disappointment. "Fine. I'm on my way." Before I ended the call, I thought to ask a blaringly obvious question. "Wait, Cara, who is it?"

Cara lowered her voice to a barely-there whisper. "I'm not supposed to say exactly, but him and Celine are in the front room glaring icepicks at each other right now. Just get here."

Shit. A kelpie.

ABOUT THE AUTHOR

Rachel Sullivan is a dog-hugger and tree-lover who writes empowering books about characters who unearth their own inner truth and follow it to freedom. She pulls from folklore, mythology, and ancient belief systems to create her award-winning stories.

When she's not writing, Rachel works in circulation and reference services at a public library. She also enjoys hiking, wine tasting, attempting to grow her own food, and reading. She lives in Washington among evergreens, animals, and three generations of women.

Visit her website: http://rachelsullivan.net/

facebook.com/AuthorRachelSullivan

twitter.com/RachelSulli3

instagram.com/rachel_sullivanbooks

pinterest.com/dog0hugger

Made in the USA
Monee, IL
24 August 2020